IN THE BALLROOM WITH THE CANDLESTICK

A **CLUE** Mystery
BY
DIANA PETERFREUND

Amulet Books
New York

Library of Congress Control Number for the
hardcover edition: 2021029310

Paperback ISBN 978-1-4197-3979-8

CLUE and HASBRO and all related trademarks and logos
are trademarks of Hasbro, Inc. © 2021 Hasbro.

Book design by Brenda E. Angelilli

Amulet Books are available at special discounts when purchased
in quantity for premiums and promotions as well as fundraising or
educational use. Special editions can also be created to specification.
For details, contact specialsales@abramsbooks.com or the address below.

Amulet Books® is a registered trademark of Harry N. Abrams, Inc.

ABRAMS The Art of Books
195 Broadway, New York, NY 10007
abramsbooks.com

Don't give away the ending—it's the only one we have.

Alfred Hitchcock, *Psycho*

1

Orchid

Vaughn Green was singing again.

Orchid McKee looked up from the textbook she had been trying, and failing, to read for the last fifteen minutes. The Tudor House dining room was empty except for her. She cocked her head to the side, wondering if she'd imagined it.

But no, that was him. And it wasn't a song she recognized, either.

Weird. She'd thought each of his songs was etched permanently in her memory. By now, she could guess the tune within a handful of notes. If the song was "Another Me," she could tell even before it began, with the halting half-strum of Vaughn's guitar that Scarlett had kept in the video for *authenticity*.

Of course it was all *authentic*—the arrangements simple, the sound tinny. He'd been making the recordings in his room with his phone instead of real recording equipment. But the fans didn't care.

The hundreds of thousands of fans.

She sat up and glanced at her phone, wondering if it was autoplaying one of the recordings. But it was silent. She swiped over to the music account.

Nothing. Well, unless you counted the fifty thousand new views since this morning. Today's top track was "Off on Another Great Adventure." Not one of Orchid's favorites, to be honest.

Vaughn hadn't gotten to go on any great adventures. He'd died in a car at the bottom of Rocky Point Ravine.

But what was this song? She couldn't make out any words, but she knew it was Vaughn. His style, his voice. Where was it coming from? She opened the door to the hall. The music went on, still faint as ever. Now, she could hear words.

And when this heart, this body, this shore, this dawn breaks
There'll be another addition to my list of mistakes.
Because I never told you all . . .
That morningfall.

Yeah, that was Vaughn all right. Half his songs were about secrets. Maybe that's why she liked his music so much.

But this song, too, was a secret. Because Orchid had never heard it.

"Hello?" she called into the quiet hall. Students didn't stick around Tudor House these days if they didn't have to. It was one of the reasons Orchid liked to study here. Being invisible was a luxury she'd lost in the past few months. If she had to hide out in the Murder House to get away from people's prying eyes, so be it.

There were a few rooms still unfilled with blood or memories.

She walked farther into the hall, listening for the ghostly strains of Vaughn's voice. It got louder as she moved toward the front of the house. The doors to the kitchen, ballroom, and conservatory were open, revealing nothing but the usual Tudor House furnishings. She listened at the billiards room door—recently repurposed as Peacock's ground-floor bed-room since the accident—and heard nothing. The library—Dr. Brown's office—was shut, as usual, but the sound wasn't coming from there, either.

"Hello?" she said again, more loudly. "Does anyone else hear that music?"

She heard a door open in the second-floor hall and then Violet Vandergraf was on the stairs, descending toward her. "Hey, Orchid. What's going on?"

"Listen," she said, shushing her.

The music stopped.

Violet cocked her head to the side. "What am I listening for?"

"It's gone! I could have sworn . . ." Orchid shook her head. "I thought I heard Vaughn singing."

Violet's eyes widened and she pulled out her phone. "Um . . . let me call Scarlett, okay?"

"That's not what I meant," Orchid said quickly. "Not for real." They didn't think she was that crazy, did they? "Just one of the songs."

Violet chuckled. "Um, I mean, yeah. Someone's always playing them now. Wasn't that your whole point in putting them online?"

Was it? Orchid couldn't quite recall what had possessed her to let Scarlett put Vaughn's recordings online. It was in the days right after his death, when everything in the world had been a gray blur. She'd been sobbing into her pillow about how everything was all her fault, and how his whole life had been stolen from him. Scarlett was trying to help. She had some experience, she'd said, with streaming video games and other content. She could help Orchid with the publicity. If everyone was going to learn the truth about Orchid anyway, they might as well take advantage of it.

Orchid's lawyer hadn't seen the harm in it, so they'd let Scarlett do whatever she wanted. Neither Orchid nor her lawyer, Bianca, thought it would go any further than their friends at school.

They'd underestimated Scarlett.

Five songs. Five hits. Scarlett was the one who kept track of the viral spread of each track, pinpointing the source and optimizing the synergy, and a whole host of other terms that made Orchid's skin crawl. Back in Hollywood, that was the sort of stuff her manager had taken care of, and Orchid had hated her manager.

A few months ago, she had killed him.

"They weren't playing one I'd ever heard," said Orchid now. She checked the lounge. Empty. That just left the study.

She wasn't going in the study.

Violet frowned. "Weird. Are you sure?"

Was she *sure*? "The recordings are *mine*, Violet. He made them for *me*."

She held her hands up. "I know that. Everyone knows it. I'm . . . I'm going to call Scarlett, okay?" She lifted her phone to her ear.

"I don't need a babysitter." Orchid turned in place, listening. "I heard it."

Violet, the phone still at her ear, also looked toward the study, then back at Orchid. "You want me to look in there for you?"

Orchid swallowed. She hadn't crossed that threshold in four months, ever since she'd found Keith inside.

They'd cleaned everything, she'd been told. New rugs, new curtains, new upholstery on the chairs. Apparently, she'd made quite a mess with that wrench. Who knew the human body could hold so much blood?

"Yes," she said softly.

They'd sealed up the secret passages, too. For real this time. No more sneaking around under this house. No more break-ins. No more secrets.

Violet looked in the study. "Empty. And Scarlett's phone went to voicemail. She must be in a meeting."

Scarlett was always in meetings these days. That's what happened when most of the student body left. All those committees with no chairperson, and Scarlett more than happy to take them on.

"I don't need Scarlett to tell me what I heard."

Violet came over and took Orchid's hand, patting it in what Orchid could only assume she thought was a comforting manner. "Vaughn's not making new music, honey. He's dead. But it's okay. My grandma still holds out hope for Elvis."

Orchid snatched her hand back. She crossed to the coatrack and grabbed her jacket. April evenings were cold in Maine.

"Orchid, I miss him, too," Violet said. "I had to do that history poster all by myself, remember?"

Orchid rolled her eyes as she zipped up her jacket. She couldn't imagine what a hardship that had been. A whole history poster. Meanwhile, Vaughn's entire life had been stolen.

"I'm going for a walk."

"Good!" exclaimed Violet, who was probably even now texting Scarlett. "Clear your head."

What went unsaid: *and stop acting crazy around me.*

Yeah, right. The problem wasn't in her head. That music had been coming from somewhere.

Outside the walls of Tudor House, though, all was still. Once upon a time, Orchid had relished the remote peacefulness on this little island at the end of the world. But then, at least, Blackbrook had been bustling, a hive of brilliant kids running around the campus, the rulers of their own dominion, constantly busy with sports and activities and whatever teenaged dramas powered student life.

The school was a shell of its former self now. First there'd been the storm, which destroyed half the dorms and flooded several classroom buildings. They would have recovered from that quickly, with no greater damage to the school's reputation than a report that the living quarters were a mite crowded for a year or so. But then there had been the murders. Even those still willing to send their precious youngsters back to a school where the headmaster had been stabbed to death by one of his own staff members had balked when, only a month after the reopening, a student had been stalked and nearly murdered in her own dorm. She'd only survived by fighting her attacker off.

In the end, she killed him, but his reign of terror had caused no fewer than three additional deaths, of staff and students both.

Orchid wondered how Blackbrook's admissions office related that story, or if they even needed to. After all, most people had already seen it on TV or in the papers. Usually with Orchid's picture attached.

Vanished Child Star's Secret Life at an Exclusive Boarding School

No Charges Filed Against Former Child Star Emily Pryce in Death of Ex-Manager

Murders in Maine: The Stalking of Former Child Star Emily Pryce

The Surprise Connection Between Emily Pryce and Viral Music Sensation Vaughn Green

Scarlett had jumped for joy over that last one. The impressions on Vaughn's channel had spiked, and never stopped.

Orchid had been dreading all the publicity, but when she saw how it helped Vaughn, she found she couldn't begrudge it as much as she'd thought. After all, the danger of people finding out where she was had always been about Keith. And Keith was dead.

Even at Blackbrook, people stared for a few days, then stopped. With the kind of money most Blackbrook kids had, celebrity wasn't all that weird. The rich and famous rubbed elbows wherever they went. A former child star? Meh, that was nothing. The fact that she'd killed a man proved more impressive. After four months, the skeleton of a student body that remained on campus had all but absorbed the shockwaves of each disaster. It was, perhaps, a self-selecting group. Those who had the stomach or the need to stay on at Blackbrook, despite the death and destruction, were those most equipped to handle it.

Like the Murder Crew. Orchid, Scarlett, Mustard, Finn Plum, and even Peacock. No one thought Beth "Peacock" Picach would be returning to campus after the accident. Blackbrook's star tennis player had been in the car with Vaughn and Keith when it plunged off the cliff into the Rocky Point Ravine. Unlike the others, she had survived the crash, but with enough damage to her body to make playing tennis this season or any other massively unlikely.

Still, she was here, on campus. Murder Crew forever.

Orchid walked across the green but heard nothing but the breeze in the budding trees, the crunch of gravel beneath her boots, and the distant crash of waves upon the rocks. Here and there, an occasional light shone from a window. There was a jogger across the quad, a knot of students reading beneath a maple, a couple kissing in the portico outside the boys' dorm.

But no more music.

She hadn't imagined it. People didn't hallucinate their dead boyfriends singing an entire verse of a brand-new song. At least, not without the benefit of heavier drugs than Orchid had ever done, even back in Hollywood.

She kept walking, out to the edge of campus, only half-aware of where she allowed her feet to take her. Oh, who was she kidding? She knew where she was going.

The cliff.

The sun had dipped below the horizon now, bathing the rocks in a reddish-purple glow. The sea rolled beneath a darkening sky, but Orchid couldn't make out any of the shimmers from the bits of glass and metal still embedded in the base of the cliff. Maybe it had all washed away by now. All traces of Vaughn.

Except his songs.

Orchid hadn't been imagining it. She couldn't have been.

Movement caught her eye on the far side of the divide. At low tide, the ravine ran dry, and clamdiggers often picked their way across the rocks in search of shellfish. This one was just completing a climb back up to the summit of the ravine on the village side. He turned to look back at Blackbrook, and the last slivers of daylight illuminated his face.

Orchid's jaw dropped.

Vaughn.

2

Scarlett

"I'm telling you, I saw him." Orchid's eyes were wide, her skin paler than usual.

Scarlett Mistry bit her lip. "And I believe that you saw . . . something." At sunset. Across the whole ravine. And in her current . . . fragile state. Scarlett wasn't about to call the school counselor about this, because Perry Winkle was kind of a jerk, but she had to nip this in the bud. "But . . . Orchid, there are always clamdiggers out at low tide. There used to be a whole club for them on campus." It had been one of the few clubs Scarlett hadn't joined, given her vegetarianism.

"It was Vaughn. I know it was."

They were sitting in the dining room of Tudor House, waiting for the other girls to join them. Although now Scarlett didn't know how good of an idea it was, given Orchid's state of mind. She'd already gotten some disquieting texts from Violet about Orchid's earlier insistence that she'd heard Vaughn singing a new song from somewhere in Tudor House. And now this?

Maybe she should encourage Orchid to call her therapist. This might be above Scarlett's pay grade.

"Violet told me what you heard—"

"Yeah, and how do you explain that?" Orchid announced, as if presenting the coup de grâce.

"I can't," Scarlett admitted. "I don't know what you heard, and no one else heard it. Maybe someone was listening to one of his songs outside, and it just sounded unfamiliar because of the way the sound traveled through the stones of the house."

Take that, Dr. Gadsden. The physics teacher had had the temerity to give Scarlett a B in physics last year. And, as she just proved, she'd learned plenty.

"It was new *words*, Scar. A whole new song."

Wouldn't *that* be nice? Scarlett had no complaints about their current levels of engagement, but a new Vaughn Green track would be just the thing to catapult the channel to insane heights. But it was unlikely. The music teacher had none, and Vaughn's cell phone, retrieved from the crash site, was toast. His teachers had told her he used the computer banks at school for all his papers, and Finn's dip into his Blackbrook cloud drive only turned up two additional recordings to add to the three he'd sent Orchid. They'd been popular, but the numbers would not be sustained without new content. It was the law of the internet.

"I know grief makes us think weird things—I know that," Orchid was saying now. "But it didn't turn me into a songwriter."

Ooh, next best thing. Emily Pryce, former child actress, now a singer-songwriter. One party Demi, another part Ariana . . .

"Okay," Scarlett said. "Let's do a thought experiment. Let's say you heard some music—some kind of music. And you went out walking at sunset to . . . well, chase it down. And out by the cliffs, you saw someone on the other side of the ravine that looked like Vaughn."

"*Was* Vaughn, " Orchid corrected.

Whatever. "What did you do? When you saw him?"

"I screamed, of course!" Orchid was gripping the edge of the carved wooden table with her hands. "I screamed his name."

Scarlett's brow furrowed. Yeah, that was going to have to stop. The tabloid stories about Orchid had been mainly sympathetic toward everyone at Blackbrook. They'd been good for Orchid's business, good for Vaughn's music. The last thing anyone needed was an article about Orchid standing on clifftops, beating her breast and screaming out her dead boyfriend's name. There was suitable mourning, and then there was certifiable.

Especially since they'd only dated for, like, a day . . . which was not a thing that Scarlett would *ever* say out loud. Orchid had a right to her feelings. As long as those feelings were good for page views. Scarlett had encouraged her to record an introduction to each song. As it was the first time Emily Pryce had been seen on-screen in years, it was enormously popular. But she hadn't been able to convince Orchid to do any more.

And maybe that was a good thing, if she was going to start ranting about ghosts.

"Then what happened?" Scarlett asked carefully.

"What do you mean?"

"Well—whoever it was, did they hear you? Did they turn around?"

"He stopped moving for a second," Orchid said. "I . . . I thought he heard me."

Sure. Ghosts are known for their excellent hearing. "And then?"

"Well, he kept going up the embankment, and then he disappeared into the trees."

"When you say 'disappeared,' you mean like, walked into the trees and then you couldn't see him anymore?"

Orchid narrowed her eyes. "Yes. I don't mean like he vanished in a puff of smoke."

"Good!" Scarlett exclaimed. "I'm just trying to figure out what we're working with here. Because you aren't talking about a real person, Orchid. Vaughn is dead."

Orchid's big, expressive, movie-star eyes filled with tears.

Scarlett sighed. "And I'm just saying that, you know, you were out there, where he died. It was dark. You were thinking about him"—obsessing about him—"and then you saw someone."

"I saw *him*."

"And when you called out, whoever it was very reasonably stopped and listened because they heard someone calling, but then when they didn't hear anything else, they just kept walking home with their bucket of quahogs."

"He didn't have a bucket," Orchid grumbled.

Gee, she sure saw that person very well all the way across the ravine at twilight. "Then what was he doing out there?"

"*Haunting me, of course!*"

Of course. Scarlett took a deep breath. "Why?"

"Because I'm responsible for his death. Because he has unfinished business. All the usual reasons. Geez, you've seen movies."

She had. And Orchid had been in them. But there was no such thing as ghosts. "Well, you're not responsible for his death, and you have probably done the most to help him with his unfinished business of anyone, so . . ."

"Anyone but you," said Orchid.

"Yes," Scarlett agreed. "I produced all his music, and I have been the architect behind all its marketing and monetization and even the images we chose for the videos. I worked my butt off for that boy and we weren't even friends." She shrugged. "And he hasn't been haunting me, so there."

Orchid groaned and put her head down on the table. "I know. I know how I sound. But I also know what I saw. What I heard. It doesn't make any sense."

It didn't make the kind of sense that Orchid would be interested in right now, anyway. Scarlett patted Orchid's head in what she hoped was a comforting manner. Her hair was a disaster, even by Orchid standards. The muddy brown dye had almost completely washed out, and the blond roots were grow-ing in, but not in any cool, reverse-balayage kind of way. Plus, it needed to be washed.

"We should color your hair," Scarlett said.

"I don't care," Orchid mumbled into the tabletop.

That's the whole problem, Scarlett thought. Add it to the list of things she wasn't saying out loud. "Well, if you don't care, then I decree we're going to color your hair. Maybe some fun color. You know, for prom. You don't have to blend in anymore."

"I don't have to go to prom, either."

"Blasphemy." But Orchid was clearly not in the mood to discuss school dances. "Why don't you go upstairs and take a long, hot shower, or do a face mask or something? You don't have to come to the meeting."

Orchid rolled her eyes. "Oh, I'm released from Prom Committee duties because I saw my dead boyfriend's ghost? How magnanimous of you."

"You're welcome," said Scarlett, not taking the bait. It was probably better to go without Orchid anyway. Scarlett was attempting to convince Dr. Brown that, reduced student population or not, they still needed to hire a band for prom. If Orchid was there she might go nuts and lobby to just play Vaughn's maudlin tunes on a loop.

Not happening. Scarlett had her eye on a hot band from Portland called the Singing Telegrams. Upbeat, peppy, and you could dance to it. She'd listened to enough of Vaughn's ballads to last a lifetime.

Scarlett marched Orchid upstairs to her room and then texted the others.

SCARLETT

> Orchid's out. Where are you, ladies? I want to present a united front to Brown on this band issue.

VIOLET

> :-(Math tutoring ran over. Be there ASAP.

Okay. So she was one woman down.

AMBER

> Sorry, Scar! Got caught up with Tanner. I'll be there soon.

Boyfriends, again. Out of everyone, Scarlett would have thought Amber was most invested in a good prom. After all, she was the only one with an actual date.

PEACOCK

Still making my way over from the
gym. Give Dr. Brown my best.

At least Peacock had the best excuse. She was still on that little scooter to support her cast, and it took forever to get around campus on that thing. Scarlett wasn't even sure why she'd come back here, especially since tennis was not happening for her this season and she still had to travel to the mainland twice a week for PT. But Peacock claimed to have her own reasons. Murder Crew loyalty, probably.

Still, it was typical. Scarlett was the only one around here that actually cared enough to get things done. Cared even more than Dr. Brown, if she was being honest. The interim headmaster was not an educator, and had no idea what made the students tick. Ever since she'd taken over, after the storm, Dr. Brown had been laser focused on halting the steady flow of Blackbrook kids—and their corresponding tuitions—out the door. To her, that meant ensuring nervous parents that the campus was safe, and making sure that the academics were up to the school's usual rigorous standards.

In both goals, the good doctor had failed miserably. Another student and staff member had died on campus during her tenure, as well as the attempted murder of Orchid, and the near-death experience of Peacock. And most of the disasters had occurred during the standardized tests. Blackbrook scores this term were lower than the spirit of the student body.

How can you study when you don't feel safe? How can you feel safe when you don't feel normal?

That's what Dr. Brown didn't understand. Canceling "frivolous" activities and clubs was no way to retain students, or make them study harder. They'd lost their dorms and their classmates. Austerity was a terrible idea. A big, lavish dance, however, might be just what they needed to remind people what they loved about this school to begin with.

Scarlett had crunched the numbers. She'd worked the angles. And now she was going to make Dr. Brown see it her way. Just like she used to with Headmaster Boddy.

Scarlett squared her shoulders and marched back downstairs to the main floor. Dr. Brown was still holding her office hours in the library, as she was still performing double duty as house proctor as well as headmaster.

And sucking as both, if you asked Scarlett. But no one had. It's like the administration had totally forgotten not only the Student Advisory Board, but the fact that Scarlett Mistry was its chair. They were botching the response to this completely. Scarlett's parents, who ran the Mistry Hotels hospitality chain, had definitely dealt with their fair share of dead bodies on their properties over the years. There'd even been a few murders, because mob bosses liked to knock each other off and also appreciated the fine amenities of a Mistry luxury property. But her parents' business was thriving, while Blackbrook was nearly dead. Because they didn't understand how to disconnect the school from the tragedies that had occurred there. They needed way better PR.

But no one ever listened to Scarlett.

She rapped firmly on the door. No response.

Scarlett had gone from mild annoyance to simmering rage. First all her friends had blown off the meeting, and now Dr. Brown had followed suit. She couldn't hold all of Blackbrook together with her own two hands.

"Come on," she hissed, jiggling the door handle. It opened. Oh.

Scarlett opened the door and peeked inside, but the library was deserted.

Well, maybe Dr. Brown was just in the bathroom or something. She must be around. She wouldn't leave the door unlocked.

She took two steps into the room. Unlike most of the people now occupying Tudor House, Scarlett had lived here long before everything had gone to hell in a handbasket. She knew what the library was supposed to look like. Say what you will about Mrs. White, Murderer—but when she was in charge of this place, it was lovely and well cared-for. Now that Dr. Brown was the house proctor, the soft candle-style sconces in the halls had been replaced with bright fluorescents, the fireplaces were boarded up, and even the leather-bound volumes of the off-limits library were covered with white boards listing school schedules and other administrative information. In the old days, the students of Tudor House could come in here and read. Now it was Dr. Brown's office, with her papers, her desk, her wardrobe, and the corner she'd walled off with a tall, decorative screen that presumably contained her bed and other personal effects.

"Dr. Brown?" Scarlett said, just in case the good doctor was asleep behind the screen. But no one stirred. She checked, and the bed was empty.

So she *had* left the door unlocked.

Well, wasn't this the opportunity of the semester? Headmaster Boddy hadn't been the world's most careful administrator. Passwords taped in desk drawers, things like that. And since Scarlett was on all the student committees, there were many times she had to be let into his office in the now-disused administration building. She'd found all kinds of delicious tidbits in his computer. With Finn's help, she'd gotten access to even more.

But Dr. Brown was a little more canny, and far more careful. At least until today. Scarlett sidled over to the big desk, which was set before the old, lead-lined picture windows swathed in what must be half an acre of red velvet drapes. She bumped the desk with her hip, and when that didn't wake up the computer screen, sighed and jiggled the mouse.

Score. It hadn't gone to sleep yet, which definitely would have required a password to get in. Dr. Brown's desktop was disturbingly neat—the screen of a Type A scientist, or a sociopath. She looked at the folders available: documents, faculty meetings, the usual administrative entry points into the school's system.

Once upon a time, Scarlett would have used these precious moments to massage her grades, but after skipping out on the SATs this winter, she'd rejiggered her priorities. Princeton was off the table—at least the old-fashioned way. Now, her only option was a celebrity slot—the kind reserved for, say, producers of major viral video hits. So what need did she have to sneak around her headmaster's computer files? What need to push so hard for Blackbrook at all?

Scarlett didn't entirely know, and that was its own kind of problem.

Her eye caught on one folder. *Vaughn Financial Claims.*

What? Was the school being sued by Vaughn's family? She took a quick glance around.

And that's when she saw it. Behind the red velvet curtain. A large, person-shaped bump in the luxurious fabric.

Scarlett shot up straight and tried to look like she wasn't digging around in the headmaster's computer. "Who's there?" she said sharply.

Still no answer. And no movement from the lump, either.

Scarlett felt foolish. It was probably just the way the drapes were . . . draping. She reached over to shift them back into place.

Her fingers touched velvet, and something else. Something large and person-shaped, which shifted, and then slid out from behind the curtains and fell to the carpet with a thud.

And for the third time this year, Scarlett Mistry found herself far closer than she'd ever wanted to be to a dead body.

This one had once belonged to Dr. Brown. Scarlett was no more an expert on corpses than the first time she'd been in the same room with a dead headmaster, but she was proud to say she was rather over the shock of it. She didn't even scream this time.

"Oh," was all she could think to say.

Dr. Brown's eyes were open, her mouth was slack, and her skin was the scary kind of pale. Scarlett stared into the woman's dead eyes, but nothing stared back.

The door to the office opened, and she looked up to see Violet, Amber, and Peacock crowding around the threshold.

"Hey," said Amber brightly. "Sorry we're la—" her words died off as she caught sight of the body.

Violet did scream.

Scarlett raised her hands. "I didn't do it!"

3

Peacock

The doctors say if I like tracking things so much, I should track how I feel in my "journey of recovery." But I've been keeping this thing for four months now, and the only notable entries are six weeks in, when they finally let me out of that stupid bed, and another month after that, when I got the stupid hip cast off and got to change from the wheelchair to the scooter.

What a waste.

Besides, the last time someone asked me to track my feelings, it was so he could figure out my housemates' schedules in order to stalk and kill them, so you'll excuse me if I find this entire exercise a wee bit triggering.

You know what else is triggering? Yet another dead person, this one in the room next to mine! How am I supposed to sleep now? At least three people were murdered in this building—no, not even in this building! ON THIS FLOOR. And now I'm just supposed to live in the billiards room like it's no big deal, just because ground-floor rooms are hard to come by since the flood?

They said Dr. Brown died of natural causes—a stroke or some-thing. But come on. Who do they think they're kidding? Did she just hide her own body inside the drapes? Of course it was murder. Because Blackbrook. And once again, because Blackbrook, people are probably going to blame me. They blamed me for Headmaster Boddy.

Never again! If tennis is out—POSSIBLY FOREVER!!!!—then I should at least do something useful with myself. I'll solve the murder myself, before anyone decides it was me again.

POSSIBLE SUSPECTS:

1. **ORCHID MCKEE,** *a.k.a. Emily Pryce, a.k.a. lying liar who lies—about her very IDENTITY. Super weird. And super fragile, lately. Violet said she's been hearing things that aren't there. Also, she's already killed once. She should go at the top of anyone's list.*

Plus, Orchid was conveniently the only one absent from our planned meeting with the headmaster. Was she worried that she wouldn't be able to act shocked enough to discover the body? After all, it wasn't like she was once some Oscar-caliber superstar. Just some cheesy kids' movie actress. I for one never saw those dumb heiress movies. Some of us have lives . . . or used to, anyway.

2. **SCARLETT MISTRY:** *Constantly arguing with Dr. Brown, which, if people's past suspicion of ME means anything, is supposedly very important. She says when she found Dr. Brown, she was already dead, but can we be sure of that? I know that if I were ever to stumble across a corpse, I'd be careful to notice things like mortal wounds on it, but she says she has no idea how Dr. Brown died. I find that suspicious. Wouldn't you at least look? It's not like it's that gross. Certainly no worse than how my legs look with all the pins in and stuff, and I still make it through PT 2x week.*

3. **PERRY WINKLE:** *Everyone knows our illustrious guidance coun-selor wishes he had Dr. Brown's job, and now, apparently he does? I mean, you wouldn't think that the job of a boarding school headmaster was something you'd kill for, but it also doesn't seem like something you'd get killed AT, and we've had two dead ones here this year alone.*

4. **TANNER CURRY:** *I told Winkle about this one, but he blew me off. Typical! Well, I'm writing it here anyway, just for further thought. I saw and heard Tanner Curry in Dr. Brown's office fighting with her yesterday, before Scarlett found her body. I don't know what about, but their voices were raised. And, as I mentioned above, everyone knows the last person seen fighting with a headmaster is definitely a major suspect in their death.*

Let's see what we see.

4

Mustard

Mustard's father always said that boredom got you into trouble. If you kept yourself occupied, mind and body, then you didn't have time to be stupid.

And since Mustard had been very, very stupid, it only followed that he had to keep himself very, very busy.

Even in the carved-out ruins of this illustrious school, there was plenty to do. Easy targets, like academics. Shockingly, Farthing Military Academy hadn't quite prepared him to hold his own on topics like literature or art history. Mustard had to hustle to catch up to his classmates on any subject that wasn't military history or war games.

Even easier targets, like hard labor. At the beginning of term, he'd been punished for his stupid infractions by getting placed on the work crew cleaning up the campus. Most of the other students on the crew had no idea what they were doing, but facilities work was part of the core curriculum at Farthing. He may not have read *The Crucible*, but he could pour concrete.

And if all else failed, there was exercise. Go for a run. Get shredded.

Do anything other than think.

Well, not *anything*.

The weather today was mild but gray as Mustard jogged along the freshly laid paths through the green. His paths, that he'd laid himself. All perfectly even. Perfectly straight.

He was feeling good. Clean, except for the sweat. Tired, which was how it should be. He had his route down cold by now, and if he timed it just right, there was no danger of seeing anyone he should not. No danger of trouble.

He jogged up to the door of his dorm, and saw Amber Frye crying on the stoop. For as long as he'd known her, Amber had been dating his roommate, Tanner Curry. He'd seen her crying before. Very few people at Blackbrook had made it through the term without tears. She'd bawled all the way through the memorial service for Vaughn Green, and Mustard hadn't been sure she even knew who the guy was.

"Oh, Mustard!" she cried as he came forward. "I don't want you to see me like this!"

That would be a first. "Hey, Amber. Are you all right? You want me to get Tanner for you?"

She sobbed and her eyes released a fresh batch of tears. "That's the whole problem! Tanner just broke up with me!"

"What?"

"He won't even tell me why!" she wailed. "I don't know what's going on with him anymore!"

Mustard understood where she was coming from. He couldn't figure out his roommate lately, either. When Mustard had first moved in, Tanner had been an easygoing prep, the kind of kid who wore boat shoes without socks and used his generous trust-fund allowance to fill their shared dorm fridge with pizza bagels. The Currys had been attending Blackbrook for generations, and Tanner's place in the school's firmament was practically preordained. He wasn't a striver like Scarlett or, well, some other people Mustard had met on campus—and though he played sports, it wasn't his life, like it had been with Peacock. Tanner played squash like he was training for business meetings at the country club. He rowed crew because it's what a Curry did. Everything was exactly what a Curry did.

He and Mustard got along very well.

But lately, things had been different. Though most of the students had been off-kilter since the storm, Tanner seemed to take everything in stride, at least until the second waves of deaths on campus. Now, he slept odd hours, and Mustard sometimes saw him in their room when he thought he should have been in class. He'd lost weight, too, though Mustard had attributed it primarily to him quitting the crew team and no longer needing to bulk up. And now he'd dumped Amber? Was there something else going on?

"I'm sorry," Mustard said to Amber. He wasn't sure what else he was supposed to do. He felt bad for her and all, but . . . it was a high school romance. Tanner and Amber weren't engaged to be married or anything. Girls made such big deals about things. Mustard heard Orchid McKee had launched a whole online music channel memorializing Vaughn Green, which . . . were they even dating? He hadn't even realized they were dating.

One time, back when he was still speaking to the rest of the Murder Crew, Scarlett had mentioned that Orchid and

Vaughn had only kissed a couple of times before he died. Was that what counted for dating at Blackbrook?

It had better not be.

She sniffled. "Don't tell him I whined to you like this. I'm . . . I'm sorry. Just, watch over him for me? He's not okay. He thinks he is, but he's not."

Mustard watched her head down the steps, her shoulders still shaking. He clenched his jaw.

Tanner was fine. The one who did the dumping was the one who was fine. Everyone knew that.

He went up to his room. Tanner was slumped on the couch, scrolling idly through his phone. Were those shadows under his eyes?

"Hey," said Mustard.

"'Sup," Tanner replied without looking up.

Everything cool?

I just saw Amber. She said you two broke up.

Do you want to talk about it?

"Just had a run," said Mustard, instead of any of those other things.

"Cool." Tanner still didn't look his way.

Mustard grabbed his towel and headed for the showers. He turned the water on hot, stripped, and got underneath the spray.

If Tanner wanted to break up with Amber, it was his own business. No one else needed to know why. Tanner didn't even need to know why. You didn't always know why you did things, and that was okay.

Showers were a tough place. You could always keep busy there, shampooing and scrubbing and such, but it was also really hard not to think. That's probably why the military recommended short showers. You don't want to spend too much time thinking when you're killing people, either.

Five minutes later, he was back in the room, his hair damp, his clothes fresh. Tanner was still buried in his phone. Mustard took in their room. His side, with his perfectly smooth bed, the blanket pulled tight on all corners, his books, notebooks, and even laptop aligned in perfect, parallel lines on the desk. And then Tanner's side, with the sloppy duvet, pyramid of empty energy drink cans, and pile of dirty clothes.

"We have to clean up in here," he said.

"Who is *we*?" Tanner said into his phone screen.

Mustard looked at him. "Okay. *You* have to clean up in here."

Tanner paused his scrolling, then threw the phone to the side. "Fine." He stood, straightened his clothes, then started chucking—trash into one bin, laundry into another.

Mustard glanced down at the phone, still lying faceup on the couch. The screen displayed a comments section—a mix of heart-eyed and crying emojis, mostly. He sidled closer, trying not to look like he was spying.

> OMGGGGGGGGGG This one's my favorite. #ripvaughnangel Gone too soon!!!!!!1!1!1!1!1!1!

> this one's about emily I know it. they were such a gorgeous couple. I wish she'd do another video.

> ikr? we know it was self-defense emily!! don't be afraid #freeemilypryce

> Lolol everyone knows this channel is run by her lawyers to help her out.

> Idiots she's not even in jail. She's at that prep school. That's how she even knew Vaughn to help him with his music.

> you people are so gullible! Vaughn isn't dead. Just watch. they're about to "find" more of his music. What a scam. lololololol

Wait, this was why Tanner had quit crew? Had dumped Amber? To follow the comments section of Vaughn Green's music channel?

Maybe Mustard wasn't the only one who needed to keep himself busy.

Tensions had been particularly high on campus ever since Dr. Brown's death. The quiet dread suffusing the campus ever since the explosion of violence around the SATs had erupted into open panic. Everyone had been waiting for the next disaster, and another dead headmaster in Tudor House felt like the start of a third wave.

Mustard knew Scarlett had been the one to find the body. Knew it because of the seven emails, three voicemails, and thirty-one text messages she had sent to him either individually or through the #MurderCrew group chat. He had them all muted on his phone—for reasons not entirely related to that horrific hashtag—but, notifications or not, he'd still read the texts. Scarlett had many thoughts about Dr. Brown's death, which was a wonder for someone who appeared to have observed so little about it.

Mustard hadn't been the one to make that point, though. It had been someone else.

So, obviously they didn't need his input.

Besides, Dr. Brown had died of unregulated hypertension. Scarlett hadn't seen anything on the body because there was nothing to see. Strokes didn't leave marks, and it was no surprise that Dr. Brown had stressed herself into an early grave. What was actually shocking is that no one else at Blackbrook was going the same way.

Mustard watched Tanner's frantic attempts at cleaning.

"I heard about you and Amber," he said to his roommate's back.

Tanner stopped and turned. He pushed his shaggy hair out of his eyes and looked away. "Yeah, well. It ran its course."

Mustard nodded. Things did that. You got it out of your system.

But Tanner wasn't finished. "I just—she wanted to go to prom and all, and I'm not down for that. They're doing another memorial. All these memorials . . . Dances are dumb enough anyway. I don't want to go to one that's also a funeral."

Mustard looked at his roommate's phone. "But you're a fan of Vaughn's music?"

"Yeah," Tanner said. "I mean, I always was. We used to play in a band for, like, five minutes freshman year. I had no idea he'd done all this stuff by himself."

"I knew him," Mustard said. "Because of the storm and stuff."

"Yeah. I remember. You had him over that time."

That wasn't exactly how it had gone, but Mustard wasn't in the mood to correct Tanner, or have him start asking questions about the rest of the Murder Crew, hashtag or none.

"All that stuff they say in the comments, about the car . . ." Tanner was saying.

"The car?" Mustard asked.

"Yeah. They were saying that manager guy—the one who tried to kill Orchid—"

"Keith Grayson," Mustard said. He knew from the group chat. And, well, the news. The man had also gone by Ash, in his role as life coach to Peacock. Now there was a real sicko.

"Yeah. They said that he killed his other clients by sabotaging their car. They wound up driving off a cliff."

Really? Mustard hadn't known that part. Orchid texted almost as rarely as Mustard himself.

"The Steelman twins. They were friends of hers—Emily's. Orchid's."

Okay, so maybe Mustard should be paying closer attention to #MurderCrew.

Tanner shrugged. "I don't know. It's weird. Amber said Vaughn drove Orchid around in that car. In Rusty's car, the day before. And then for it to go off the cliff like that, just the same . . ."

"How did he sabotage the car?" Mustard blurted. "With the Steelman girls?"

Tanner's brow furrowed. "I don't know."

"Because I saw Keith." He'd helped load him in Rusty's car. "And if he wasn't dead already, he nearly was. So if you think he grabbed the wheel or whatever—"

"No," said Tanner. "I don't think that."

Peacock had no memory of what happened in the moments before the crash. But Mustard had never suspected foul play. It had been a foggy morning, and Vaughn was probably driving distracted—he'd just witnessed his girlfriend brain a dude with a wrench. Also, he'd been upset already. Raging at Mustard about covering up Rusty's murder . . . Although, that hadn't exactly been what he was shouting about. Actually, it might have been the opposite. He'd said they'd accused someone of murder? Mustard wasn't entirely sure. It had all happened so fast.

And if he couldn't remember that, it was little wonder Peacock couldn't remember a crash off a bridge into a ravine in which she was the only survivor.

"Maybe he'd already sabotaged the car," Tanner said now. "Because he thought Orchid might be in it."

"Like, cut the brake lines?" Mustard asked. "On the off chance Vaughn was going to give Orchid a ride and go careening toward a cliff?"

"I don't know, man. It's Blackbrook."

It certainly was.

"It's just—Vaughn died in a car crash. Vaughn's parents died in a car crash. Vaughn's—" He broke off, shaking his head. "It's a lot."

It certainly was that, too. "Accidents."

A lot of accidents. But it happened that way, sometimes.

Tanner shook himself all over. "Sorry. I got real dark. Let's do something."

At the very least, a change in subject. "Okay. What?"

"I don't know. A party?"

Mustard looked around their barely tolerable disaster area. "Here?"

"Yeah. Meet some new girls . . ." Tanner trailed off.

Mustard didn't blame him. Even before the murders, Blackbrook was a small campus. These days, it was tiny. That's why you had to be so careful with what you did, and who you did it with. Most girls left on campus were so tight with Amber they'd throw a drink in Tanner's face before consenting to be his rebound.

"Maybe invite freshmen?" Mustard suggested. Though an evening entertaining a gaggle of freshmen girls in his dorm room sounded worse than a month of KP duty.

Tanner didn't seem to relish the thought, either. "How about a boys' night?" he suggested. "Movies, pizza . . ."

"Cool." It had been ages since he and Tanner had just hung out. "There's a Rocky Point guy on the cleanup crew who could get us beer."

"Awesome. Seven?" Tanner had his phone out and was jabbing away. "Just add anyone you want to the invite."

Wait, what? Mustard's phone buzzed in his pocket. He looked at it.

> Movie night @7 Chez Tanner/
> Mustard. Avengers or Ocean's 11.
> Vote below!

Below that appeared three pizza emojis, a film strip, and a witch's cauldron Mustard presumed was code for "brew."

Mustard checked to see who else Tanner had invited. A few of the guys Tanner played squash with, some rowers, a couple other students Mustard vaguely knew, and then . . . yep.

Crap. He should have said something to Tanner. Though saying something was the entire problem, wasn't it?

His phone buzzed again. This time, it was a private message.

PLUM

> Um . . . movie night? What the hell?

5

Plum

At six fifty-six that evening, Finn Plum sat in his dorm room desk chair, twirling in circles and staring at the ceiling.

It was a pretty boring ceiling. There was the chunk missing from the drywall that looked a bit like a kangaroo mouse, and then the three small, perfectly round holes where Jin, his old roommate, had once launched pencils skyward. Before his parents had yanked him back home to Beijing.

Where it was safe.

If Finn were to die right now, like so many Blackbrook people before him, would he be happy that this was the last sight he saw? Would he regret spending this, his last night on Earth, sitting alone and staring at a dorm room ceiling?

He looked at his phone. Six fifty-seven now. And no new messages.

Of course not. There had been no new messages from Mustard for months. Not to Finn, and not on the #MurderCrew group chat, either. No messages, no phone calls, not a single email, and for such a small campus, it was amazing how little Finn managed to actually see him around.

Unless he made a special point of visiting the construction areas, and even then, Mustard was really good at not making eye contact.

Six fifty-eight. Finn wondered if the other guys would choose *The Avengers* or *Ocean's 11*. If this was the night you were going to die, what would you want your last movie to be?

Your last meal?

Your last kiss?

Sometimes Finn wondered if Vaughn Green's life had flashed before his eyes as he went over that cliff. If he'd thought of all the music he'd never be able to make. Scarlett and Orchid had done well by Vaughn, no denying that, but it still sucked. If Finn were to die tonight and people still went ahead and developed his dye formula and made millions, he supposed it would be better than never having accomplished anything at all, but he wouldn't get to enjoy any of it.

And if you didn't get to enjoy it, what was the point?

Of course, the last time he made that argument to someone, it hadn't gone over very well.

Seven o'clock. The party in Mustard and Tanner's room had officially started.

Finn resumed staring at the ceiling. He was not going to go unless Mustard texted him back. Which wasn't going to happen anyway, so he should probably think of something else to do with his evening.

Not that there was much else to do. Scarlett was busier than ever with her path to online domination. He'd never been close to Orchid, and it felt a bit weird to try to make friends with the former movie star now that everyone knew who she was. First of all, he didn't want to be some celebrity hound, and besides, it was hard to really get to know someone *after* you'd seen them bash a man's brains out.

Orchid used the #MurderCrew group chat only slightly more than Mustard did, anyway. Which left Finn, Scarlett, and Beth to talk among themselves.

He could call Beth, he supposed. He'd spent many nights with her this spring playing board games—the only kind of game she could play in her casts—in the Tudor House billiards room. It had gotten to the point where they'd figured out that they each had a decided advantage in a particular type of game—Beth would beat Finn's pants off in fast-paced card games or other things that required quick thinking and quicker actions, and get bored stiff by the kind of long-running games Finn favored, the ones where you built castles or towns or civilizations with twenty different kinds of pieces.

For a while, he'd wondered if he and Beth might get back together again, and once, after a particularly well-played round of Jenga, he'd thought about kissing her, but then he just . . . hadn't. Were they in the friend zone now? And if he could get to that point with Beth, who he'd been hung up on since freshman year, then why was he still checking his phone every five seconds to see if—

The phone buzzed on his desktop.

Finn grabbed it.

MUSTARD

Yeah, well, it was Tanner's idea.

Tanner's idea? Like, Tanner knew about them?

> **What is that supposed to mean?**

Mustard hadn't told Tanner. He wouldn't . . . would he?

Mustard wasn't responding, which was typical. Finn tossed the phone aside. He'd promised himself not to play these games anymore.

But then it buzzed again, and Finn sighed. The game was on.

MUSTARD

> It means I wasn't the one who made the invite list.

Finn knew a person couldn't actually growl a text message, but somehow Mustard managed it. He could just hear it, could just see the furrow on Mustard's brow as he fought with himself. Always himself, although he acted like he was fighting other people.

MUSTARD

> Anyway, are you coming?

FINN

> To the party I was accidentally invited to? Pass.

He had a busy evening planned of staring at the ceiling and trying not to think about Mustard.

Time was, he'd spend his free nights hidden away in the chemistry lab, working on his secret side project. But the sad

— 39 —

truth was, he'd gone as far as he could with the dye without more industrial equipment. What he really needed was to sell the formula. Take the money and run. However, it proved harder to call up people at chemical companies and sell them your valuable formulas than Finn had anticipated. Ever since he'd arrived on the Blackbrook campus, he'd heard the legend of Dick Fain, the famous former Blackbrook student who had created an industrial glue and made millions off it before he was even out of high school. But Finn had no idea how he'd managed it.

Plus, he couldn't risk any of the faculty at Blackbrook hearing about his work and trying to take a cut.

His phone buzzed again. Finn ignored it for five whole seconds.

MUSTARD

You weren't accidentally invited. Tanner wants you here.

FINN

Tanner.

Mustard wasn't the only one who could convey tone through a text.

MUSTARD

Yeah.

We invited a bunch of people, but Tanner pissed off his old crew buddies or something

FINN

> Wait, you want me to come to this party because no one else will? Sounds better by the second.

Another long stretch of silence.

MUSTARD

> Sorry I asked.

Finn scowled.

FINN

> Okay, I'm coming.

Sometimes, he really hated himself. Or he hated Mustard. Or something.

The weather had warmed significantly in the past week. Finn didn't even bother with a jacket as he made his way over to Mustard and Tanner's dorm. He took the stairs to their floor, then knocked on the door to their room.

Even when Mustard answered the door, he didn't meet Finn's eyes.

"Hey."

This was such mistake.

"Hey." He edged past him, being careful to not so much as brush up against his shoulder, and inside. Tanner was slumped on the couch, scrolling through his phone. The TV was queued up to play a Marvel movie. There was an untouched pizza sitting in its box on the coffee table, and a six-pack of beer beside it.

Some party.

"So! What are we watching?" Finn grabbed a slice of pizza and sat down on the couch next to Tanner. Next to Tanner, thank you very much. Mustard could find a place to sit elsewhere.

"You know what I don't get?" Tanner said, his eyes on his phone screen.

Finn glanced over—wait, was that Vaughn Green playing the guitar?

"When I was with Amber, all the guys would complain I didn't see them enough. And now I dumped her, and they are doing some stupid crew thing? Without me?"

Wait, Tanner broke up with Amber? How had Finn missed this piece of campus gossip?

"Well," Mustard said from his place on the windowsill, which was about as far as he could get from Finn without climbing outside, "you did quit the team."

"Yeah, because . . . whatever," Tanner said, and tossed the phone aside. "I can't win."

Finn watched as Tanner grabbed a beer and chugged. He gave Mustard a look that Mustard pretended not to see.

Tanner burped. "But at least we're not dead, right? That's an accomplishment at Blackbrook." He popped another beer and passed it to Finn. "Cheers."

Finn did not like beer. He turned and held the can out to Mustard. "Beer?"

Mustard started to reach for it, but the second his fingers touched Finn's the can slipped from his grasp and clattered to the ground. Both boys froze rather than chance moving closer to each other to grab the can. Meanwhile, beer spilled all over the hardwood.

"Anyone getting that?" Tanner asked.

"Yeah." Mustard stood and snatched the can off the floor, then set off into the hall in search of paper towels.

"We throw the best parties," Tanner said, and slumped back into the couch cushions.

Finn was very tempted to leave. He should never have come. He was just . . . repeatedly stupid when it came to Mustard.

He wished the other boy would just tell him the rules. For months now, Finn thought it was simple: No Contact. No talking about what had happened, no acknowledgment of each other out in public, no nothing.

No wonder he came running the first time Mustard asked to see him, even if it was to this pathetic event.

Mustard returned with wads of paper towels from the restroom, and Finn nearly jumped out of his seat.

"Sorry," he said quickly. "I thought maybe it was the dorm proctor."

"Quit a few days ago," Tanner said. "You know, when they found *her*."

Dr. Brown.

"You can't pay people enough to work at Blackbrook."

"So you guys don't have one at all anymore?"

"Nope," said Tanner. "We got an email from Winkle saying he was just over in the freshman hall, if we needed him. And you know, keep on the straight and narrow." He was onto his second beer. "But I've got soldier boy over there for that."

Finn looked at Mustard, who was scrubbing and scowling in equal measure.

"Straight and narrow," he echoed. Loudly.

Mustard lobbed a wad of beer-soaked towels at the garbage can. Then another, and a third. *Whomp. Whomp. Whomp.*

Mustard had excellent aim. Finn remembered how, in the intake file he and Scarlett had stolen from the administration, it said he'd started hunting when he was four.

"Doesn't matter, anyway," Tanner said now. "This school is done for."

Finn did not disagree. He was planning on begging his parents to let him drop out as soon as they were all home for the summer.

"But that's going to be a problem," he said, "For Curry Chem."

"Why?" Finn asked. Not that he would be willing to approach Curry Chem. There were too many of their execs on the Blackbrook board.

Tanner shrugged. "Blah blah, patent licenses. Curry likes the work that comes out of Blackbrook. That's why they make sure they have so many people on the board. No school, and that *special relationship* comes to an end."

This was exactly what Finn was afraid of. If he had to split the rights to his dye with Blackbrook, then Blackbrook could force him to sell the work to whoever they chose, and at the rates the school agreed were fair. The school, with all their board members who also worked for Curry.

"Is that why Dr. Brown was sent in to be headmaster?" he asked. "Because she was a Curry exec?"

Tanner didn't say anything for a long time. "I don't know what she was sent here to do. I don't even know if she did, in the end."

"To fix things," said Finn. That's what she said when she was yelling at them.

Tanner raised his head and looked Finn right in the eyes. His expression was haunted. "Oh yeah. Cause things are fixed for sure."

And then he opened another beer.

Oh, right. Tanner Curry, of the Curry Chemical Currys, probably knew Dr. Brown long before she'd shown up on campus.

Finn sat back, his brow furrowed. "I'm sorry," he said. "I hadn't thought about the fact that you probably knew her."

"Since I was born," he said, between gulps. "And I was probably the last one to see her alive, too. She dragged me in there the morning she died to tell me in no uncertain terms how disappointed they all were in me. I keep thinking if we hadn't fought—" he stopped talking, then burped.

"Tanner," said Mustard, coming forward. "Man—"

"It's fine!" Tanner slammed down the can and swiped at the air in front of him. "Just—let's not talk about it, okay? If I'm not going to talk about it with my *girlfriend*, I'm certainly not going to—" He cut himself off and his face went pale, his eyes widening. "Oh, God, I'm going to be sick."

Then he lunged for the door and stumbled out.

Finn looked at Mustard, who was looking at the door. "You want to go after him?"

"No," said Mustard dryly. "I'm pretty sure he wants to be alone to puke. And cry. I would."

Finn nodded. Him too.

But now there was another problem. Finn didn't know exactly what the rules were between the two of them, but if there was a list out there, the first thing on it would be *Do Not Be Alone Together.*

He remembered the last time they were alone together.

It hadn't gone well. It had been a week or so after Vaughn's death, when they'd all returned to campus and tried to pretend their lives would get back on track. And it had started out fine, all whispers about how much they'd missed each other, Mustard's hands, and his shoulders, and the kind of rough, breath-stealing kisses Finn thought only Mustard was capable of—and then Finn had opened his big mouth, and that was that.

No Contact.

"I had no idea," Mustard was saying. "Amber even told me he was going through a rough time, but I thought she meant crew and stuff. I should have put it together, but he never said anything—"

"People don't always say what's going on with them," Finn said. "*Mustard.*"

And then Mustard did look at Finn, for one brief, glorious moment. Except it wasn't glorious at all.

"Don't," Mustard warned.

"So . . . we're just never going to talk about it, then?"

"Yeah," Mustard snapped. "Never works for me."

Finn took a step forward. "Well, it doesn't work for me."

Mustard stumbled back, looking for a second as graceless and drunk as his roommate. "Tanner's coming back any second, and I know *you* don't care about stuff like that, but—"

"You don't know what I care about!" Finn blurted. He glared at Mustard. Screw this. He was out of there.

In the hall, Finn got his bearings, then headed toward the bathroom to say good-bye to Tanner.

But the bathroom was empty. He looked for a pair of feet under the stalls, listened for the sound of retching, but nothing. The door opened behind him.

He turned and saw Mustard coming in behind him.

"I got a text from Tanner," Mustard said. "He went for a walk to clear his head."

Finn nodded. "Okay, well, I'm going to—"

"Wait." The word escaped from Mustard half-broken, very battered. "Just . . . wait."

Finn swallowed, and waited. In the bathroom. There was a drip in the sink. He could hear the pipes running water to other floors.

"Look," Mustard said at last, "you can do whatever you want to. You can be whatever you want. But that doesn't mean I can."

Finn snorted. "That's such crap."

"What did you expect? That you could just tell everyone and I'd be cool—" He stopped talking as the door opened and another student walked in.

Finn rolled his eyes and grabbed the door. This whole thing was a huge mistake.

Mustard followed him out into the hall and cocked his head at him to return to his room.

No. *No.* No. And then Finn followed him anyway.

But as soon as they were alone in the room, Finn started talking. "First of all, I didn't tell *everyone*. Like I said, I came out to my parents and my brother. Because I love them and they are my family. And they don't even know you so what difference could it *possibly* make—"

Mustard looked horrified. "*And* your brother?"

"Yes. He's a junior at Eli. And I told him my business, not yours."

"Your business," Mustard drawled coldly. "The great personal revelation you learned while hooking up with some guy named Mustard. No way that'll get back to me. How do you not get this? *Your business* doesn't exist in a vacuum."

"It exists even if you don't speak to me for four months," Finn snapped. "Even if I don't ever find another guy I like ever again. I'm bisexual."

"Shhh!"

Oh for crying out loud! Finn took two steps forward and put his hands on Mustard's shoulders. When the other boy didn't move, he leaned in for a kiss.

Mustard drew back.

There. There was the answer. Finn pushed him away, glaring angrily. "You know what? Don't call me again. Not for anything."

And then he made toward the door again. This time, he wasn't going to be talked out of it.

"Plum," Mustard called. "Wait."

Nope. Finn paused and turned. "What now?"

"What did you tell Scarlett?"

"Are you kidding me?" He wasn't going to dignify that with an answer. Let Mustard talk to Scarlett—or not—himself. This was over. For good.

6

Orchid

"Six months," Amber wailed, scooping chocolate ice cream directly from the carton. "Six months and just like that, it's over. How dare he?"

"What a jerk," Violet agreed. She was hogging the strawberries and cream, but Orchid didn't want to make a big deal out of it.

Scarlett nodded sympathetically and took another scoop of mango sorbet from her plate.

Orchid was slowly making her way through her dish of butter pecan. They were all sitting around, letting their hair dye process and eating junk food. It was Scarlett's idea of a girls' night, and as far as Orchid was concerned, it was more depressing than if they'd all just stayed in their rooms and sulked. Like pink hair was going to cheer her up?

She hadn't gotten six months with Vaughn. She hadn't gotten six days. Not really. They'd had those weeks on opposite coasts, texting each other in the wee hours of the morning. They'd had that one makeout session in the ballroom, that one night cuddled close on a hospital bench. And yet here she was, acting as brokenhearted as Amber.

Seeing ghosts.

Scarlett thought Orchid was crazy, and maybe she was right. When they'd read *Romeo and Juliet* in English class, everyone had made fun of the two leads, killing themselves over a romance of a few days. And here she was, acting just the same way.

Maybe Juliet hadn't killed herself because she was so in love with Romeo. Maybe she just felt guilty that all those people died because of her.

"You know," said Peacock, who, like Amber, was eating her mint chocolate chip right out of the carton. "After what Finn did to me freshman year, I wanted to kill him. For, like, two years."

The other girls looked at her.

Her eyes went round. "What? I didn't, *obviously*. But I wanted to." She took another big spoonful of ice cream. "So, you know, Amber. Feel your feelings. All of them."

"Beth," Scarlett warned.

"What?" Peacock asked.

"I don't think we encourage people to have murderous feelings. Especially not at Blackbrook."

Peacock shrugged and stabbed at her ice cream.

Orchid bit her lip. Did she have murderous feelings? She was, after all, a murderer.

I can't let you become a murderer.

She didn't know if she'd felt anything at all in the moment she'd attacked Keith with the wrench. Hadn't thought, hadn't felt, just acted. He'd been trying to choke her to death, and then he'd miraculously let go and turned around, and she'd taken her only chance.

Open and shut self-defense, her lawyers had said.

But she barely remembered it at all. Not like the other night, when she'd seen Vaughn Green on the other side of the ravine.

Which meant she was crazy, right? That she could recall a figment of her imagination with perfect clarity, but the most momentous experience of her life was mostly a blur?

"He's all torn up about Dr. Brown. She was practically his godmother, did you know that? But he won't even talk about it."

Peacock made a sound like *harrumph*.

Some people didn't want reminders of death. After the accident, Orchid had her lawyers ask about Vaughn's body. She knew money was tight for him, and wanted to make sure there was enough for a funeral. But all her lawyers found out was that his family had collected the body, and they were keeping the memorial private.

They clearly didn't want to invite the girl who had been responsible for his death.

After the ice cream, the girls all rinsed and blow-dried their hair, and oohed and ahhed over the results. Peacock had done blue tips again, and Scarlett had put in precisely one deep-red streak. On the bottom, where it barely showed. She argued that since she'd had to bleach it out first, she was the only one making a permanent commitment. Violet had chosen bangs over color, and they'd highlighted Amber's hair. Orchid had allowed her friends talk her into a purply-rose color, to match her fake name.

It looked nice enough, but she'd dyed her hair too many times in her life to really be shocked by the results. Red when she'd been a child star, a muddy brown when she'd been in hiding at Blackbrook. She supposed orchid hair suited her better than the flame-colored locks she'd worn for the heiress movies. As soon as Scarlett let them, Orchid headed upstairs, where she spent several minutes examining her new pastel tresses and marveling over the fact that she'd agreed to do it, after all these years of trying to stay as hidden as possible.

But hiding was no longer an option. After the accident, there had been a week or so of paparazzi presence—mostly on the mainland, waiting outside her lawyer's office or the court-room. Blackbrook had locked the campus down, and Orchid never went anywhere. Soon enough, they'd given up.

The other kids had whispered and pointed and stared for a few days. And then they had stopped. There were other, more important concerns when it came to being a student at Black-brook, like passing advanced chemistry—and not getting killed.

Before bed, she checked Vaughn's stats again. So many hits, so many comments.

Orchid had gotten really good at not reading the com-ments. The ones where people liked Emily were fine, but even the few that attacked her—for becoming Orchid, for having anything to do with Vaughn—hurt so much she could barely function afterward. It made her feel cheap and dirty, like when she was still a little girl in Hollywood, and she'd had to deal with the comments from grown men. But she couldn't stay away from the site entirely. She liked watching the numbers go up. Liked seeing how many fans he had.

Orchid went to bed listening to Vaughn singing, and when she woke in the middle of the night, it was as if he'd whispered the answer in her ear:

Of course! That was why he was haunting her. His family!

When her lawyers had delivered the news, she'd been too overcome with guilt to think about it, but now it seemed clear as day. Vaughn had always told her that his parents and grandmother were dead, but he must have some family—some distant family who had collected his body and buried it. Some heirs who technically owned the rights to Vaughn's music. Rights that she and Scarlett were stepping on by posting it online.

She needed to find them and make it right.

The next morning, before Scarlett could wake up and talk her out of it, Orchid got dressed, including sturdy walking shoes, and set off for Rocky Point. It was a cool, clear day, and the sunlight glittered on the sea and burned away all the morning fog. Orchid's hair looked a very bright pink this morning, so she pulled it back and covered it with a hoodie. She didn't see anyone else on campus, except for Mustard, who appeared to be completing some kind of marathon, from the look of his sweat-soaked thermal. He did little more than nod to her as they passed each other on the sidewalk.

Orchid was relieved. She didn't want to argue with anyone. She had to do this.

She had never before walked into the little village of Rocky Point. Sometimes, the school van would carry kids in for excursions, and she knew lots of students who had made the hike. Vaughn did it every day, she supposed.

But she never had.

Along with the hoodie, jeans, and hiking boots, Orchid wore sunglasses, as if she really were an undercover movie star. When she finally made it to the village, she stood for fifteen minutes outside the Rocky Point hardware store and food mart, willing herself to go inside and talk to a clerk.

Finally, she saw a woman approaching the store on foot— clearly a local. When the woman exited a few minutes later with a cup of coffee, Orchid approached.

"Excuse me, I was wondering if you could give me directions?"

The woman eyed her, her expression unreadable. "Maybe."

"I'm looking for the Greens. The, uh . . . the family of Vaughn Green? Do you know where they live?"

The woman snorted. "Would have thought you'd know a thing like that, Miss Pryce."

Orchid's gaze dropped to the asphalt. This was exactly what she'd been afraid of.

But then the woman seemed to take pity on her. She pointed up the road. "Third left, second house down. With the blue shutters. His brother's probably home."

Orchid's heart stopped beating. "His *brother*?" she sputtered.

"Yeah," said the lady, with an incredulous shake of her head. "Oliver."

And then she walked off, leaving Orchid reeling.

Had Vaughn ever mentioned a brother to her? All that time, she'd heard of dead parents and a dead grandmother, but he'd never once mentioned a brother. Come to think of it, she had no idea at all who Vaughn lived with. But it had to be someone, right? They didn't just let kids live alone.

You live alone, idiot.

But Orchid's emancipation had taken lawyers and a for- tune to enact. Vaughn had to have some kind of guardian.

It must be this brother—this Oliver. Maybe he was some much older stepbrother or something who had gotten saddled with custody after Vaughn's grandmother died. They obviously weren't close at all. Orchid would swear she'd never heard Vaughn say his name once.

Three streets and two houses later, she stood in front of a dilapidated double-wide with peeling paint and a sagging porch. There were empty window boxes and what looked like the remains of a garden out front. There was no car in the driveway.

Maybe the brother wasn't home.

She knocked on the door. No answer.

Vaughn's house. His guitar was in there. His books. His clothes.

She took a deep breath and twisted the knob.

The door opened.

"Thank goodness for small towns," Orchid whispered, and stepped inside.

The place was a disaster. Ancient furniture was buried under piles of newspaper clippings, and dusty shelves crowded with old knickknacks were hidden behind tacked-up printouts of even more. Articles about the accident, about Keith and Blackbrook and Vaughn and . . . her. She saw her face winking out of shadowed corners—usually old red-carpet photos from when she'd been twelve, but the occasional publicity still and a few grainy shots of that time she'd had to appear in court. There were dirty plates lying around, and the place smelled musty, like dampness and old books.

The decor was old-fashioned, ornate dining chairs and ceramic figurines, and Orchid realized that this house must have belonged to Vaughn's grandmother. Either that or this brother of his had very grandmotherly taste. There was a cluster of family photos on the wall behind the TV. Orchid drew closer.

"Oh God," she whispered, when she saw a picture of Mrs. White. She was younger then, but it was her, smiling next to another young woman as they worked in a garden. Another picture of that woman with a little girl, and half a dozen of that girl at various ages as she grew into a pretty and serious-eyed young woman. Orchid recognized her face. She must be Vaughn's dead mom.

Then a picture of the same woman laughing in front of a Christmas tree with a huge pregnant belly. Orchid stepped down the row.

The next picture showed two babies sleeping side by side in little matching onesies. And then another, of two toddlers staring up at the camera with serious eyes. By the time she got to the third set, when the boys were older and their faces had settled into the features she knew so well, the bottom had dropped out of Orchid's reality.

What was she looking at?

What was she looking at???

Two identical boys riding bikes. Two identical boys digging for clams. Two boys side by side, in a double frame for school pictures, looking so much alike you'd think it was just Vaughn in two different shirts . . .

Orchid gasped.

"Don't be afraid," said a voice at her back. Vaughn's voice.

She whirled around and he was standing right there in the room, his hands raised. Real. *Real.*

"You're—" she blurted. "You're—" *Vaughn Vaughn Vaughn Vaughn Vaughn* . . .

"Oliver," finished the boy. "Vaughn's twin brother."

Vaughn was a twin?

7

Orchid

don't understand," Orchid whispered, staring at the mirage before her. "Vaughn didn't have a twin."

The ghost of Vaughn Green frowned. "I assure you, Vaughn had a twin. Do you think he told you everything because you made out once or twice?"

"I—" Orchid shook her head wildly. "I—"

"Don't be afraid, Orchid." He shoved some papers off the couch. "Have a seat, I'll explain everything."

There was really no other choice. Wordlessly, Orchid took a seat. The couch cushions were dingy and sunken, but she wasn't sure her legs could support her much longer.

Vaughn had *lied* to her. All those weeks of sharing intimate texts, that one precious night in Tudor House. His music . . .

This was impossible. She was in a nightmare.

The ghost of Vaughn Green shifted piles of paper to make more room on the couch, and Orchid clasped her hands in her lap to keep from trying to touch him. His buzzed hair, his sharp jaw. Was he thinner than Vaughn? Did Vaughn have those shadows under his eyes? Was all of that just what happened to you in the four months after your brother had died?

Oliver. *Oliver.* Some older stepbrother he lived with out of necessity was one thing, but how could Vaughn have never mentioned a twin?

He sat across from her, well beyond arm's reach. "Can I get you anything? I don't have much, but I think there's some tea . . ."

He trailed off, but she said nothing. Just stared.

"I'm so sorry," she said at last, as her eyes began to sting. "I'm so sorry. You look just like him."

"Yeah," he said, his tone clipped. "That's why it worked."

"Why what worked?"

"The scam."

She shook her head in confusion. "What scam?"

He blinked at her. "Wow, you still don't get it! I guess we were way more careful than I thought." He laughed, but there wasn't a shred of humor in it. "The scam we were pulling on Blackbrook. We were both going, at once. Both of us, on Vaughn's scholarship. Taking every class we could, pretending to be the same person."

Orchid could not believe her ears.

"That's why we couldn't mention having a twin. We couldn't talk about the other brother—about me—at all. People would ask what he was doing, or want to meet him, and the whole thing would fall apart."

"Both of you?" Orchid was still working to wrap her brain around this. She remembered once that Scarlett had told her that Vaughn was taking a ridiculous number of classes. That she had no idea how he'd found time to study so hard. Well, now they had their answer. "Wait," she said, as things began clicking into place. "My history class. You'd act like you didn't know me—"

"The system wasn't perfect," Oliver said. "We didn't share enough. We'd seem flaky or forgetful. That's why we could never make friends. It was hard enough keeping our schedules straight."

Orchid leaned back, staring at him in utter disbelief. And then another, more disturbing realization floated up. She felt sick to her stomach. "Who—who was I *dating*?" she asked weakly.

Oliver took a deep breath and looked down at his lap. "Vaughn," he said. "You were with Vaughn."

"Always?"

He groaned in frustration. "What kind of sickos do you think we are?"

The kind that pretend to be a single person, Orchid wanted to say. But she was still in shock. After all, her dead boyfriend was sitting across the couch from her. Or, sort of her dead boyfriend? She was very confused.

"Who was the musician?" she asked now. "Both of you?"

"No, Vaughn. He took after our parents like that." Oliver's face was grim and set.

Right. The musicians who had died in a car wreck while on tour. They ended up having everything in common, in the end. "Who was with us in the storm?"

"Vaughn!" Oliver shouted. "Well, mostly Vaughn. I tried to steal his spot in the afternoon and he fought me for it. Gave me a black eye so I couldn't go back. But I gave him a bloody nose."

Orchid remembered the bloody nose. This was incredible.

"How long are we playing twenty questions?" Oliver spat at her. "You didn't know I was here, so what were you planning on doing after you broke into my house?"

"I—I was looking for Vaughn's family—"

"After four months, you come looking?" That laugh again. Smug, humorless. "Not in too much of a hurry to pay your respects to your boyfriend's family."

"I'm so sorry," she said. "I didn't know—"

"And now you do," he cut in. "Now what?"

Now what, indeed? She took a deep breath and then, very carefully, she reached out and touched his arm. Not Vaughn's arm. Not Vaughn's sweatshirt, though she could swear she'd seen it on him before. Oliver.

He looked down at her fingers as if they were some alien thing.

"I'm so sorry," she repeated. "I'm so sorry about your brother."

His lip trembled, then drew into a tight line. For all the tears she'd shed over Vaughn these last few months, she knew they were no match for what this boy must have gone through. Alone. But he didn't have to be alone anymore. He may not be ready to cry in front of her, but she could still try to help him.

She owed it to Vaughn.

Emboldened, she went on. "What are you going to do . . . Oliver? If you were taking classes at Blackbrook, you're not enrolled in the local school. What are you going to do about school?"

He was still staring at her hand on his arm, and she took it back. He followed the movement with his eyes, then slowly, his gaze traveled up her body to her face. And when he spoke, his tone had softened.

"I don't know. We didn't plan for this. The idea was to get our diploma, win two scholarships to college, accept them both, and get out of this town, once and for all. Once we were in college, I could 'change my name' to Oliver, and move on with my life."

Wow. It was diabolical, and also brilliant. Whose idea had it been, Vaughn's or Oliver's? "Would that even work?"

"We'll never know now, will we?" Oliver shrugged. "I can't go back to Blackbrook. I can't be Vaughn full time when Vaughn is dead. I'm nobody now. I have nothing."

Orchid wanted to touch him again, but she didn't dare. This wasn't right. Here she thought she had been suffering, but she hadn't even scratched the surface. This boy had lost his twin brother and his whole life plan in one fell swoop. He'd spent four months alone in this wreck of a house while she and Scarlett had made his brother into a star.

She wiped ineffectually at her eyes, but the tears kept coming. "That's why I'm here," she said at last. "It's the music. Vaughn's music."

His eyes met hers again, interest lighting up the coppery green depths.

"I realized we didn't really have the rights to it. His family—you—it's your music. Legally, it's yours, and every-thing we've been doing with it—"

"You're actually doing something with it," Oliver said. "More than he ever did."

There were acres of bitterness fenced inside that sentence.

Orchid thought about the months Oliver had spent alone in this house, far more haunted than she had ever been.

"No one would hear about it if it weren't for you and Scarlett."

She raised her eyebrows in surprise. "How do you know it's Scarlett?"

"Of course it's Scarlett," Oliver scoffed. "I know how she operates."

Right. Right. He knew them all. He was pretending to be Vaughn half the time. This was going to be hard to wrap her brain around.

"And even if I didn't, I watched you all put it together. I saw Scarlett interacting with the fans online. You know how hard it's been all these months not to say anything in the group chat?"

Again, she looked at him in disbelief. "You're on the group chat? The #MurderCrew group chat?"

"You all never took me off it—took Vaughn off it."

"But Vaughn's phone was destroyed in the crash!" cried Orchid. How many times had she heard Scarlett lamenting that fact, about all the potential recordings that had been obliterated along with Vaughn's life.

"Yeah, well, we both have access to his account, for obvious reasons." Oliver took his phone out of his pocked and pulled up the #MurderCrew chat.

It felt strange, somehow, knowing he'd been on there all those months, eavesdropping on them talking about Vaughn's death, and Scarlett's campaign for Vaughn's music, and Orchid's defense, and Peacock's recovery. Oliver was a stranger.

Except . . . he wasn't? If his story was to be believed, half of the things they all thought were Vaughn had been Oliver all along!

She felt faint. "I think I might need some tea after all."

Oliver went to the kitchen to find clean mugs, and Orchid tried to catch her breath. It had been weeks since she'd had a full-fledged panic attack. Maybe the time had come.

She thought about the lyrics to Vaughn's songs. Always about secrets, about lying about who he was, about feeling torn in two. She had thought it was about the struggle of being a scholarship student, at living halfway between the life of a Rocky Point townie and a Blackbrook kid. Turns out, it hadn't been a metaphor at all.

He had a whole song entitled "Another Me." Orchid squeezed her eyes shut in mortification. He'd basically been screaming the truth, and she hadn't heard him.

That night, in the ballroom, when she'd kissed him!

I believe when you really care about someone, it's easy to see the truth of who they are.

Except she hadn't seen that. Orchid had probably paid more attention to Vaughn than anyone at Blackbrook, and she hadn't picked up a fundamental truth about his identity.

She looked at the kitchen, where Oliver was messing around with a saucepan of water.

Was this really the truth? It seemed incredible. Outrageous. But, what possible purpose would it serve for Oliver to lie to her about something like this? Besides, it was the only thing that explained why Vaughn had never told her about his own twin brother.

It still knocked her sideways, though. Even Orchid, who had spent three years hiding her true identity, could hardly fathom what Oliver claimed he and his brother had done. Orchid had a fortune at her disposal, she had lawyers and accountants to help her set up fake IDs and shell companies from which her fake parents could pay her bills.

She looked around the dingy old house. These boys had pulled off a far more massive scam, with nothing. How could they have gotten away with something like this for three years without anyone at Blackbrook realizing what they were up to?

Unless people *had* realized it, and were helping. Mrs. White and Rusty were both close to Vaughn—and Oliver, she supposed. They were from Rocky Point, and they had to have figured it out. Maybe they had been in on the scheme from the beginning. Rusty could have fudged their work-study requirements so it hadn't interfered with their class schedules, and Mrs. White—

Well, was there anything the woman wouldn't do? She'd murdered the headmaster over a development plan—

A chill stole across Orchid's skin as the thought occurred to her. If it even had been the development plan? It had always seemed out of character for the old hippie to snap and stab a man, even if he was threatening to knock down the house she'd lived in for decades.

But maybe that wasn't why Mrs. White had killed Headmaster Boddy at all. Orchid remembered how frantic Vaughn had been, that night during the storm when he'd recognized the knife that Mrs. White had used. He'd been terrified of something that he'd never quite explained to Orchid.

Had Mrs. White killed Headmaster Boddy because he'd discovered the Greens' secret? If Vaughn were exposed, then he'd certainly be expelled. His entire future would be destroyed. Mrs. White—his godmother—would want to protect him from that. Maybe she would even kill for it.

Orchid started in her seat as he returned to the room, a steaming mug in each hand. "I hope you don't take milk in your tea," he said. "We—I—don't have any."

She stared at him, unblinking. It was Vaughn. His voice, his walk, the sheepish, apologetic half-shrug he gave her as he set the mugs down on the scratched surface of the coffee table.

"It's fine," she said. She wasn't sure she could taste anything right now anyway.

Oliver sat down next to her again—much closer this time. Did he smell like Vaughn? Did she dare breathe him in?

"I know it's a lot to take in," he said.

All those nights, she'd listened to Vaughn's songs knowing he was gone forever, and it was her fault. Her sweet, gentle, poetic boyfriend.

The one who'd lied to her every single day.

The one who hadn't been upset by the revelation that she was not who she claimed to be. At the time, she'd been amazed at how cool he was with it. He'd known she was Emily Pryce and just sort of . . . shrugged it off. But duplicity was in the very air Vaughn breathed. So what if Orchid had changed her identity? At least she didn't have to share it.

She was so confused.

"I—I'm just trying to figure it out," she stammered. "When was I with Vaughn and when was I . . . with you?"

He shook his head and grabbed his mug of tea, possibly more for something to do with his hands than anything else, as he, too, made no attempt to drink it. "You'll make yourself crazy with that kind of stuff. I know I have, and I've been living this life for years."

And now he had no life at all.

She looked at him. *Vaughn.* Gaunt and tired, maybe, but still the boy she remembered. Sort of.

"It's hard to be a twin, you know?" Oliver said into his mug.

Orchid shook herself free. This wasn't Vaughn, and she had to remember that.

He went on. "You want to be distinct from your brother so much that sometimes you end up clinging to something that's artificial. You pursue things not because it's what you really want, but because what you want more than anything else is to be *different*. One decides he wants to play music like his parents, so the other one won't even sing carols at Christmas. One is determined to cause trouble, so the other thinks he has to be good enough for both of them."

She laughed at that, in spite of herself. "So, were you the good twin or the bad twin?"

But Oliver gave her very serious look. "I don't know. I think it depends on your definition."

If someone had asked Orchid before, she'd say that Vaughn had to be the good part of any configuration. But it turned out that she didn't know him as well as she had thought.

Maybe the person she'd known wasn't even Vaughn.

"I think I have the same definitions as everyone else," she said.

"That's what everyone thinks," Oliver says. "But, come on, *Orchid McKee*. You don't even have to read half the press about you to know that's not true."

He wasn't wrong. She had killed a man. She had lied to everyone. She was the reason this boy's brother was dead. All she had to do was look at the comments section on Vaughn's channel. For every ten people who posted in support of her, there was one or two who believed *she* was the one who deserved to die.

If anyone should be furious with her right now, it was Oliver. But here he was, bringing her tea and telling her secrets that even Vaughn hadn't revealed.

"Untangling which parts of my personality are things I chose for myself and which part I chose so I could be different from my brother is going to take a long time," Oliver said now. "I can't be the person I was when I was living a half-life with him. The plans we each had are ruined. There's no going back."

Orchid's breath caught in her throat. "No," she said carefully. "There's not. What's done is done. That's what I've had to accept these past few months. Everything I did, every choice I made—I can't take any of it back. But I do want to fix things going forward. That's why I released Vaughn's music. I thought it was a tribute to him. But I didn't think things through. It doesn't belong to me." Oliver was in a bad situation. She could at least help him there. "It belongs to you."

Oliver looked at her again, and for the first time, she saw something approximating a smile on his face.

8

Scarlett

Scarlett could not believe her eyes, and her ears seemed to be proving a little untrustworthy as well. This was way too much to take in this early on a Saturday.

Besides, she'd already come face to face with one dead person this week. She really didn't need to meet another.

She sat in the sunlight of the Tudor House dining hall, the remains of her breakfast on the table in front of her. Before her stood Orchid, who had criminally pulled back her new pink tresses into a messy bun under a hoodie, and a person who had just confessed to an even more monstrous cover-up.

"I'm sorry," Scarlett said, holding up her hands. "You've been on the group chat for months now and you never bothered to tell us?"

"Yes," said this—this person, this Oliver Green. Wow, the resemblance was uncanny. Of course, identical twins were called that for a reason, but she had never really put it to the test.

Then again, it was possible she was always dealing with this one. Her brain hurt just thinking about it.

"I didn't know how to tell you," he went on. "I didn't want to freak you out."

"Hmm," said Scarlett. She looked at Orchid. How was she taking all of this? More traumatized than usual?

But Orchid seemed, well, if not okay, at least calmer than the last time she and Scarlett had discussed this topic. And at least she knew she was no longer seeing ghosts.

Not real ones, anyway.

"I don't think the group chat is the real issue here," Orchid pointed out.

Easy for Orchid to say! She hardly ever talked on it. Scarlett tried desperately to recall if she'd written anything unflattering about Vaughn in the last few months on #MurderCrew. Almost definitely, if she was being honest. There was little love lost between the two of them.

Or maybe there was little love lost between Oliver and her.

"So which one of you made my life a living hell for the last few years?"

Oliver blinked at her innocently. "Um, Vaughn?" he suggested uneasily. "I mean, I hope I didn't do anything to put us at odds."

Scarlett pursed her lips. "Okay, so we've got the nice but useless twin. You aren't Orchid's boyfriend, you don't play music—"

"Scarlett!" Orchid exclaimed.

"What? Why did you bring him here?"

Orchid shook her head in disbelief. "Because Vaughn has a secret twin brother who it turns out we all know and who we have been stealing from by producing Vaughn's music without his consent." She glared at Scarlett, who pouted.

Oh. That.

"About the music—" Oliver began. He started digging in his ratty pockets. Lack of care for personal appearance seemed to be a Green family trait. He pulled out a flash drive. "Here."

Scarlett took the piece of plastic. "What's this?"

"It's a song. Vaughn's song. There might be more, but I had that one."

"Haven't you heard of the cloud?"

Oliver frowned. "I—I didn't know how to get it to you. I thought maybe mail it, anonymously . . ."

"Oh, yeah, after the year we've had, that's a great idea." She rolled her eyes. Were they sure he wasn't the creepy twin?

"Scarlett!" hissed Orchid.

Oliver sighed. "It's called 'Morningfall.'"

"Wait," said Orchid now, turning to Oliver. "Did you say 'Morningfall?' Like, *Because I never told you all, that morningfall?*"

Scarlett had to hand it to Orchid. Her singing voice was not half bad. They really needed to get her to release a video. The fans would eat it up.

Oliver ducked his head. "Yeah."

Orchid's eyes burned like fire. "Have you been sneaking on campus and playing this song outside Tudor?"

Oliver's jaw was set, his shoulders hunched. "I probably should have mailed it anonymously, huh?"

"Oh my God. You *are* the creepy twin!" Scarlett pinged the flash drive off his head and it clattered on the table. "I spent hours trying to convince Orchid that she wasn't being haunted. Turns out, she was. By *you!*"

"What did you want me to do?" Oliver ducked away. "Just

"Just announce myself on the group chat, like, hey guys, my brother's dead but I'm still here, want to be friends?"

"Why not?" Scarlett replied. "That's essentially what you did this morning."

"That's not fair," said Orchid. "I sought him out. I went to *his* house."

Yes, nice and early, so as to be sure that Scarlett couldn't have stopped her. Which she almost definitely would have tried to do.

Though, if Scarlett were being honest with herself, this was actually a useful turn of events. The channel desperately needed new content, and she could probably milk four or five videos out of a lead-up to a new song. And an identical twin added a delicious dimension to the story! Too bad Oliver wasn't a musician. He could have a ready-made career.

"Are you sure you don't play?"

He narrowed his eyes at her in a way she found disturbingly familiar. Maybe he was the one she'd always fought with. "Yes, I am."

Hmm. "Want to learn?"

"Scarlett!" Orchid begged. "Leave him alone!"

Scarlett frowned. She *would* have left him alone. She would never have known he was around. But if he was here, and handing over new Vaughn Green music, then they should try to do as much with it as they possibly could.

"This is huge, Orchid. Don't you get it? We can tease out a huge revelation, we can do countdown videos, and then we can have *Oliver* introduce the new music! His brother's music!"

"I'm not doing that," said Oliver.

"Are you kidding me?" asked Scarlett. "Why not?"

"Just—take the song, okay?" He swiped the flash drive off the table and held it out again, pushing himself away from it as if it smelled bad. "Take it and do whatever you've been doing. I recognize that you're doing a good job and all, but I don't want to be involved."

"That makes no sense."

Orchid took the flash drive, then put her hand over Oliver's. "It makes perfect sense. He was your brother."

Oliver pulled away from her as if her touch burned. He took a deep, shuddering breath.

"This is hard, I know," she continued in a soft voice. "I haven't wanted to do any videos, either, despite pressure from *certain people*."

Scarlett crossed her arms over her chest. "Yeah, well, I only stopped bothering you about it because your lawyer said it probably wasn't the best idea."

"You have a lawyer?" Oliver asked her.

"Well, yeah," Orchid admitted, ducking her chin to her chest. "I killed a guy."

"Lawyer*s*," Scarlett corrected. "There's the criminal one, and then there's her business team."

Oliver took this in, his gaze hardening. Then he nodded curtly. "Might want to get some new ones. They let you produce songs that don't belong to you."

"I'm sorry," Scarlett scoffed, "didn't you *just* say you didn't want to be involved?"

"That doesn't mean he's giving up his rights," Orchid said. "Oliver and I have come to an agreement."

Scarlett whirled on her friend. "Wait, what? Without talking to your lawyers?"

"The lawyers you apparently didn't consult before putting the songs online to start?" Oliver asked.

Oh, yeah. That was the Vaughn she remembered. Scarlett wondered if this was the one who'd kept her from tearing down the boathouse. Or maybe both brothers were equally terrible.

"We're going to keep producing Vaughn's music," Orchid said. "And we'll get a cut of the profits. But we're giving everything we've made on it so far to Oliver, and in return, he's not going to sue us for infringement."

"Sue us?" Scarlett snapped. "With what lawyers?"

This time, Orchid didn't cry out *Scarlett!* She just rubbed her temples in frustration.

Scarlett stepped around the table and up to Oliver. "Maybe you should think about the trouble you can get in for defrauding Blackbrook. We know what you did now."

"I'm sure they are going to rush to punish a poor young man who just lost the only family he had left in an accident the school is arguably responsible for," Oliver replied, deadpan. "Come on, what we did is nothing compared to the carnage that Keith guy unleashed on the people of this school."

Scarlett stepped back.

Oliver, however, wasn't finished. His eyes narrowed with rage. "But I sure do appreciate you threatening me over the rights to my dead brother's music. I'm glad you haven't lost all your cutthroat tendencies, Scarlett. You'll need them if you really want to make Vaughn a star."

"I don't!" she shot back, and he flinched. "I wanted to do a favor for my friend Orchid, who just so happened to be really broken up over the death of your brother, and feeling very guilty about him not ever getting his music out into the world. I had no idea it would get so popular and make the kind of money it has."

Well, almost no idea. Scarlett could hardly help being good at her job, could she?

"And how much money is that, exactly?"

Unbelievable. Scarlett looked at Orchid for confirmation. Orchid bit her lip and nodded.

She sighed, wishing more than anything she could tell him that it was none of his business. "Twelve thousand dollars."

Oliver's blinked. "*What.*"

"Would be more if we had more videos." If she could convince Orchid to record something, they'd go gangbusters. And at least that would be their property, and they wouldn't have to share with this jerk.

"That's . . . a lot," Oliver mumbled.

Scarlett lifted her shoulders. "It's okay." She knew music channels making ten times as much. Ones with steady streams of content.

He gave her a disgusted glare. "Maybe to you, Manhattan. Or Hollywood over there," he added, gesturing to Orchid. "But it's more money than I've ever seen in one place."

She decided it would be best to keep her mouth shut.

"Look," he said, his tone brusque, "I understand that you have done a lot of work here. So I'll give you two thousand of what you've made so far, and you can have fifteen percent going forward, okay? Like a real manager."

"Are you insane?" she cried, appalled. "I've devoted months to this. It's been my life."

"No!" Oliver said. "It was my *brother's* life. His life's work. I appreciate what you did, but it's not yours."

"Scarlett," Orchid tried. "He's right."

He may be right, but that didn't make it fair. Oliver may have inherited Vaughn's music, but it was Scarlett who had made it worth money. "Just last night, I moderated a two-hour discussion in the comments section about guitar techniques. Do you want to know how many pictures of finger calluses I was forced to look at?"

Orchid buried her face in her palms. Oliver put his hands in his jacket pockets and fixed her with an imperious look.

"Then you can have nothing. It's your choice, Scarlett."

It wasn't a choice at all. This person who was not Vaughn knew her way too well. She wasn't going to let go of her new project, even if Oliver only let her keep the scraps. It wasn't about the money. It was a springboard into other things. Like her family starting out in this country by buying a run-down motel and turning it into a multimillion-dollar hospitality business. First Vaughn Green's online videos, and then total entertainment domination. Scarlett could see it all.

Let Oliver have his measly ten thousand dollars. He could use it to buy a new pair of pants.

"Fine."

He gave her a smug, self-satisfied smile.

She thought she hadn't liked Vaughn. But it was definitely this guy she hadn't liked all along.

"Oliver," Orchid said gently, "why don't you come upstairs with me. I'll get you a check, and those other things we talked about."

"What other things?" Scarlett exclaimed as they turned to leave.

"None of your business," Oliver called over his shoulder.

Hey! That was her line! Scarlett followed them out into the hall. Orchid made for the stairs, but Oliver crossed to the door of the library and touched the yellow caution tape stretched across the door.

"So you found her in here?" he said to Scarlett without turning around. "Dr. Brown?"

"If you've been keeping up with the group chat, you know all the details."

"Not *all* the details," he said. "It's not like you took pictures."

"Eww," she said. "Why would I take pictures?"

"For evidence." Oliver turned around and shrugged, sticking his hands back in his pockets. "It's Blackbrook. You never know when there's going to be more murders."

Sicko. "They said she died of a stroke."

"Is that what they said?" He leaned forward. "Tell me, Scarlett: What does a stroke victim look like? Were her eyes bloodshot? Was there any bruising on her face?"

"What do I look like, a medical examiner?" Scarlett said. "I was too busy being in shock."

"I haven't forgotten the details of the dead bodies I've seen," he replied coldly. "I had to identify my brother, cracked skull and all."

The door to the billiards room opened, and Peacock backed her little scooter out into the hall. She was dressed in her current uniform of old gray sweats slit up the legs to fit her cast and boot. She rearranged herself on her scooter and looked up to see the three of them.

At the sight of Oliver, her expression changed to one of pure shock. "Whoa . . ."

"Hey," said Oliver, casually, and went back to caressing the library door.

Peacock's free hand floated up, her finger pointing at Oliver as her mouth dropped open. She looked frantically at the girls as if to confirm that they, too, were seeing the apparition. "Um . . . *Vaughn?*"

Oliver seemed to remember himself. "Oh, right. Sorry." He waved. "I'm Oliver. Vaughn's twin brother."

"Oh!" Peacock's expression softened, thought she still peered intently at his face. "I had no idea Vaughn had a twin brother."

"No one did," grumbled Scarlett.

"I'm Beth," said Peacock. "I was—I was in the car—"

"He knows, Beth," said Scarlett.

"Yeah, I know," said Oliver. His gaze traveled down over her various bandages, scars, and casts. "You're looking . . . better."

That sounded weird, but then again, he'd been watching her recovery on the group chat, same as the rest of them.

But Peacock didn't know that. "Better than what?" she asked.

"Better than my brother." He pushed off the door and headed for the stairs. "That check, Orchid?"

Orchid cast one last, concerned look at Scarlett, then hurried to catch up with him on the landing.

Scarlett approached Peacock, who had gone rather pale. "That's not what he meant," she said in a low voice.

The other girl was gnawing on her lip. "Oh no?"

"He's on the group chat, through Vaughn's account." That was a version of the truth, anyway. Scarlett and Orchid could figure out how and when to tell the others about the Greens' scheme some other time. "He's seen all our messages, including the pictures you've been posting."

"What a creep." Peacock shuddered. "He's really nothing like Vaughn, is he?"

Scarlett watched Oliver disappear with Orchid upstairs.

"No," she said. "He's not."

9

Peacock

ELIZABETH PICACH'S ~~RECOVERY JOURNAL~~
INVESTIGATIVE NOTEBOOK

POSSIBLE SUSPECTS

1. TANNER CURRY: *Moving him up a slot, based on Amber's description of his recent behavior. He's acting weird. Maybe all this grieving over Dr. Brown is hiding a guilty conscience. Besides, what were they fighting about, anyway? And why did he quit the crew team? I would kill to be able to play tennis this season.*

2. OLIVER GREEN: *Possible motives: 1) His brother was killed due to negligence under Dr. Brown's administration.*

2) Townies like to kill Blackbrook headmasters. This is a fact.

3) He's a creep.

Evidence: Really, <u>really</u> interested in who found Dr. Brown's body and what shape it was in. Practically molested the police tape over the library door when he was here. See #3, above.

Of course, this all might be moot. All the school administrators left alive are convinced Dr. Brown died of natural causes. Probably because THEY don't want to believe they could be next.

3. PERRY WINKLE: *Not ready to take him off my list, but honestly,* *killing the headmaster to get the most fatal job in Maine seems like a bit of a stretch. Staff here are dropping like flies. No one wants this job.*

Besides, I've got an appointment next Monday to talk to him about my concerns, and I really don't want to be murdered. But what am I supposed to do? No one here is taking Dr. Brown's death seriously. Assuming the school is safe in the wake of a surprise death is what got us into trouble last time! Remember: they said Rusty died of natural causes, too. A week later, there were three more bodies.

And me.

Full disclosure: seeing Oliver was very strange. I don't even like listening to Vaughn's music. Why am I alive and he is not? Why am I alive, if I can't do anything I want to do?

I can't remember what happened in that car. Did Vaughn get distracted? Did the brakes give out? Did I say something to him? Was I the last thing he saw before he died? Could I have stopped it? Could I have saved us?

Sometimes I dream I'm in the car, and I jump out in time. Sometimes I dream I'm the one behind the wheel.

I used to dream of tennis, but now all I can think about is death.

10

Plum

The door to Finn's dorm room was unlocked. That was weird. He never forgot to lock the door. Finn stuck his keys back in his pocket and turned the knob.

"Ah, Phineas," said Perry Winkle, who was sitting at Finn's desk chair, his hands folded politely in his lap. "So glad you made it."

"What are you doing in my room?" Finn demanded.

Winkle chuckled, his bright blue eyes crinkling up at the corners. "Another part of the student handbook you seem unfamiliar with. *School administrators reserve the right to enter and inspect student rooms for possible contraband or other conduct violations at any time.*"

Oh, Finn was familiar with it. It's why he was always very careful not to hide his contraband in his room. If it wasn't in your possession, there was plausible deniability.

Not that his system was perfect. Sometimes he lost his work in flooded underground tunnels, for instance.

"Oh." He kept his tone as casual as possible as he set his backpack down on Jin's old bed. "Well, look around, I guess."

"I have," said Winkle. He was dressed, impeccably as always, in a tan suit with a pale blue and gold Fair Isle sweater vest. Finn thought maybe it was time to ban sweater vests entirely from his wardrobe. "You keep your room very neat, Phineas."

"Yes," he replied smoothly. "I'm a model student."

"Very stark," Winkle went on, looking around the bare walls and empty desktop. "Almost . . . monk-like."

Finn shrugged. He'd had a poster or two up in his old dorm in Dockery, but he'd never bothered redecorating here. He was only in this dumb freshman dorm because his old one had flooded. Jin had made an effort, but now Jin was gone, too. "So?"

"But you're not a monk, are you?"

Well . . . recently, he'd been a bit more monk-like than he wanted.

"You're a scientist."

Oh. Phew. Finn was having a tough time keeping track of all his secrets.

Except not totally phew, because Winkle went on. "And yet I don't see a lot of work around here. No field journals, no lab notebooks . . .

"Yeah," said Finn. "Academics at this school have really gone in the toilet lately. Maybe you should look into that, *headmaster.*"

Winkle smiled, and it wasn't a nice one. "Where are your notebooks from last term, Mr. Plum?"

"I don't know. Recycled?"

"Where are your *other* notebooks?"

Finn made sure to look confused. "What are you talking about?"

"I think you know."

He made his eyes go wide and innocent. "No, sir, I really don't. I'm just trying to get through the semester, same as everyone else." And then get out.

Winkle pursed his lips. "It has come to my attention that you engaged in some very interesting research last term."

"Well, that was before my chemistry teacher quit—"

"*Extracurricular* research."

Finn shook his head. "Sorry, man. I don't know what you're driving at."

"Enough!" Winkle said, standing. He jabbed a finger in Finn's direction. "You're not dumb, Phineas, so don't act like it. You have a formula for some sort of industrial dye, developed at Blackbrook, and you've been keeping its existence hidden from the administration."

Finn kept his mouth shut. But his mind was racing. How had Perry Winkle figured things out so quickly? He'd been very thorough about erasing Headmaster Boddy's notes on Finn's dye during the storm. After four months of Dr. Brown never bringing it up, he'd assumed he was in the clear.

"Now, seeing as you're such a clever boy, I know you understand how our policies and honor code work."

"Going to kick me out?" Finn asked, amused. "Go ahead. My parents already said they'd find me another school next year." Or maybe he'd take a gap year and jump straight into college.

"No, I'm not. I'm going to give you a chance. You and I both know this school is done for. I don't blame you for not wanting your rights tied up in this swamp. But you're in a bind, unless . . ."

"Unless what?"

"Unless you are willing to strike a deal with Curry Chem for your formula."

Wait. Winkle wasn't here on behalf of the school? "You work for Curry?"

"I'm a consultant," he replied. "I work in crisis management."

"I thought you were a guidance counselor."

"Yes," said Winkle. "Guidance through a *crisis*. Which I think we can both agree this school is in. But I'm board certified in psychology, and I know all about adolescent stressors. I understand where you're coming from, Phineas. It's your invention and you're proud of it. But you've bitten off more than you can chew."

Finn felt his stomach sink. The guy wasn't wrong. He hadn't yet figured out what he was going to do with his invention, beyond hide it from Blackbrook. And he had hidden it well. Dr. Brown hadn't found anything out about his dye in all those months.

Actually, now that he thought about it, it was weird that Mr. Winkle figured it out in a few days on his own. Unless Curry Chem had been tipped off by an actual Curry—like Tanner. And the only way Tanner could have found out about it was—

Mustard.

"I want you to turn over any materials you have for evaluation," said Winkle. "And engineers from Curry will decide if it's worth anything. If so, you accept our offer and I'll pretend you never touched it at Blackbrook."

Somehow, Finn doubted the valuation or the offer would be anything remotely competitive.

"But if not," Winkle added, "then you'll be tied up in the lawsuits that will soon bog down this school for decades. You'll never sell anything." He leaned in. "And honestly, I'm not sure if transferring schools is going to work, either, what with the honor code violation that's going on your record if you don't comply."

"What?" Finn whispered.

"It's not like most of your teachers are still around to verify your grades."

He wasn't kidding.

"I don't have anything," Finn said quickly. "I don't know what you heard, but it's just gossip—"

"You have something," said Winkle smugly. "Or you would have denied it long before you heard my offer." He tapped his temple. "Trained psychologist, remember?"

Then he brushed past him and headed toward the door. "You have three days to magically recover whatever research you may have forgotten about, or I'm afraid you'll be in violation of our honor code and we'll file a lawsuit to prevent you from selling your work anywhere else."

"Come on, man!" Finn called. "It's nothing!"

Winkle paused, turned, and tapped his finger on his chin. "So you're saying it's not very valuable? I'll pass that message along to the Curry accountants."

And then he was gone, leaving Finn scowling in his empty, monk-like bedroom.

He took out his phone and swiped to Mustard's texts. For a second, Finn considered sending another *what the hell?* text his way. But what was the point? If Mustard had leaked the secret, then he knew exactly what he was doing, and why.

No, he needed real help. He needed Scarlett.

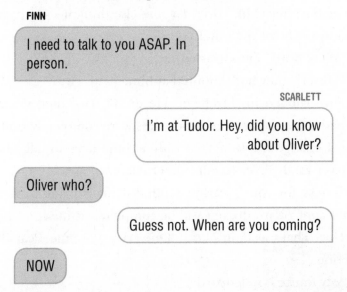

FINN

I need to talk to you ASAP. In person.

SCARLETT

I'm at Tudor. Hey, did you know about Oliver?

Oliver who?

Guess not. When are you coming?

NOW

He made it over to Tudor in record time. His room was giving him the creeps now, anyway. For all he knew, Winkle had installed a security camera.

Scarlett answered the door. "Come in," she said in hushed tones. "He's still here."

"Who?" Finn asked.

"Oliver!" She shoved him into the lounge, where Beth was on the sofa, her legs elevated, scribbling in a notebook.

"Hey, Beth," he said.

"Hi." She waved her pen at him, but didn't look up.

"Who is Oliver?" he asked Scarlett. "Your prom date?" She was slammed these day with prom planning.

"As if," Scarlett said, her voice dripping with disdain. "He's upstairs with Orchid right now."

"Doing who knows what," Beth chimed in. She tapped her pen against her chin. "Does anyone else think it's weird she's making a play for the other twin?"

"What twin?" Finn insisted.

"Oliver!" they both shouted at him.

Finn rubbed his forehead. He didn't have time for this. He had three days before his dreams were completely ruined. "Can I change the subject? I didn't come here to talk about whoever Emily Pryce has decided to date."

"Lucky for you," Scarlett scoffed. "But if I don't get this under control, my dreams will be completely ruined."

Hey! That was Finn's line. "One crisis at a time, Scar. This is serious."

"My future is in jeopardy!"

"*My* future is in jeopardy!" he shouted back.

From her place on the couch, Beth laughed. Loudly.

They both turned in her direction.

"Sorry," she said. "I was just thinking about how lucky you two are to still have futures."

Finn ducked his head in mortification. "Beth, that's not what I meant . . ."

"What?" Beth replied. "Your future *isn't* in jeopardy?"

"I . . ." He couldn't finish that phrase. Not to Beth, who was holding her scarred wrist gingerly. Who had one leg in a big cast and the other in a walking boot. But playing a game of Who Has It Worst wouldn't suddenly put Beth back on the tennis team, and it definitely wasn't going to help him figure out what to do about Winkle's threats.

Finn frowned and muttered to Scarlett. "She's not okay, is she?"

Scarlett gave him a look. "Is anyone at Blackbrook?"

So Finn put on the face he wore for every sad, sorry game night he'd endured with Beth over the past few months. The somber, sympathetic friend face. "Beth, remember what the doctors said. You just have to give yourself time to heal. You won't know what you're dealing with for several months—"

She rolled her eyes. "Yeah. I just sit here and wait for a few months before I find out whether or not my future is ruined. Easy-peasy. Carry on."

He nodded. "Thank you. Now, Winkle—"

"Except," Beth went on, her tone a little manic, "people are still dropping like flies on this campus. It's tough to say if any of us even *has* a future. After all, Vaughn didn't. Scarlett's entire project depends on someone else having everything taken from him."

Scarlett crossed her arms defensively. "You say that like I was the one who did it."

"I don't know who *really* did it," Beth said. "That's the problem. Technically, it was Vaughn who did this to me, but why did that happen? Because Orchid killed Ash—I mean, Keith? Because the school didn't protect us from a deranged stalker? Who is really to blame? And the murders keep coming."

"Are you talking about Dr. Brown?" Scarlett asked. "That was natural causes."

"You can kill someone without sticking a knife in their chest," Beth said. "There's more to this death than Winkle and the rest of the administration is letting on."

"You sound like Tanner," said Finn. "He was all about blaming himself the other night. He said if they hadn't fought, maybe she'd still be alive."

"Now, see, that's interesting!" Beth said, pointing her pen at him. "Because I did hear them fighting the other day. So maybe he meant, maybe if she had kept her mouth shut, he wouldn't have had to kill her?"

"What?" Finn asked, appalled. Beth thought Tanner was a killer? The only thing that kid ever destroyed was the dorm bathroom after chugging a six-pack. "No! I think he meant maybe if he hadn't stressed her out so much, she wouldn't have had a stroke."

"If she even did have a stroke," Beth mused darkly. "After all, this is Blackbrook."

"Now you sound like Oliver!" Scarlett exclaimed.

Who the hell was this Oliver person they kept talking about?

But before he could ask, Beth went on. "I'm the one who heard the fight, and let me tell you, it wasn't pretty."

"Why didn't you say anything before?" Scarlett asked.

"What, like, in front of Amber last night?" Beth made a face. "No way. She was already so upset, I wasn't about to start asking if she thought her boyfriend was a murderer."

"So what were they saying?" Finn asked. Maybe they were discussing the conundrum with Curry Chem and the student patents. Tanner had certainly seemed concerned about them the other night. Maybe concerned enough to get Mustard to spill the beans about Finn's dye.

"I couldn't understand most of it," Beth admitted. "And it wasn't Dr. Brown doing the yelling. Just Tanner. But I did hear him say something about a cover-up."

"Cover-up . . ." Scarlett repeated. "Like the school was covering up a crime?"

"They *did* cover up a crime!" said Finn. "They said Rusty's death was natural, and it wasn't." Maybe Dr. Brown's wasn't either.

"Why would Tanner kill Dr. Brown for covering up Rusty's murder?" Scarlett asked.

"I never said Tanner killed Dr. Brown." Finn said. "I know that dude. He's not a killing type."

"Neither was Mrs. White," said Scarlett dryly.

They should call Mustard, Finn thought, in spite of himself. If they were discussing Tanner, he should know. "Maybe we should ask Mustard. Should I post to the group?"

"No!" cried Scarlett quickly. "I may need to edit it."

So she didn't want to tell Mustard? Finn was confused. He certainly wasn't going to be the one to call Mustard, especially after last night, but if the others were floating his roommate as a potential killer, Mustard had the right to know.

The door to the lounge opened and Orchid came in. Other than her hair being dyed a bright lavender-pink, she looked more drab and colorless than usual. "Well, he's gone."

"Who?" Finn asked.

"Oliver!" all three replied.

Finn rubbed his temples. "Nice hair, by the way. All of you. Did I miss a meeting?"

"This was Tudor House girls, not Murder Crew," Beth replied.

"Thanks," said Orchid, touching her bright tresses.

Scarlett, however, was all business. "What did you give him?" she demanded of Orchid.

Orchid stood stiffly, her chin raised, her lips pursed, as if expecting a fight. "The money, like we discussed."

Scarlett made a little strangled sound in her throat.

"It's his, Scarlett. He's Vaughn's brother."

"Wait," said Finn. "Vaughn had a brother?"

"Keep up!" Scarlett hissed, and then she returned her attention to Orchid. "What else? You were up there an awfully long time."

"Yeah, well . . . we had a lot to talk about." Orchid's shoulders were hunched, her hands clasped in front of the latest in a series of shapeless gray hoodies. It would never cease to amaze Finn how someone could have all the money and resources in the world, like Emily Pryce, and still insist on dressing the way she did. Not even Scarlett's influence had rubbed off on her.

"I just *bet* you did," Scarlett said meaningfully.

"It's not like that!" Orchid exclaimed. "I had things of Vaughn's. After he died, I found something that belonged to him. Belonged to his family."

"Where?"

"The boathouse. There were these old letters from the time his grandmother had lived at Tudor. Did you know her name was Olivia Vaughn?"

"Well then, their mother wasn't particularly creative with baby names, was she?" Scarlett said, her tone dripping with disdain. "What did they say?"

"Stuff I felt bad about reading, to be honest," said Orchid. "About how his grandmother was sent to Tudor when she got pregnant. Her boyfriend followed her and enrolled in Blackbrook, but then they broke up anyway. He abandoned her and the baby when Olivia refused to give it up for adoption. And then he went on to work for some chemical company."

"Well, that is the Blackbrook way," said Finn ruefully.

She hugged herself. "That whole family—it's like tragedy after tragedy."

For real. No wonder Vaughn only wrote sad songs.

"So Vaughn was keeping things in the old boathouse," Scarlett said. "Now I understand why he didn't want the campus beautification committee to knock it down. What else is in there?"

"Boats?" suggested Peacock.

Orchid shrugged. "I don't know. I haven't been back. There was all kinds of old equipment when I was there a few months ago. Computers and lab equipment and stuff. I guess the school was storing it there after the flood."

"That doesn't make any sense," Scarlett said. "That thing's a shack. It's hardly protected from the elements."

Finn frowned, too. After the flood, a lot of school equipment had gone missing. His chemistry lab had lost a scanning electron microscope.

All of a sudden, Winkle, the dye, the issue with Curry Chem—none of it seemed remotely important. Finn snapped back to a night four months ago. The night before the accident, when he'd gone looking for Mustard and found Tanner and Vaughn having a very serious discussion about . . . something. Then, later, when Finn had told Vaughn about the fight in the tunnels the night Rusty died, he'd freaked out and run off. And then the day after that, right before they'd witnessed Orchid attacking Keith, he'd confronted Finn about what he knew about the tunnels, and . . . murder? Definitely something about murder.

Maybe Vaughn and Tanner had a scheme to steal supplies from the school, and were hiding them in various places on campus—the tunnels, the old boat shack. Why Vaughn would do such a thing was obvious, but Tanner was more of a mystery. The Currys had serious money. Still, Finn knew a little bit about the thrill of sneaking around and breaking rules. Maybe Tanner wanted to live on the edge, too.

And then what?

Rusty caught them, perhaps? Had the altercation Mustard overheard in the tunnels that night not been between Rusty and a townie at all, but between Rusty and Tanner?

Maybe Tanner was the killing type, after all.

Vaughn probably wouldn't have murdered the fellow townie janitor, but maybe Tanner had, when he'd been caught red-handed. And with the influence of the Curry family at Blackbrook, they would have indeed covered up any evidence that would have led back to their son. They would have insisted the school announce that Rusty died of natural causes!

And months later, Tanner would be eaten up inside due to guilt. Being a killer could do that to you.

"Ladies," he said, slowly, carefully. He needed to think about how best to deliver this information to the others. Mustard had been in the tunnels the night that Rusty had been killed. No one knew that but him. "I think we need to have a #MurderCrew meeting. All five of us."

"You mean six," said Scarlett. "Turns out, Oliver's been in our chats the whole time."

"Vaughn's brother?" Finn asked. "Why?"

Scarlett groaned. "Sit down, Finn. You're not going to believe this."

11

Peacock

POSSIBLE SUSPECTS
1. **TANNER CURRY**
2. **OLIVER GREEN**
3. **FINN PLUM**

FINALLY.

I thought no one else was going to pay any attention to this stuff! I'm out here, on my own, solving mysteries and taking names.

And yes, I'm going to say it: thank goodness for Finn.

Unless, of course, he's casting all this suspicion on Oliver and Tanner in order to cover up his own misdeeds. After all, Finn was the one who found Rusty's body. He won't tell us how he knows about the fight in the tunnels. And he's still determined to hide his experiments from the Blackbrook administration. Maybe all of this is just projection so we won't find out he's the real murderer.

No. A person wouldn't do that, would they?

But this Tanner connection is interesting, especially given what we are learning about Vaughn. Or is it Oliver? Whatever, the Greens.

Apparently, one or both of the twins was stealing computers and lab equipment from Blackbrook. And Tanner might have been involved, too. If so, then maybe Rusty wasn't killed by ~~Ash~~ Keith in the tunnels after all! Maybe it was Tanner!

If Finn is right, then there might be more to this situation than anyone thought. Amber said that Tanner is always moaning about the things his family expects of him and how they've been so disappointed in him lately. And Scarlett said she saw a file on Dr. Brown's computer called Vaughn Financial Claims. If the administration caught them in the act, it provides motive, timing, everything!

Did Tanner kill Rusty and make Blackbrook cover it up? If so, he must have been relieved when Vaughn—the only person who could have connected him to whatever happened in the tunnels— died in that car crash. If Blackbrook was covering up a murder by the son of a prominent family, they must have been relieved, too. Everyone assumed it was Keith, especially after what he did to Orchid and Rosa.

And me.

Keep on subject, Beth!

Questions to be answered:

* Who killed Dr. Brown, and why?

* Does Tanner know about Oliver, or were he and Vaughn working alone?

* What part does Oliver play in all of this?

We need to find out, and in a way that doesn't put any of us in danger. I, for one, have spent far too much time around murderers this year.

Scarlett, Finn, and Orchid are going down to check out the boathouse. I'd go, too, but it's tough to get down there on the scooter.

I said I'd talk to Mustard while they did that, but Finn didn't think it was a good idea. Not really sure why.

12

Mustard

Mustard came back from the shower—his second today, but who was counting?—shook the last droplets of water off his close-cropped hair, and checked his phone.

Three new messages from Plum. Typical. He stormed out the other day, and now he wanted to talk about it.

Or *not* talk.

Mustard set his jaw and swiped through to see the messages.

PLUM

Call me ASAP. We need to talk.

Called it. They *didn't* need to talk. Talk wasn't going to fix whatever their problems were. And neither was doing anything else.

PLUM

Srsly. Call me.

Whatever. He'd tried to work it out with Plum. Tried to come to some new understanding of what had happened between them last winter. But that's not what the other boy really wanted. No, instead Plum had this whole coming-out fantasy mapped for the two of them. Maybe Plum's entire family in New York was throwing a party. Getting a cake with rainbow icing.

No way.

PLUM

> PS: If Beth reaches out to you before we've had a chance to talk, believe me, I didn't tell her anything. Just . . . Call me and we can figure out what to say.

Mustard groaned. Just great. Now Peacock knew? That girl had zero filter.

The phone buzzed in his hand again. He checked the ID.

Peacock was calling him!

He threw the phone down on the bed like it was a live scorpion. It buzzed for a minute, then went silent.

He breathed a sigh of relief.

A minute later, it started up again. Perfect. Figured that Plum would tell his ex-girlfriend that he and Mustard made out a few times, and the very first thing she thought to do was call Mustard for all the gory details.

When Peacock called the third time, Mustard decided it wasn't too early for another run. He took the stairs two at a time and burst out of the boys' dorm onto the sidewalk—

Where stood Peacock, one casted leg kneeling on her little scooter, phone pressed to her ear, and eyes lifted to his bedroom window.

"Oh, there you are!" she exclaimed brightly. "It would have

taken forever to go upstairs with this thing. Thanks for coming down. They really need more ADA compliance around here, don't you think?"

"Sorry, Peacock, I can't talk right now." He turned on his heel and headed in the direction of the nearest set of stairs. Hopefully, she would not be able to follow.

"This will just take a minute." He could hear her rolling after him. "I need to talk to you—"

"You know," he called over his shoulder, "people keep telling me that, and it's never a good idea!"

"—about Tanner," she finished. "And Vaughn."

He stopped. That was not what he was expecting. He turned around. "Tanner and Vaughn? What?"

"Well, you're Tanner's roommate. Were he and Vaughn close?"

Mustard thought about Tanner scrolling obsessively through the comments on Vaughn Green's music channel. "They were in a band together freshman year. Didn't last long. I never got the impression they hung out much after that." Green was likely too busy with janitorial work.

"Finn said he saw Vaughn in your room talking to Tanner the night before he died."

Mustard shrugged. "Okay, maybe they were friends." It would certainly explain Tanner's morbid obsession with the crash. "What of it?"

Peacock wheeled closer. She'd redone the blue streaks in her hair. "You don't think they were *more than friends*, do you?" she asked, raising her eyebrows.

Mustard reeled back. "What? No! I mean . . . wasn't Vaughn dating Orchid? I thought Vaughn was dating Orchid." Although, people could like both boys and girls, as Finn had become so fond of telling everyone all the time.

Oh. That's what she was getting at. *Dammit, Plum . . .*

"Look, Peacock, I don't know what Plum said to you, but . . ." He trailed off at the strange expression on her face.

Peacock stared at him, her brow furrowed. "What?"

Mustard was extraordinarily confused. "What?"

"I don't think they were hooking up, you moron. Wait, do *you* think they were hooking up?"

He would genuinely prefer not to get into a discussion about two boys hooking up in his dorm room. "What are you talking about then?"

"I'm talking about *murder!*" Peacock threw her arms in the air. "You know, the relentless parade of corpses on this campus? The fact that we can hardly go a month around here without tripping over a killer? The fact that the deaths have started up again and no one seems to care but me?"

Mustard just stared at her for a second, the twin emotions of relief and bewilderment washing over him. Then, he scrubbed his hand through his hair and sat down on the stoop. It probably shouldn't come as a surprise that Peacock was obsessed with death. A few months ago, she'd stared it right in the face. He'd seen stuff on the #MurderCrew chat about her nightmares, and how Plum would go to her room at night and stay with her until she fell asleep.

Plum did that a lot, actually. Not that Mustard was keeping track.

MUSTARD

"Well, you're wrong about that last thing. Tanner seems to care about Dr. Brown's death a great deal."

"Amber said he's totally freaking out about it."

"Well, Amber's perspective might be a little off, given that they just broke up."

"Mustard," Peacock goaded.

He sighed. "Yes. He's been talking about it a lot."

"And why do you think that is?" she pressed. "Maybe he's got something to do with it. I hear that murderers often become obsessed with the crimes they commit."

Where had she heard that? A crime show on TV? Mustard refused to play detective again. It never worked out well.

"I mean, it's probably because Dr. Brown is an old friend of his family's from Curry Chem," he said.

"And Vaughn? Is he obsessing over Vaughn's death, too?"

Yes, actually. But he wasn't alone there. Vaughn had thousands of fans who discussed it constantly online. Tanner had told him a bunch of their theories during his drunken stupor last night, after he'd returned from his walk. The conspiracies ranged from aliens to a cabal of Nashville executives intent on squashing the next country music star because he was from New England.

It was a little nuts. And so was the idea that Tanner could have anything to do with Green's death.

"Vaughn died in a car crash." He glanced at her casts and scars. "I believe you were there?"

Her eyes narrowed to tiny slits, her mouth to a hard line.

"Okay," she said coldly. "Then what about Rusty?"

A chill stole across his skin. "Rusty?"

"Finn said there was a chance that Rusty wasn't killed by As—I mean, by Keith in the tunnels under the school. That it was someone else."

Oh, Plum had said that, had he? "What else did he say?"

"That's all."

Another wave of relief. Finally, Plum's message suddenly made a lot more sense. He hadn't been telling Peacock about *them*—only about what Mustard had said happened in the tunnels the night Rusty had been killed.

At least Plum could keep his mouth shut about *some* of Mustard's secrets.

"You think it might have been Tanner?" Mustard shook his head. The voice he'd heard that night in the tunnel was not Tanner's. "What would Tanner have been doing in those tunnels? And what reason would he have to kill anyone?"

Peacock smiled in triumph, and then laid out a whole theory that the rest of the Murder Crew had apparently been concocting this morning about Tanner, Vaughn, and a bunch of stolen lab equipment. It was pretty outlandish, and not just because Tanner was a trust-fund baby with millions of dollars at his disposal and no need to steal anything. All one had to do was look at how tricked-out their dorm room was.

And then came the piece de resistance, which turned the entire conversation from the type restless boarding school kids had on the weekends right into the type of conspiracy theories usually limited to online comments sections.

Namely, all this nonsense about "Oliver Green."

Eventually, Mustard held up his hand to stop her. "Let me

get this straight. Vaughn has a secret twin brother who he was trading places with?"

Peacock nodded vigorously. "Yes! They were both attending Blackbrook on Vaughn's scholarship. Isn't that wild?"

He snorted. "Are you sure you haven't been breathing in too many fumes from that hair dye?"

"Mustard, we all saw him! Orchid tracked him down on Rocky Point and he came to Tudor today. He's on the #MurderCrew chat because Scarlett never bothered to take Vaughn's number off. He just never revealed himself because of the scam he and his brother were pulling on the school."

Mustard sat back. "Whoa."

Okay, maybe some of those online comment threads had a point. This wasn't quite aliens, but a secret twin brother was still way out there.

"But!" Peacock went on, eyes alight. "Maybe the true reason he never revealed himself was so we wouldn't find out that their *real* scam was stealing lab equipment from Blackbrook and selling it on the black market!"

Mustard wasn't sure how much used beakers and laptops went for, but he was pretty sure that Vaughn Green's music channel made more than that now. His talent was the real goldmine, but he'd had to die to make any money off it. And the story still didn't implicate Mustard's roommate.

"So what makes you think Tanner was involved in any of this?" Mustard asked. "Maybe it was just the twins."

"Because Tanner—" Peacock began, and then her mouth snapped shut. "Omigod, there he is!"

Mustard looked and saw his roommate hurrying across the green. He looked—well, he looked weird. *Haunted.* He wasn't walking, but he wasn't quite running, either. And he had a big envelope in his hands.

"Okay," said Mustard, standing. "I'll talk to him."

"Wait!" Peacock put out her hand and grabbed his arm. She had a surprisingly firm grip for someone with her arm in a brace. He guessed all that physical therapy was paying off. "Don't let him know we're on to him!"

He glared at her and shook himself free. "I think I can manage a little discretion." Unlike some people he could mention. "We should meet up . . . the five of us."

She nodded. "I'll tell Scarlett to set it up."

Mustard followed Tanner into the dorm and upstairs to their room. He was only a few steps behind him, but didn't call out. Instead, he waited until his roommate had opened the door to his room and gone inside. Then, he hurried to the door and stuck his palm in the jam to keep it from closing all the way.

Maybe Mustard wasn't entirely done with playing detective, after all.

He peeked into the room through the slit in the door. Tanner had emptied the contents of the envelope onto his desk—a sheaf of papers—and was sifting through them as if he was searching for a particular piece of information.

Well, Mustard wasn't going to learn what it was from here. He pasted a casual expression his face and opened the door wide.

At the sound, Tanner jumped a mile. Well, that wasn't exactly the behavior of an innocent person, now was it?

"Hey, man," Mustard said. "Everything okay?"

"Soldier boy," said Tanner, breathless. "You scared me!"

Scared him . . . by walking into his own room? "What's up?"

"Nothing," he mumbled, and started gathering up the papers and shoving them back into the envelope.

"What are those?"

"Nothing!" Tanner shouted, and then dropped the envelope. The papers slid all over the floor. The one that drifted onto Mustard's shoe was a photocopy of an envelope. It read:

Olivia Vaughn

Tudor House

Rocky Point, Maine

Mustard picked it up. He met his roommate's eyes. They were bloodshot and hollow. Probably to be expected, given Tanner's drinking the previous evening. "Are you okay, Tanner?"

"Give me that!" He tried to snatch the paper from Mustard's grip, but Mustard had a pretty firm grip. He whiffed, then stumbled, then appeared to give up entirely and collapsed on the bed.

Mustard decided to take that as a no.

"What is this?" he asked, waving the sheet.

Tanner rolled over and sat up, putting his head in his hands. "I don't know. It was in my mailbox at the student union just now."

Mustard picked up another sheet, this one also a photocopy of an old letter, from someone named Richard, and handed them both over to Tanner. "Mean anything to you?"

"Unfortunately, yes," Tanner grumbled. He grabbed

the envelope and pulled out another sheet. This one had a sticky note pasted on the page, scrawled over with thick black marker.

Here's the proof. Make up your mind or be part of the problem.

"This mean something in particular?" Mustard asked him.

"It means I'm being haunted," Tanner said.

Mustard was very quickly reassessing his opinion on the rest of the Murder Crew's crazy theories. "By Dr. Brown?"

Tanner was silent for a long moment. "By Vaughn Green."

That was a marvelously common sentiment these days. "What do you mean?"

Tanner hesitated for another twenty seconds. There had never been so much sustained silence in this room. "The night before he died, Vaughn came to see me."

"That's what I heard," said Mustard.

"You heard?" Tanner raised his eyebrows. "Vaughn talked to you?"

Mustard shook his head. "Plum said he saw Vaughn here that night."

And now Mustard remembered something else. In all the chaos of that morning, before the bloodshed and the car crash, Green had driven to campus to pick a fight with them. He'd chased Finn and Mustard across the lawn in front of Tudor, demanding to know what they'd claimed to have seen in the tunnels that night.

Tell me, punk! Before you start accusing people of murder!

He'd never really thought of it again. After Vaughn's death, who he had mistakenly thought Mustard and Finn were accusing of murder didn't seem to matter much anymore. Besides, it had been Keith who'd killed Rusty in those tunnels.

Right?

Mustard looked carefully at his roommate.

"Do you want to tell me what you two talked about?" Mustard asked. "I didn't know you were friends."

Tanner took another deep breath. "We weren't. At least, I didn't think we were. He as always so busy with work-study and his music, and I had crew and . . . Amber. I didn't even know he was dating that Orchid girl until later."

"No one did."

"He was acting so weird," Tanner admitted. "Asking me all this stuff about my dad and Dick Fain. They'd been friends here, you know. My dad was pretty instrumental in convincing Fain to sell his glue formula. Soon after, the company went from being Northeast Chem to Curry Chem. Barely out of high school and my dad was this total business superstar."

"And so was Fain, right?"

"For a year or two, and then he died." Tanner looked away.

"So what was Green asking for?"

"I don't know. I don't know if *he* knew. He was asking if Curry had all the rights to the glue, or if they split it with the Fain estate, or Blackbrook, or whatever."

"How does it work?" Mustard asked. He knew that Blackbrook had restrictive rules on student work, but he thought those were put in place after Fain's invention, when they realized what a goldmine it had been.

"Well, Fain died without a will, so my dad and the rest of the board managed some legal tap dancing to have the patent assigned to Blackbrook, who turned around and licensed it to the company."

"Sketchy," said Mustard.

Tanner shrugged. "That's business. But it only works because Fain had no heirs to fight over his estate." He looked down at the letters. "But Vaughn said that was wrong. He said he had proof that he was an heir to the Fain estate, and he wanted me to put him in touch with someone who could help."

Somehow, Mustard doubted that anyone at Curry Chem was interested in helping some Rocky Point scholarship kid mount a claim against them for any part of the Fain glue fortune.

"What did you do?" Mustard asked.

"Not much," said Tanner. "I mean, Vaughn died the next day."

Yeah, Mustard could relate to that feeling. "So you just let it go?'

Tanner kept his eyes in his lap. "What does it matter? Vaughn is gone, and he said his parents were dead. That's why Orchid is putting up all his music or whatever." He shook his head. "But . . . I don't know. If all that's true, then where did this mail come from? How does someone know what Vaughn and I talked about that night?"

Mustard frowned. He'd told Peacock that he wouldn't tell Tanner about their suspicions. But that didn't mean he couldn't tell his roommate about their other discovery. Besides, it was clear from this conversation that whatever was going on with Vaughn and Tanner was about a lot more than just some lab equipment.

"I think I know where it came from," he said. "Vaughn has a brother—Oliver."

Tanner paled. "A brother? He never mentioned that."

"Yeah, apparently that was a thing. It was a huge secret or something—"

"Does he live on Rocky Point?" Tanner had jumped to his feet.

"I think so," said Mustard. "And if Vaughn was an heir, then his brother would be, too—"

"I have to go talk to him," said Tanner, jumping to his feet. "Right now."

"Do you want me to come with you?" Mustard asked.

"No, soldier. This is a solo mission." Tanner grabbed the envelope and his backpack and headed out the door.

It was funny. Mustard would have thought that learning the origin of the mysterious letters would help calm Tanner down, but he seemed more haunted than ever.

13

Scarlett

Surprising no one—but least of all Scarlett—the boathouse was empty of everything except boats, a few buckets, and some long, moldering coils of rope.

"I swear, this place was full of lab equipment and laptops a few months ago," Orchid declared.

Scarlett didn't doubt it. She may have doubted the whole ghost story, but Orchid had been right about that. Well, almost.

"That was a few months ago."

"True," Finn added. "Plenty of time for Tanner to fence whatever they had stashed here."

"Tanner," mused Scarlett. "Or someone else." She turned to Orchid. "Maybe the thief wasn't Vaughn. Maybe it was Oliver."

After all, who was more likely to be robbing the school? The trust-fund kid or the townie who was stealing half a scholarship?

"If I were Oliver," said Finn, "I'd want a backup plan to this crazy scheme of the two of them both going to college on different scholarships. Like, how would that even work? Wouldn't the schools find out that they'd enrolled in two different places?"

Scarlett considered this for a moment. Applicants had their high schools send transcripts and recommendations with their applications, but as far as she knew, it was up to the students to respond to acceptance letters. Did colleges even compare class rosters? Had anyone ever tried this scam in the history of college applications? "I don't think it's a scam anyone has ever thought of pulling before. How often do you get identical twins pretending to be a single person, let alone doing so to get a scholarship to college?"

"This is moot," said Orchid, slicing her hand through the air. "Vaughn's dead and Oliver's not pretending to be him anymore, so who cares whether or not their wild plan would actually have worked?"

Scarlett shrugged. It was a useful thought exercise, if nothing else. If colleges weren't poised to sniff out that particular scam, were there other loopholes someone much more skillful than Vaughn Green might exploit? For example, someone like her?

Scarlett's makeup SAT scores weren't much better than her practice test, and she knew a Blackbrook diploma didn't carry the same cachet it used to. Who cared if you were getting all As in English when your English class now consisted of an ill-trained sub showing videos of teen movies based on the works of William Shakespeare? Princeton was becoming ever more unlikely, and she'd been so busy with Vaughn's music the last few months, she'd barely had time to notice.

But Finn, at least, was willing to get back on topic. "Now I'm wondering . . . who was it I caught in Tanner's room that night? Oliver or Vaughn?"

Orchid shrugged. "I've been asking myself that question all day. Was it Oliver or Vaughn who said this, who did that—"

"Was it Oliver or Vaughn you were in love with?" Scarlett prompted.

Orchid said nothing, which was practically worse than outright denial. Ugh. Why had she put all her eggs in the Vaughn Green basket? Now months of Scarlett's hard-won success was going to go right into Oliver's wallet, and she would be left with nothing.

Unless she could get Orchid back on her team. Maybe her friend wouldn't be so quick to hand everything over to Vaughn's brother if they knew for certain he had a criminal past.

"What did he say to you?" she asked Finn.

"Honestly, Scar, I don't remember. You know, on account of all that murder and violence that happened the next morning?"

Fair enough. Scarlett hadn't always done so well coming in contact with dead bodies. Maybe the difference was that Keith wasn't dead. Not yet, anyway. For Scarlett, that whole mess had just been another problem to solve. Keith was bleeding out on the floor of the study? Find first aid and get him to a hospital. Orchid had delivered the killing blow? Call her lawyers, set up an argument of self-defense. Those were the kinds of tests Scarlett was truly good at.

And this, too, was a problem with a solution. Scarlett just needed time to work it out. "Then all we know for sure is that one or both of the Green boys were involved with Tanner in some kind of thievery on campus."

"Excuse me!" Orchid cried. "We know nothing of the sort! We know one of the Green boys was talking to Tanner the night before Vaughn died, and we know this shack used to have a lot of expensive equipment in it."

"And Olivia Vaughn's letters," Scarlett pointed out. "Which connects this equipment to the Greens."

"It could just as easily connect to the crew team," said Orchid. "Oliver said he'd never seen those letters before in his life."

"Oh, and he's got a great track record when it comes to telling the truth!" Scarlett was disgusted. "You're just going to defend him—both of them!—no matter what."

She couldn't believe Orchid. One look at a surviving Green, and the past four months just vanished. *Scarlett* had been the one by her side every second. The one making sure she worked with her lawyers and the media, the one keeping the worst of the internet comments at bay. The one who had engineered the entirety of her dead boyfriend's current success!

"Well, I'm not going to start accusing people of theft or murder based on such flimsy evidence!" Orchid declared. "Rusty was killed by Keith. Dr. Brown had a stroke."

"I don't know if I'm sure of that anymore," said Scarlett, crossing her arms.

"What's next?" Orchid scoffed. "Mrs. White didn't really kill Boddy?"

"Maybe." Scarlett shrugged one shoulder. "Maybe we were wrong about everything when it came to Vaughn Green."

Orchid stared at her in shock. "What are you saying?"

"I'm saying as long as we're going with wild speculations,

how about this one? Headmaster Boddy found out about Vaughn and Oliver's scam the night of the storm, and one of them—maybe both of them—killed him."

Orchid's chest was rising and falling rapidly. Her face had gone ghostly pale.

"And Mrs. White, their godmother, took the fall."

"Oh my God," whispered Finn.

But Orchid said nothing, which Scarlett knew meant that she'd already considered this possibility.

Scarlett went on. "I lived in Tudor House for two years. I knew Mrs. White pretty well, and she never seemed like a murderer to me."

"How about me, Scarlett?" Orchid breathed. "Do I seem like a murderer to you? Because that's what I am."

"No, I just—"

"You just nothing. You said enough. You've always hated Vaughn and now you hate Oliver."

"I didn't even know Oliver existed until this morning!"

"And you've already accused him of multiple murders!"

"Ladies," said Finn, stepping between them. "Let's just dial it back a bit. We've all had a lot of information thrown at us today. We need to take some time to analyze it."

"You analyze the data, professor," Orchid said, seething. "I'm out of here." And then she turned on her heel and marched out of the boathouse.

"See?" called Scarlett at her retreating back. "You might have left Hollywood, but you still act like a diva!"

And then the boathouse was quiet, with nothing but the creak of old boards and ropes. Scarlett didn't even know if she believed what she'd just said about Oliver, but she sure as hell knew she didn't like the guy. First the schools' computers and microscopes, and now her entire music channel? He may not be a murderer, but he was definitely a thief.

"Well," said Finn, who couldn't quite hide his smirk, "You sure told her."

Scarlett couldn't take him right now, on top of everything. "I do *everything* for *everyone* around here, and no one appreciates it. She says I hate Vaughn, but I'm the one who made him a posthumous rock star. His stupid brother wouldn't even have that check she just gave him if it weren't for my months of hard work. I had to moderate a forum discussion on finger calluses last week."

"What check?" Finn asked.

"Are you not listening to me? *Finger calluses!* It was disgusting." Hundreds of closeups of people's hands, with shiny, angry red grooves marring their skin. Who knew playing the guitar meant bodily mutilation?

"It sounds disgusting," he agreed. "But what check?"

She gave up. "Well, it's technically Oliver's music, isn't it? Since he's Vaughn's closest living relative. So we were producing it illegally, and Orchid and Oliver came to some kind of agreement about how to settle that."

"I hope it included paying you for your trouble."

Ah, there was the Finn she knew and loved. Always quick to figure out the angle. She missed the old days, when they'd been an unstoppable pair. "It did. Fair market rates."

"Good. I wish I'd let you handle my business last year. The way things are going now, I'm going to lose all of it."

Then he told her about his recent visit from Perry Winkle, and the threats the new interim headmaster had made.

"If you ask me, the real thieves at this school are the administration and Curry Chem," he finished. "If Tanner or the Greens really were stealing a few laptops from the school, it's chump change compared to what the officials are getting away with. Tanner even told me the other day that if the school goes under, Curry stands to lose a lot because of the friendly agreements they've forced student inventors to broker with them."

"I don't get it," Scarlett asked. "Why didn't you sell your formula months ago, before the school got wind of it?"

"Because then they'd learn about it anyway, and I'd have a lawsuit on my hands."

Ah, yes, like with Oliver and the music.

"Besides, I'm not so good with the sales part of things. I needed a Scarlett of my own." He gave her a shy smile, the kind she knew he'd scientifically calibrated to come across as charming.

She was not charmed. If he'd just been honest with her last fall, they could have made a mint from his formula! Now she had to deal with Oliver Green, and Finn was going have all his work co-opted by Curry Chem and their manipulative contracts. What was with Blackbrook boys and their endless lies?

Well, Orchid might fall for it, but Scarlett would not.

"I now see why you wanted to talk earlier," she said, "before all this nonsense came to light."

"Yeah, but I get that we don't have time for all that now."

"Don't be silly," said Scarlett. "I am excellent at multitasking. How do you think I run so many student clubs? I can solve murders and fix your problem. And plan prom, too."

"This is a lot more complicated than a student club. I don't know if we can beat them this time."

"You're wrong," she said, "as you so often are."

He opened his mouth as if to object, then wisely shut it again.

Good. Finn worked best when he took her directions and ran with them. This was the proper order of things. The real problem, as Scarlett saw it, is she hadn't been given all the information. Oliver was an unknown quantity. Had she been aware of his existence, she could have factored it into their plans. Heck, she could have made it work to her advantage. People just needed to tell her things.

And that went for Phineas Plum, too.

"Here's the deal, Finn," she said. "You didn't tell me about your dye, which was a mistake. And now we have a mess to clean up. But you're still not telling me other things."

He blushed all the way into his hairline. "What?"

"You said you knew there was a fight in the tunnels the night Rusty was killed, but you never said how. What were you doing in those tunnels?"

"I was . . . looking for my dye."

"Lies."

"I was! You know I was!"

"No. What I know is that you hadn't been able to get into the tunnels before you and I broke into the secret passage in the study. At which point, if you recall, Rusty was already dead." She definitely remembered his corpse falling on her head.

And then she remembered something else. That the very-much-dead Rusty had a bloodstained note on him. One that had been signed with a set of initials belonging only to herself and—

"Mustard," she said, as she put it all together.

"What?" Finn said, turning even redder.

"Mustard was the one in the tunnels the night Rusty died!" she exclaimed. "What was he doing there?"

"Looking for my dye," Finn said.

"Stop lying!"

"I'm not!" he shouted back. "Mustard knew I'd left the dye in the secret passage during the storm and couldn't get to it once they sealed the entrances. He bribed Rusty to go into the tunnels and try to get in the back way. But then—something went wrong. There was someone else down there. Mustard never saw him, and we were going to go to the police the morning of the SATs, but after everything that happened, it seemed pointless. We figured the voice he'd heard fighting with Rusty was Keith. Case closed."

But was it? Were any of these cases closed? Vaughn or Oliver killing Headmaster Boddy and letting Mrs. White take the fall made a lot of sense, especially with the size of the secret they'd been guarding. But Dr. Brown was trickier. After all, neither of them went to Blackbrook any longer. She thought of the file she'd spotted on Dr. Brown's computer: *Vaughn Financial Claims.* At the time, she'd figured it was about a wrongful death suit Vaughn's family must be pursuing against the school.

But Vaughn's family was . . . Oliver? So if he was suing, then did Blackbrook know about him? It made no sense.

And Finn's story wasn't finished. He turned and walked a few feet away, then came back, his hands clenched at his sides. "Scarlett, I have to tell you something else."

"Okay." She steeled herself. Given the revelations of the day, she had no idea what her friend was about to hit her with.

He straightened up to every inch of his height. "I'm . . . bisexual."

Scarlett blinked. She thought it was something important, like murder. "Oh."

He let out a breath, and slumped. This had clearly been a big deal to him. She should react more.

"Thanks for telling me." She placed her hand gently on his shoulder. "I mean it."

"Well, in the spirit of honesty . . ."

"Right." She furrowed her brow. Why was he bringing this up now? Scarlett couldn't say she had been expecting it, but honestly, she always had to take a moment to reorient herself whenever she learned about people's romantic interests. It seemed like such a waste of energy. Like a few months ago, when she figured out that Mustard had a thing for—"Wait, does this have anything to do with Mustard?"

The blush came back. "Why do you ask that?"

"Because he has a crush on you." She'd put it together the night she and Mustard had gotten in trouble with Dr. Brown.

His expression turned to one of shock. "How—how do *you* know that?"

She shrugged. "Because I'm smart? And observant? And he bribed Rusty to get your dye back?"

Again, Finn relaxed. "Okay. I mean, that's actually how I figured it out, too."

He'd figured it out already? "Finn, are you two *together*?"

"No!"

Well, that was a relief. Scarlett would far prefer to imagine that there was a person besides herself on this campus who could pay attention to something other than their libido.

"I mean—not really."

Scratch that.

"We made out a few times. But not in months, because he's—he's not really cool with it."

Yes, so Scarlett had gathered. Unlike Finn, who seemed ready to march in a Pride parade. "Have you told anyone else? Have you told Peacock?"

"No," Finn said firmly. "And you can't tell her, either, okay?"

"Of course not!" Scarlett was offended by the very idea. She liked her secrets just where they were, thank you very much. "But I thought you and she had been spending all this time together recently—"

"Yeah, not like that," Finn said. "I know I used to be really hung up on her, but we're just friends now. She needs a friend. She's still struggling from the accident."

"I know," said Scarlett. "But I can only handle so many crises at a time."

"Beth isn't your responsibility."

She snorted. "She doesn't sound like she's yours, either."

Scarlett knew that Peacock's parents had gotten her a team

of doctors for her various injuries, but her trauma lingered, and after her experience with "Ash the life coach," Peacock reacted in a strongly negative manner to any suggestion she consult a therapist for her mind and not just her body. Orchid had even set her up with Orchid's psychologist in Hollywood, but Peacock had blown her off in favor of more scribbling in her ever-present notebook.

"And you should think about telling her anyway," she went on, "since you guys are such good friends now."

He shook his head. "No. I'm not going to risk it. Look how fast you connected me to Mustard. He would freak."

"Peacock wouldn't guess."

"You did."

"Yeah," Scarlett scoffed. "But I'm a genius."

If only everyone else would realize it, too.

14

Orchid

The rest of the weekend passed without anyone getting any answers. Well, except for Scarlett: She did manage to book the Singing Telegrams for prom, which Orchid only found out about because in order to secure them for the high school dance, Scarlett had apparently promised the band a two-song livestream of the event on Vaughn's channel. Like all of Vaughn's other fans, Orchid got a push notification of the announcement.

The #MurderCrew group chat was dark, too. Apparently, no one felt like chatting now that they knew Oliver had been silently observing all their texts for months. For all Orchid knew, the others had set up a secondary group chat and left both her *and* Oliver out of this one.

Actually, that would be just like Scarlett.

Amber had gone home for the weekend, Violet was cramming for a history makeup, and Peacock had progressed from a notebook to a full-fledged diagram laid out on the billiard table with photos she'd cut from the yearbook and a ball of yarn she'd swiped from Mrs. White's forgotten knitting basket in the corner of the study. Orchid wanted no part of that.

But she didn't want to be alone with her thoughts, either, and that's where she was left, from Saturday afternoon through Sunday and, once again, when class let out on Monday afternoon.

Vaughn, how could you?

Last winter, when Keith was threatening to strangle Orchid in the study, he told her scary things about Vaughn. Scary, delusional things she'd figured at the time were little more than an attempt to be cruel in the moments before he killed her. Stuff about how Vaughn sneaked around in the tunnels, about how he visited Mrs. White in prison, about how he was the most dangerous person she knew.

What a good liar he is! The parts he plays . . . he's a better actor than you are.

She hadn't believed Keith. But obviously some of what he'd said was true. Vaughn was indeed a liar—he'd been lying to all of them about Oliver, about their bizarre plan to impersonate a single student at Blackbrook. What if the other things Keith had said were true as well? Vaughn obviously did a lot of sneaking around Blackbrook. Maybe he *was* visiting Mrs. White.

Maybe Orchid didn't know him at all.

She realized now that these past few months, as she had been helping Scarlett produce Vaughn's music, she had erected in her head a sort of imaginary Vaughn. Her imaginary boyfriend, who was poetic and romantic and sweet and gentle. The real Vaughn was someone else entirely.

The real Vaughn might not entirely have been Vaughn. Not always. Oliver had denied it every time she asked, but she didn't know what to make of the connection she felt every time they had touched—in his home, in Tudor. Was it only that he looked so very much like Vaughn, and that she wanted him to be Vaughn with every fiber of her being?

Or at least, to be the person she'd constructed in her fantasies?

If she were speaking to Scarlett, she probably would have been talked out of the very foolish thing she did next. But she was not, and so she took out her phone and typed out a text.

ORCHID

> I don't know how regularly you are checking this account, but I also realize I don't have any other way to get in touch with you.

The reply was swift.

VAUGHN

> I'm here.

If only! She knew it wasn't him. She *knew* that. It was just Oliver on Vaughn's account. But seeing his texts, like they used to come this winter when she was in California and he was in Maine and they'd texted each other like crazy, long before either of them had been willing to admit anything resembling feelings—well, it broke something inside of her.

It was Oliver, but that was enough.

VAUGHN

> How are you?

Scared. Lonely. Confused. Concerned. Furious, and not sure if it was at Oliver, Vaughn, or the world in general.

ORCHID

I don't know. It's . . . a lot.

VAUGHN

Yeah, try living it for years.

I miss your brother.

There was a long pause on the other end.

VAUGHN

I miss him, too. I didn't realize how much I would.

What a strange thing to say. Vaughn was the only family Oliver had. Of course Oliver would miss him!

VAUGHN

We didn't always get along. Actually, we almost never got along. What we were doing—it made us hate each other. I couldn't be myself because of him, and I imagine he felt the same way.

ORCHID

You mean he resented you because he had to share his life with you?

Another pause.

VAUGHN

> Vaughn definitely resented
> everything he had to share.

It couldn't have been easy for either of them. For years, Orchid had avoided making friends at Blackbrook, terrified people would guess her secret. She imagined it was much the same with Vaughn and Oliver. All those times she thought Vaughn was being rude in history class, it was just Oliver keeping her at a distance—keeping everyone far enough away not to realize who he was.

When your very identity is the thing you have to hide from the world, what other response is there but to start hating who you are?

ORCHID

> But you don't have to share
> anymore.

Wow, had she really just typed that?

VAUGHN

> Means a lot less when it's only a
> reminder that your brother will never
> get the thing he wanted all his life.

Right, the music. Of course, he was talking about the music. She supposed the money she had given him was cold comfort in the face of not having a Blackbrook diploma and a scholarship to college, of not having your brother, yet knowing that he did, in fact, have what it took to be a very successful musician.

ORCHID

> I think he'd be happy knowing you're still working to help him achieve his dreams.

VAUGHN

> I hope so.

She bit her lip and pressed the phone to her chest. What was she thinking? This wasn't Vaughn.

Another text buzzed through.

VAUGHN

> What are you doing right now?

She didn't know. Orchid imagined her therapist would have lots of questions. Her relationship with Vaughn might have been a healthy, normal thing for her to do, but this? Anything but.

VAUGHN

> Are you busy?

Oh. That. Her fingers flew.

ORCHID

> No.

VAUGHN

> Can I come see you?

Orchid's breath caught in her throat.

ORCHID

> Yes. Please.

Her therapist would have many, many questions. Orchid herself had many questions, but she didn't allow herself to ask any of them. Instead, she changed into a nicer pair of jeans and a body-skimming top. She brushed her teeth and her hair and she even put on lip gloss.

It would take Oliver half an hour to walk here from Rocky Point. But she ought to go down and wait for him in the hall anyway, because heaven forbid Scarlett got to him first. In fact, she ought to do a sweep of the entire ground floor.

It was clear. Even Peacock had abandoned her elaborate diagram this evening. And who knew where Scarlett had gone off to? But it wasn't Tudor House, and for that, Orchid was grateful.

She didn't need anyone else asking questions.

As she stood in the hall, peeking out the long windows alongside the front door, she thought she heard a noise from the kitchen. Maybe someone was here after all? Orchid rounded the stairs and headed toward the back of the house.

The kitchen was empty, but the back door near the pantry was unlocked. Orchid locked it. Could never be too safe at Blackbrook. She cast a glance at the pantry. The secret passages were sealed now. Really, truly sealed.

But she had heard something. She no longer thought she was experiencing auditory hallucinations. She hadn't been wrong about "Morningfall." She wasn't wrong about this.

Back in the hall, Orchid noticed the ballroom door was open, and when she approached the threshold, it was to find Oliver inside, standing near the chaise and looking very seriously at a guitar that rested on a stand near the wall. He looked—well, he looked like Vaughn. He wore a pair of work pants and faded boots and a red hoodie pushed down off his head. She wondered if they used to share clothes. If they smelled the same.

"You just feel free to let yourself in?"

He raised his head, one half of his mouth turned up. "I was letting myself into this house when you were still in Hollywood."

Good point. "So you know where Mrs. White kept her spare keys?"

He chuckled. "No. I have a key."

Of course. Orchid remembered Keith telling her about how Vaughn sneaked around the campus, even around this very building. She thought of the cache she'd seen in the boathouse. She thought of the storm, and how they'd searched for an intruder hiding somewhere in the mansion's rooms.

"I don't think that's how it should work."

"Yeah, because Blackbrook works the way it should."

She came farther into the ballroom, shutting the door behind her. "What are you doing in here?"

He looked away. "Visiting. This was Vaughn's favorite room."

"Because of the music?"

"Because this is where he kissed you." He patted the back of the chaise.

Orchid's throat went dry. "He told you?"

Oliver looked at her again, his expression impossible to make out. "Would you like me to apologize on his behalf?"

"No." She drew closer—not quite to the chaise, but only a few steps away. And that reminded her. "You should know, the others are formulating a theory about you."

"Oh yeah?" He sat down on one side of the chaise. There was plenty of room beside him. It was a clear invitation—one Orchid was determined to ignore. "What is it?"

"You're not going to like it."

"I didn't expect I would."

She took a deep breath. "They think you, and your brother, and Tanner Curry, were part of some kind of theft ring. That you were stealing equipment from Blackbrook and hiding it in the old boathouse to sell."

"Huh." Oliver appeared to consider this. "Tanner Curry? What possible reason would that guy have to steal things?"

Not exactly a denial. She walked the last few steps to the chaise. "And they think you murdered Dr. Brown. And maybe Rusty. And maybe even Headmaster Boddy."

He looked almost amused. "Why stop there? Maybe I murdered my grandmother. Maybe I murdered Dick Fain."

Orchid actually didn't know how Dick Fain had died, but she was pretty sure it was long before either of them had been born. "This isn't funny."

"No, Orchid, being accused of murder is never funny, and I should know. Vaughn thought I was a killer, too."

She looked down on him in horror. "He didn't!"

"He did. We fought about it on his last night on Earth. He accused me of the most horrible things. He hated me so much . . ." His voice caught.

"I'm sure he didn't hate you," she said, though the words felt stale in her mouth.

I can't let you become a murderer. I just can't.

Those were the last words Vaughn had ever spoken to her. Was he so upset about her having killed Keith because he already had a killer close to him?

"No you're not," Oliver replied coldly. "You're not sure because I'm not sure, and I've been thinking about this a lot longer than you have. Maybe he did hate me. Maybe he died thinking—" he broke off.

"What?" she whispered.

He shook his head. "My brother never would have been there that morning if it weren't for that fight. If it weren't for me. So if you're going to make a list of the people I've killed, you should probably start with him."

15

Orchid

Orchid had only met Oliver a few days ago—well, *really* met him—and yet she felt like she might understand him more than anyone else alive.

Don't be silly, she wanted to say to him. You didn't kill Vaughn. I did.

It was for her that Vaughn had loaded Keith in the back of Rusty's old car and taken off like a bat out of hell. It was because of her that he'd been driving like a maniac toward the bridge to Rocky Point.

He died because of her.

But she didn't say that. She just stood there, looking down at the top of Oliver's head and thinking that even this—the whorl of his hair over his scalp—was too much like Vaughn's. Did even their hair whorls match? How could she begin to catalog their differences when she didn't know which of her memories were of one twin and which were of the other?

Was Vaughn always Vaughn with her? In text, in conversation, in person?

The first time she'd kissed him, here in this very room, had he been Vaughn? He must have been. They went straight from there to the hospital to look after Rosa, and then from there back home to Tudor, which was the last time she'd kissed him.

Whoever she had kissed—it had only been one boy.

Had that boy been Vaughn?

"Sit down," Oliver requested.

Orchid didn't think she should. She began to move back, but he caught her hand. A charge, almost electric in its intensity, ran between their fingers, and the next thing she knew, she sat.

"Well," he said, staring down at their hands.

She snatched hers back. "Well."

"What do you want to know?" He looked at her, and she flushed a deeper pink than her hair.

So many things. So many, many things. Right now, one of them was whether or not he kissed like Vaughn. "The truth."

"Tall order."

Yeah, no kidding. But she could start small. "I just accused you of a whole host of crimes. Are any of them valid?"

"Some."

He was exasperating. "Which!"

His voice was soft and he was once more looking at her hands. "Not the ones that would make you mad, Orchid."

"So you were stealing laptops and microscopes and hiding them in the boathouse." At least that wasn't a violent crime. At least it made a kind of sense. At least it was forgivable . . . unlike murder.

"Steal from the rich and give to the poor?"

"You aren't Robin Hood!"

He gave her half a smirk. "That's what you think. I'm actually a really good shot."

That morning, after the hospital, the boy she had kissed had told her the same thing—that he'd learned to hunt, growing up in the wilds of Maine. Of course, both twins could have learned.

This wasn't Vaughn. This wasn't Vaughn.

And he wasn't telling her the truth.

"And Tanner?" she pressed.

Oliver snorted. "Tanner's got his own thing going on, trust me."

That wasn't an answer. "So you weren't working together to steal from Blackbrook?"

"When?"

That was it. She began to push herself to her feet.

"Wait." This time, his hand closed around her arm, the rough skin on his fingertips scraping the tender inside of her wrist. "I'll tell you whatever you want to know."

She swallowed thickly and shook herself free. "I think you'll tell me whatever you think I want to hear."

"What's the difference?"

"Whether or not it's true!"

Oliver was quiet for a long moment. "Lots of things are true at once. You're Orchid McKee. You're also Emily Pryce. One being true doesn't make the other one false."

"Spoken like someone with a lot of practice pretending to be someone he's not."

Oliver didn't deny this, either. "What do you want me to say? That pretending to be my brother nearly destroyed me? Because I think it did. I think it destroyed both of us."

"What do you mean?"

"It made Vaughn into the primary twin. Nothing I ever did mattered. And—and I think it ate away at my soul to pretend to be him, day after day, year after year. I resented that whatever I did, it was Vaughn getting the recognition. I hated the sound of his name. I hated being called it. After a while of that, I started hating him, too."

Orchid's heart was pounding. In her case, being someone else had finally set her free. But she could see how a false identity could be a set of shackles instead.

"And it also destroyed him. I think we both knew on some level that in order for it to work, neither of us could have a life—a real life. We couldn't have friends. We couldn't have—you—" He hesitated. "I mean, he couldn't."

"Yes. Vaughn couldn't." Her breath came in short sharp bursts. The boy sitting across from her wasn't Vaughn, right? He wasn't the boy who had kissed her, who had sent her songs, who had guessed who she was across an entire continent.

"Vaughn couldn't," he repeated. "But neither could I."

But did he want to? Orchid had promised herself no questions, but it was almost as if by setting the reasonable ones aside, she'd allowed the wild ones to take root and spread everywhere.

Maybe Vaughn wasn't the person she'd thought he was. But maybe that was a good thing. Her Vaughn—her sweet dead boyfriend, the one who had given up his life to help her—was far too good for a person like Orchid. She was a liar. A killer.

But this person . . . Oliver. He wasn't Vaughn. He admitted that he was a liar. That he was a thief. He hadn't even denied that he was a murderer, either.

Perhaps that was why she was drawn to him. Not because he looked like Vaughn, but because he looked like Vaughn and yet so clearly wasn't Vaughn. Wasn't her sweet, gentle, innocent boyfriend.

"There were things we each wanted that were at odds with the plans we'd made. One wanted to uncover the truth behind a family mystery. The other just wanted to make music and friends. We'd never seen eye to eye, but we started becoming enemies instead of partners. The last few months of his life were—they were horrible. All we did is hurt each other."

"Oliver . . ." Her hand rested on his knee, but he ignored it.

"Vaughn was the golden child. Vaughn was the good twin. Vaughn was the one I had to pretend to be. And if he was the good one—what did that leave me except to be bad?" He squeezed his eyes shut and took a deep, shuddering breath. "No wonder I believed—no wonder he hated me."

"It doesn't have to be that way anymore," Orchid said softly. "You can be yourself now. You don't have pretend to be anyone else. You're free."

"I'm not free. Look at me, sitting here with you. I successfully avoided you for months and now it's like I can't keep away."

"I know," she breathed. "I feel that way, too. Why is that?"

"I don't know," he admitted roughly. "I'm afraid to ask myself that question."

She felt exactly the same way. Her chin dipped on a nod. But she had to know. She took a deep breath, then met his eyes. "I know you said you don't want to play the game of when it was you and when it was him, but—I swear, it's all so confusing. I don't know how well I know you, but I feel like it must be better than you are letting on."

"Orchid—" he began. "I can't."

Couldn't he? "Then promise me—promise it was always Vaughn with us."

The corner of his mouth quirked, and again he said, "I can't."

She didn't know who moved first, or maybe she didn't want to know, but suddenly they were kissing.

Kissing Oliver was nothing like kissing Vaughn. Where Vaughn had been gentle and even hesitant, Oliver was eager and aggressive. He kissed her like he'd been wanting to do it forever, and Orchid kissed him back just as hard, because even if he wasn't his brother, Oliver was close enough.

Within minutes he had her flat on her back on the chaise, his weight pressing her into the cushions, his hips settled between her thighs. And even though Orchid had been moving toward this since the moment she'd first texted him, she wondered if she should put the brakes on after all.

"We shouldn't," she protested weakly, because it felt like someone should be saying it.

"Why?" he murmured, his mouth moving over her throat. A thrill coursed through her body. She clutched at his back.

She had no answer. It felt too good and nothing had felt good since she had bashed out Keith's brains four rooms down the hall. She arched her back into his touch and moaned as his fingers slid up under her shirt, then gasped when she felt him pop the button on her jeans.

"Um . . . Vaughn . . ." Orchid panted, but she was pulling him closer, even as she said it.

He raised his head, his greenish brown eyes staring down at her with a hard, flinty kind of gleam she'd never seen on the face of his brother.

"Vaughn's dead, baby."

And then he kissed her again, rough and punishing, which was probably what she deserved after calling out the name of one brother while the other was snaking his hand inside her jeans. But, oh God, if he stopped, she might kill someone.

Again.

She reached up and gripped his jaw, locking their lips together, because if she had an excuse to talk she'd probably stop this whole thing. It was a horrible idea. Deeply wretched. Downright evil.

And so, so good.

Since Orchid had come to Blackbrook, she'd isolated herself from everyone, male and female, until the storm. And then Vaughn had come along, and he'd been so sweet, and so kind, and she'd allowed herself to believe for a time that she could be like that, too. That she could deserve him, and a new life, and all the perks that came with it.

But that was a lie. She was Emily Pryce, a liar, and now she was a killer, and if that meant she was going to sleep with her dead boyfriend's brother on a couch in the empty ballroom, then so be it.

Her phone rang in her back pocket, buzzing hard enough that they both felt it.

Oliver lifted his head.

"I don't care," she breathed. It was probably just Scarlett, wanting to know where she was, as if Orchid would tell her.

"You really don't, do you?" he said, his tone half contemptuous, half disbelieving.

She hooked her leg around his back and pulled him closer to her. "Don't stop."

So Oliver didn't.

The phone went off again. Buzzkill. She yanked it out of her jeans and moved as if to toss it aside, but she caught the ID on the screen. Bianca.

Her lawyer?

"Wait." She scrambled up. "I have to take this."

Oliver sat back on his knees, his chest rising and falling rapidly, his pupils wide, his clothes in as much disarray as hers.

She pulled her arms back into her sleeves and adjusted her bra with one hand as she swiped the screen with the other.

"Bianca? What's up?" She hoped she sounded casual. But why would her lawyer be calling this late? Why was her lawyer calling at all?

"Emily, hi." No nonsense, as always. And they'd apparently slipped back into "Emily." Maybe Orchid should desist with her new name altogether. "I'm sorry to call so late. I've just received word that Linda White has been released on bond. I thought you should know, given your history."

"What!" Orchid hissed into the phone. She stood, yanked her pants back up around her hips, and walked a few feet away. "I didn't know that was an option?"

"Yes, well, there was a bond set, back when she was arraigned. Pretty low for a confessed murderer, actually. She wasn't viewed as a threat, despite her assaults on you and the other students." She could practically imagine the lawyer rolling her eyes, as if chiding Orchid for not having had her on retainer last winter. "We never revisited the topic, because it seemed unlikely that anyone would pay the bond—"

Orchid whirled around to stare at Oliver, who was still on the couch, putting himself back together. "But someone did," she said into the phone.

"Yes. It was paid, and White was released from custody earlier today, pending sentencing. We should talk about next steps. I want you to feel safe—well, as safe as anyone can feel at Blackbrook . . ."

She stared at Oliver, breathing hard. He gave her a questioning look.

No one was safe at Blackbrook.

"But I suggest filing a restraining order if you feel like there's any danger."

"It's fine," she said flatly. "What's done is done."

"I wouldn't say that—" Bianca began, but Orchid clicked off. She slid the phone back into her pocket.

"What was it?" Oliver asked.

There was only one person in the world with the money and the desire to release Mrs. White from jail: her surviving godson, Oliver Green.

"Did you use the money I gave you to bail out Mrs. White?" Orchid asked him.

Oliver met her gaze. "Yes."

"Not even going to bother lying about it?" she scoffed.

"Why would I deny what you know is true? Why would I deny doing it? Old women don't belong in jail."

"Mrs. White is a murderer."

"You're a murderer, too," he said with a shrug. "I don't automatically hate you for that."

But I do . . .

Orchid's jaw clenched. "Get out."

He laughed, and it was a horrible sound. "Who died and made you the queen of Tudor House?" He cocked his head. "Oh, that's right: *everyone.*"

Orchid shut her eyes and shook her head. She could not believe what she'd just done, how close she had come to doing something much worse. "I want you out of here. This is done."

I can't let you become a murderer.

Those had been Vaughn's last words to her. But she had become a murderer. And so much more, besides.

Vaughn had died protecting her. But she hadn't deserved it. Hadn't deserved him.

Oliver stood and finished fastening his pants. Orchid kept her eyes averted, like she hadn't just had her hands all over him.

"I want you to ask yourself what exactly you think I did wrong here," he said now. "Have you ever even seen the inside of a jail? It's horrible. And not like, a rough Hollywood set, where the craft services table is just offscreen. Really, truly horrible."

Orchid swallowed and said nothing.

"Do you know what it's been like for her all those months? She's going to go to a real prison soon, and that's going to suck, too, but at least I can give her this. She can get her affairs in order. That's all she wants."

Orchid was sure that Headmaster Boddy had wanted things in his life, too. But he didn't get them. He didn't get the chance to get his affairs in order, either. And Mrs. White had drugged Mustard, and hurt Karlee and Kayla, too. She might have killed Orchid.

"Isn't that what you want?" Oliver pressed. "You're out here, living your life, pretending nothing happened . . ."

"I'm not pretending anything!" she snapped.

That funny half-smile twisted his features again. Vaughn had never smiled like that, as if things were only amusing if they hurt. "Yeah, right. This was all pretend. Don't lie."

Lie? She wanted to vomit.

Oliver shook his head at her, but she wasn't sure if he was disgusted or just disappointed. Her own emotions wavered between the two as well. But at least he was leaving. At least she had that.

"Is she staying with you?" Orchid couldn't help but ask him as he headed for the door.

"Why?" Oliver asked. "Think I should throw a dinner party, invite the whole crew?"

"No," she replied coldly. "I think you should watch your back."

16

Mustard

This meeting of the Murder Crew was a mistake. Mustard picked that up right away.

The five of them had gathered in the billiards room of Tudor House, which was the first error. The room was currently serving as Peacock's bedroom, since her injuries meant she couldn't easily navigate the stairs to the upper rooms. She'd definitely put her own stamp on it, though—from the shelves lined with her tennis trophies to the massive poster board over the pool table covered with what she was calling evidence of murder. Mustard wasn't entirely certain how he was expected to respond to this. On one hand, yes, things had been pretty rotten at Blackbrook. But on the other, didn't anyone else notice that the school's former tennis star had gone entirely off the deep end?

And that was before she started dragging his roommate into the conspiracy.

"So you're saying he just disappeared?" Peacock demanded of him.

"No, I'm saying he went home for the weekend," Mustard said, frustrated. "Which is not suspicious."

"Weekend's over," Scarlett pointed out. "And he hasn't reappeared."

Her cell phone dinged again. It was doing so approximately every two or three minutes, to commemorate every thousand new views on Vaughn Green's latest song, "Morningfall." Mustard had heard it all over campus today. It was a catchy song, if not exactly to Mustard's tastes. Vaughn had indeed been talented, though if the lyrics were anything to go by, kind of screwed up. Of course, that was to be expected, given the enormous secret he'd been hiding. He supposed now that Oliver Green had come out of the woodwork, the world would soon hear every last ditty his brother had ever recorded.

Mustard would give Scarlett this: she sure knew how to create a spectacle. But the constant bell ringing was incredibly annoying. That was problem number two.

"You might not be aware of this," he told her, "but normal people often need personal time to deal with the death of a loved one."

"A loved one? Dr. Brown?" Peacock sounded skeptical. "Not with the fight I heard."

"You can fight with loved ones," said Plum, as if he needed to contribute something—anything—to this pointless conversation.

That—right there—was the third problem, and the most pressing one of all. Mustard had been doing pretty well avoiding Finn Plum all weekend. He hadn't passed him on campus, he'd kept his distance in the dining hall, and it was a particular point of pride that he'd left Plum's messages unread on his phone since they'd first come in.

But now, in person—well, he was just so Plum-y. Mustard remembered the day of the storm, when Plum had come into this very room, soaked to the skin. Mustard had lent him the shirt off his back. He remembered the night they'd spent in bedrolls on the floor on opposite sides of this very billiard table. He remembered how moonlight through the tall windows had cast long shadows on the other boy's slim back. He remembered most of all another dark room and other shadows, and a soft little kiss on the corner of his mouth.

Why? Why was *that* the kiss that had gotten lodged in his brain? He'd done much more with that other boy at his old school. He'd wanted to do much more with Plum, but then Plum had gone and started talking about his *family* and acting like what he wanted was to be Mustard's *boyfriend* . . .

Which was ridiculous. Because even if he did want a boyfriend—which he did *not*—Mustard knew Plum was not a good boyfriend to have. Just ask his exes—or ex? Mustard still wasn't precisely sure what had been going on with Plum and Scarlett. But he'd definitely screwed over Peacock freshman year. Everything had ended poorly, because Plum was a selfish, self-centered jerk, which was precisely what he'd proven by opening his big mouth to his family and making this all about him, about his *coming out* story.

Wasn't it?

"So were you able to find out what they argued about or not?" Scarlett was asking him.

What? Oh, right, Tanner. Mustard straightened his back, as if he was about to respond to a sergeant, then stopped himself. Scarlett was not in charge here, no matter what she liked to think.

"Tanner's not a murderer."

"That's not an answer to my question."

"Well, it'll have to do."

"Watch out, Mustard," said Peacock, "or we'll start to wonder what it is you have to hide."

He couldn't help it. He looked at Plum. Plum looked at his shoes.

His face heated with anger. "Look, that's what I came here to tell you. Whatever tree you're barking up, it's the wrong one. If Dr. Brown was murdered, it wasn't by my roommate. And that whole theory about him and Vaughn Green stealing stuff from the school is nonsense as well. Tanner's a Curry. He's got more money than anyone here, excepting maybe the movie star over there." He nodded in the general direction of Orchid McKee, who had been sitting completely silently with her arms crossed over her chest throughout this entire meeting. You would have thought she'd checked out completely, except for the way she twitched a bit when he said her dead boyfriend's name.

"I beg your pardon," Scarlett said. "Do you know how large my parents' hotel chain is?"

Mustard blinked at her. "The real question is: do I care?"

Scarlett's phone dinged again. Every time it did so, Orchid sank deeper into her seat. Pretty soon, she'd be disappearing altogether. She clearly hadn't thought this all the way through.

Girl obviously had no use for her own fame anymore, but hadn't realized that by producing and promoting Vaughn's music, she was not only consigning him to her same fate—even posthumously—but also dragging herself back into the spotlight.

He sincerely hoped she wasn't looking at the comments sections. People on the internet were accusing her of way worse things than murder.

"It's clear he doesn't care about any of this." Peacock was on her feet, or at least on one of them. She clomped toward him, waving her arm within its brace. "You're just going to defend Tanner."

"He didn't do anything!"

"Oh, and is that the final word on the subject? Mustard says Tanner didn't do anything and now the case is closed?"

"If you had any real evidence, other than you overheard them arguing—"

"That was plenty enough for you to start accusing people last time!" she said, seething.

"Beth," Finn said. He came forward and put a hand softly on her arm. "It's okay. Why don't you sit down?"

"I've been sitting down *for months!*" she shrieked. "And people are still dying on this campus, and next it could be one of us. It already *was* one of us. And it was almost me! And no one knows who was really responsible, and no one is going to pay for what they did, and why won't anyone listen to me? Why won't you listen!"

"No one else is going to die," Finn said.

"You don't know that," she growled at him. "I promise you, Finn, more people are going to die before all this is over."

Finn blinked at her, eyes wide. "Okay. Let's go sit down, all right? Come on, I'll get your . . . feet elevated. I'll make you tea."

"I don't want tea," she grumbled as Finn led her back to the sofa and got her situated. "I want *justice*."

Mustard frowned. She was unhinged. They all were.

"You know what I think?" he began. "I think this is all some fantasy you girls have cooked up to distract from what is really going on."

"That's not true!" Peacock snapped.

"Oh yes it is!" He jabbed a finger at her. "You flipped last year when someone suggested you might have had something to do with Boddy's death just because people overheard you fighting, and now you're accusing Tanner of the exact same thing. And you two"—he turned to Scarlett and Orchid—"are making baseless accusations against him to protect your new cash cow, because it's glaringly obvious who actually had the means and motive to steal from Blackbrook."

"You mean Vaughn?" Scarlett said, raising one sculpted eyebrow. "I don't think it was him anymore. I think it was Oliver."

"From what I heard, there's not much difference."

There was a bark of startled laughter from the couch.

"You're right." Orchid was making some kind of face, but Mustard couldn't tell if she was holding back laughter or tears. "I—I mean, you're right that it was Oliver, with the stolen goods, in the boathouse. He told me himself."

"He *what*!" Scarlett whirled to face her friend, seething. "*When?*"

Oh, interesting. This was clearly not something the two of them had discussed ahead of time.

"See? You don't even know which story you're going after!" He threw up his hands. "This is ridiculous. What are you even trying to accomplish here? A revenge scheme against Tanner for dumping Amber? You're going after him out of some kind of female solidarity? Why do girls always do stuff like that?"

Scarlett must have grown bored glaring at Orchid, because she turned around and directed her Medusa-level stare at him. "I'm getting a little tired of your casual misogyny."

Mustard shook his head, incredulous. "I'm not a misogynist."

She rolled her eyes. "No one admits to being a misogynist."

Not in Mustard's experience. "Believe me, I know plenty of guys who would."

"And they are just as bad as ones like you, who insist they aren't misogynists, but then still say things like 'girls always act like this' and 'a girl couldn't do that.'"

"Maybe you just don't have enough experience with women," suggested Plum.

Mustard turned to him, his eyes narrowed to angry slits. "What did you just say?"

"I mean," Plum added quickly, "that you spent your whole life at these all-boys' schools. Maybe what you think girls do or don't do isn't based on actual observations, but instead on faulty assumptions."

The last thing Mustard needed was Plum getting all scientific on him.

"This isn't an assumption, professor. I'm sitting here, looking at Peacock's suspect list, and there's not a single girl on it. You call me a misogynist, but why is she only accusing *men*?" Of this supposed murder, which probably wasn't even a murder.

"Men kill way more people than women," Peacock stated.

"Not in this house." He cast a pointed glance at Orchid, who didn't so much as change her expression.

Scarlett stepped between him and Orchid. "Orchid isn't a murderer. She killed a man in self-defense. You'd think with your military background, you'd know the difference."

"I do know the difference. And that's why I'm not going to spend too much time worrying about who you all think killed Dr. Brown, because I think it wasn't a person at all. I think it was just stress, like the authorities said."

"The authorities also said Rusty died of exposure," Plum said softly to his back.

Mustard didn't have a good response. Because he'd let the authorities at Blackbrook say that last winter, even though it wasn't true, and Plum knew it. It was the most cowardly thing he'd ever done.

Wasn't it?

He turned to look at Plum. Really look at him, for the first time in days.

And the other boy stared right back. As usual, he was completely unashamed. Mustard wondered what that must be like. It gave him the license he needed to do all the sketchy things he did, but it also let him just . . . just *be*.

Last winter, during the SATs, Mustard had walked out to go to the police and tell them what he'd heard that night in the tunnels. And Plum had come after him. There'd been no reason to do it, and plenty of reasons not to. But Plum had said *We go together. Murder Crew forever* and put his hand in Mustard's, and Mustard was weak . . .

"Let's table this for now," Scarlett announced, and somehow Mustard dragged his gaze away from Plum's. "I think we've talked about Tanner enough for one day. We should discuss another suspect." She tapped a new section of Peacock's poster. "Oliver Green."

No sooner had she said his name than the door to the billiards room opened and in walked the boy in question.

"Never let it be said I don't know how to make an entrance." He smiled, but it didn't reach his eyes.

Mustard stared. He'd been told about Oliver's existence—heck, he'd been the one to tell Tanner—and he'd even gotten advance warning that the Green twins looked enough alike to be able to pretend to be one another on campus for two years without anyone becoming the wiser, but it was still eerie to see him walking around four months after his brother's death. The close-cropped hair, the coppery green eyes, the beat-up jacket and boots—every detail was the same.

"Hi, guys," he said. "Nice to see the crew back together again."

Peacock gaped. "Have you been listening at the door this whole time?"

"Define *whole time*."

"Don't you knock?" she asked angrily.

"No."

Mustard was impressed. He may look like Vaughn, but this Green didn't act anything like his brother. This was the guy he'd sent Tanner to? Somehow, he thought he'd be just like his brother. But of course not. Those letters had the tone of a ransom note.

This Green wasn't here to make friends.

"He doesn't ever knock," mumbled Orchid from the couch. "He has a key."

Oliver smirked at her, and she visibly cringed. He finished his quick survey of the others, sizing each of them up in turn. Or at least, that's what it looked like. But Mustard noted that when Green got to him, he didn't exactly make eye contact. Mustard had promised himself he was done playing detective, but this mystery intrigued him. It wasn't just the wrongness of Oliver standing there, looking for all the world like a dude who'd been dead for months. It was something else. His hands stayed jammed deep in his pockets and his stance was rigid, as if he hadn't yet decided whether to fight or to flee.

Oliver shrugged. "I figured if you were going to speculate about my various crimes, I should at least be a part of the conversation."

17

Scarlett

Scarlett smiled at Oliver. He thought he was so smart, so sneaky. He thought he could get the better of her just because he and his brother had managed to lie to them all for years. But he no longer had the element of surprise on his side.

Step into my web, little fly.

"Speak of the devil," she said easily. "I'm glad to see you finally showed."

"What?" At last Orchid rose from the couch. "You *invited* him here?"

It was about time that she entered the conversation, too. Scarlett was sick of her friend's one-word answers, especially when she knew perfectly well that Orchid had more information about the Greens than the rest of them combined. "Of course I did. He's Murder Crew, too."

The others were staring at her in unabashed shock.

"But . . . he's a *suspect*," Peacock said weakly.

"Since when has that ever stopped us?" Scarlett said. "In fact, I think it was Oliver here—pretending to be Vaughn, of course—who reminded us that we were all possible murder suspects in this very house during the storm. It was *Oliver*—not Vaughn—who made us all suspect you of killing Headmaster Boddy, Peacock."

Peacock made an indignant little squeak.

Oliver's eyes widened in appreciation. "True! That *was* me! How did you guess?"

"I'm a genius, that's how," she snapped. "Once I knew there were two of you it became very easy to tell you apart."

"Did it?" He smirked at her.

She planted her feet wide and put her hands on her hips. "I've got some questions for you."

Her phone dinged in her pocket. "Morningfall" had been by far their most successful song release. She'd been watching the numbers climb all day, and set the notifications on her phone so she could keep track of things even in class. People had been desperate for a new tune from Vaughn for weeks, if not months, and Oliver had provided precisely that.

It was too bad he sucked so much.

She'd spent the whole weekend disentangling Vaughn Green from Oliver, trying to figure out which twin was which. There was a lot of evidence—years of battles and arguments with her, to start—plus all the videos she'd uploaded to the channel, where she got to see Vaughn's sheepish fumbles with his guitar, his shy introductions to songs that he was sending his crush, Orchid, his quick temper and frustration when he made mistakes in the recordings Oliver had handed over, the sadness and yearning that undercut each song.

Vaughn had never made sense to her before. He'd scared her in a way no one else on campus did, and now she understood why. It wasn't just that he was a liar. Lots of people here were: Orchid had lied about her identity, Finn had lied about his little science experiment, Mustard was standing right there in the room with them lying to himself about Finn, and Scarlett noticed all of it. Their lies made sense. They were protecting themselves. But Vaughn's lies had confused her. Everything about his behavior had confused her.

Now it didn't. The issue had been that Vaughn wasn't always Vaughn. Sometimes, he was Oliver. And if she wanted to keep their new business on track, Oliver was the person she had to deal with now.

"Are you going to give us straight answers?" Scarlett demanded.

"Sure." He shrugged a shoulder. "I've got nothing to hide anymore. All my secrets are coming out these days. It's very freeing, I must say."

"I can only imagine," she replied with false sweetness. "Let's begin. Did you steal supplies from Blackbrook to sell?"

"Yep," Oliver admitted matter-of-factly. "And stored them in the boathouse until I could unload them."

"Just you?" she asked, though she was pretty sure she knew the answer.

"Well, it wasn't your boy Tanner," he said, casting a glance at Mustard. "And it wasn't my brother, either. May he rest in peace." This last bit was added almost as an afterthought. He was awfully callous about the death of his brother. His brother, who was paying all his bills.

"Did you kill Dr. Brown?" Peacock broke in.

"No!" he scoffed. "Why would I do that?"

"Did you kill anyone else?" Scarlett asked quickly, before Peacock got them off track.

"Be specific."

Scarlett gaped at him. "Specific? Like you can't keep track of all the people you've murdered?"

"Sure," he said again.

Liar. She almost said it out loud. There was a brittleness to his indifference. So his brother was dead, so he was a thief and a liar, so they were accusing him of murder—it all skimmed the surface of this guy standing in their midst, his hands in his pockets like he hadn't a single care in the world. But the attitude was fragile. If she pressed in the right place, she could crack it.

Scarlett took a deep breath. "Did you kill Headmaster Boddy?"

The bomb dropped in the middle of the room. She heard Mustard's harsh intake of breath, saw Peacock's astonished expression. And most of all, she saw the flicker of fear in Oliver's eyes. Orchid and Finn might have been expecting it, but Scarlett knew it would come as a surprise to the others. This was one question she couldn't figure out on her own, and she wanted to be surrounded by witnesses before she asked. Oliver couldn't kill all of them, could he?

He swallowed before he spoke again. "You know, Vaughn thought I did. The night of the storm."

That wasn't what she was expecting, but she wouldn't let it derail her line of questioning. "Was he right?"

His eyes slid over to Orchid. "What do you think?" he asked her.

"I think you're disgusting," Orchid said, hugging herself.

"Not last night you didn't." He winked at her suggestively.

Scarlett forgot what she was doing completely. She turned to her friend, aghast. "*What.*"

Orchid cringed.

Oh. My. God. Scarlett wanted to scream. Months— *months!*—she had devoted to protecting Orchid's good name in the court of public opinion. She had shielded her from every insensitive internet comment, had made sure that only the most sympathetic of takes had been published to Vaughn's channel, had cast Emily Pryce as a hopeless romantic devoted to the memory of her dear, departed, struggling songwriter boyfriend—only to what? Have Orchid completely muck it up right when they were on the brink of stardom?

What in the actual—

"What did you *do*?" she shouted at Orchid.

Orchid's lips were a pale, thin line. "I think you should ask him what *he* did last night."

Every eye in the room turned from Orchid to Oliver.

"Well?" Scarlett demanded.

His mouth smiled, but his eyes did not. "Other than get to third base with a movie star?"

Orchid gasped and her hands dropped to her side. "Second! *Second!*" She looked at all of them. "Just second, I swear."

"*Just* second?" Scarlett couldn't believe what she was hearing.

"Eww," said Finn. "Still eww."

She was pretty sure that's what all of Vaughn Green's fans would think, too. Emily Pryce could *not* hook up with her dead boyfriend's twin brother. Especially if he, too, was a killer. That

wasn't good gossip, it was TV-movie, tabloid-trash, career suicide. Why hadn't Orchid warned her about any of this? They
may have been arguing the last few days, but Scarlett needed to
be kept up to speed with what was going on. She couldn't have
facts just dropped on her head like this. Scheming was impossible with misinformation.

"And that's not what I meant." Orchid crossed her arms
again. "I meant the *other* thing you did."

"Jeez, there's more?" asked Mustard. He rubbed his
temples.

"He used the money from Vaughn's music to bail Mrs.
White out of jail."

"Sure did," Oliver said blithely. "And I'd do it again."

Scarlett felt rage bubbling over within her. Everything was
spinning out of control. Mrs. White had been released? Orchid
and Oliver had hooked up? Why wasn't anyone listening to
her! She couldn't take this anymore.

"Answer the question," she stated. "Did you kill Headmaster
Boddy?"

"Do you mean, did I stab him in the chest?" Oliver's brow
furrowed, as if he was trying to remember.

What kind of answer was that? Her phone dinged again.

"What is that sound?" Oliver asked.

"None of your business," she snapped. Except it was. It was
literally his business. Of all the things she could have staked her
reputation on, it had to be his stupid dead twin's stupid music.

"It's the counter on Vaughn's channel," volunteered Finn.
"Every thousand hits on the new song."

For an instant, Oliver's face changed. The mean, smug

expression slipped, and surprise—real surprise—flashed across his features.

She didn't know why, though. Did he think the money had just materialized out of thin air? Still, it was interesting to see something could still wipe the vicious smirk off his face.

"You put it up already? How many hits does it have?"

She was not about to hand over her phone. "Over my dead body."

Mustard sighed. "Here." He held out his phone, displaying the music. Vaughn's voice, all tinny, spilled from the speakers.

And when this heart, this body, this shore, this dawn breaks
There'll be another addition to my list of mistakes.

Oliver reached for the phone with trembling fingers, then frowned, and shoved his hands back in his pockets.

Scarlett narrowed her eyes. This, too, was interesting. "You've seen it though, right? I mean, that's the video you gave me."

"I—" he swallowed. "I don't look at the channel."

But he was just fine with cashing the checks. "Why?"

He glared at her. "What do you mean, why? Because it's my dead brother on there, that's why!"

"May he rest in peace," Scarlett repeated back to him. Oliver flinched.

Mustard clucked his tongue at her. "Come on, now. Let's not get nasty."

"Nasty!" Scarlett shook her head, incredulous. "I'm not the one bragging about sexual exploits with my dead brother's girlfriend."

"Yeah, exactly," Mustard said. He spread his arms like he was ready to physically separate them. "Whatever . . . happened there, it's clearly complicated for everyone. And they obviously regret it, right?"

"I definitely regret it," grumbled Orchid.

"See?" Mustard said. "People sometimes do stupid stuff like that. Because . . . hormones. It doesn't mean anything."

Finn snorted.

"Excuse me!" Peacock sliced her hand through the air. "We're talking about murder here. Not hooking up, or how many hits Vaughn's new song has."

Oliver shook himself and turned his attention back to Scarlett. "Yeah. Did you ask me to come here tonight just to accuse me of murder?"

"Well, I thought it best to be surrounded by witnesses if I did."

"Linda White confessed to killing Boddy," he said.

"Yes, she did. But maybe she was taking the fall for the real killer." She lifted her chin. "Someone very important to her. Someone who is now more than happy to help her—say, get out of jail?—in exchange for her silence."

"Why would I kill the headmaster?" He was still dodging the question. "Either of them?"

"Because they discovered your secret. The one about you and Vaughn."

He thought about this for a minute. "You're right. That is a good motive."

"But is it accurate?"

"What are you asking? Would I stab a dude who found out the truth about me and my brother? Seems a little impulsive to me."

"I beg your pardon?"

"I'm not impulsive," Oliver went on. "That was Vaughn."

"Don't you dare," Orchid whispered harshly. "Don't you dare suggest that Vaughn killed Boddy. He was horrified by what happened to the headmaster. I was there. I saw it."

"Please," drawled Oliver. "You don't know if it was Vaughn or me with you that night."

"I—" Her mouth snapped shut.

Oliver turned his attention back to Scarlett. "Do you?"

"Do I what?"

"Know if it was Vaughn or me?"

Scarlett couldn't honestly say for sure. She had been chasing Finn and Peacock through the flooded campus.

"Guess you aren't as much of a genius as you thought." He shook his head, as if disappointed. "I'm not so impulsive as my brother was. I make plans. Real plans. Plans that are even now coming to fruition. Plans you could not possibly understand, Scarlett Mistry, but you are lucky to be just a tiny part of them."

She narrowed her eyes. "I am not a part of your plan."

"Really?" He looked amused. "Then who is producing all of Vaughn's music for me? I would never have had the money to get Mrs. White out of jail without your help."

Scarlett began to feel sick.

"What about Tanner?" Mustard said all of a sudden. "How does he fit into your plan? Did you send him those letters about Dick Fain?"

Oliver turned to Mustard. "I think Scarlett put it well when she said, 'none of your business.' "

"What letters?" Scarlett asked.

Orchid buried her face in her hands and groaned.

Wait . . . *those* letters? "The letters Orchid had? The ones from your grandmother and her old boyfriend? They were from Dick Fain?"

"Yes they were."

That meant . . . That meant . . . Scarlett felt faint. The letters were about what his grandmother planned to do with the baby she and the boyfriend had together. If what Oliver said was true, then Oliver was Dick Fain's grandson. Which meant the money Orchid had given him for Vaughn's music was chump change. If he got his hands on the Fain glue fortune, Oliver Green could buy and sell this entire campus.

She was cooked. She should have just stuck to prom planning.

Oliver laughed mirthlessly. "I think we're just about done here."

"No we're not!" exclaimed Peacock. "We still don't know who is guilty!"

"Blackbrook is guilty," said Oliver. "And Blackbrook is going to pay."

18

Peacock

**ELIZABETH PICACH'S ~~RECOVERY JOURNAL~~
INVESTIGATIVE NOTEBOOK**

POSSIBLE SUSPECTS

1. **OLIVER GREEN:** *Okay, so it's DEFINITELY Oliver, right? Everyone in that room saw the same thing. Even Orchid, and I guess she hooked up with him or something? Which . . . weird. She's WEIRD. So . . .*

2. **ORCHID MCKEE:** *That girl is TWISTED.*

3. **TANNER CURRY???:** *It does kind of seem like a stretch, now. But then again, he skipped campus.*

As for Oliver, I don't know. He left Tudor House, but if he has a key like Orchid said he does, we're not even safe in our own beds. Because if Oliver doesn't come in here to kill us, Mrs. White might.

I hate this feeling.

19

Plum

When Mustard left the billiards room after the meeting, Finn expected him to turn left and exit the house as well. Instead, he turned right.

Finn looked at the girls, but they were distracted—Scarlett and Orchid were fighting, and Beth was scribbling in her little notebook, lying with her legs elevated on the edge of the bed. As soon as Oliver was gone, they didn't seem to care what the other boys were doing.

But Finn cared.

He slipped out of the room just in time to see Mustard force the handle on the door of the conservatory and vanish inside. Finn knew that Dr. Brown had closed up the conservatory after Headmaster Boddy's death—a strange choice in Finn's opinion, given that it wasn't actually where the man had been killed, but only where Mrs. White had attempted to hide the body. But he supposed it was still a crime scene, and, unlike the hall of Tudor House, it could be closed off without restricting access to the rest of the house.

Quickly, he made his way down the corridor to the conservatory and peeked inside. Mustard was standing over the bloodstain they'd never fully cleaned off the floor, his brow furrowed. His hands were crossed over his chest, his arms testing the resilience of his T-shirt sleeves. Moonlight filtered in from the huge windows along the outside of the room, dancing over his broad shoulders and casting deep shadows across his face.

He was so hot.

It was almost a relief, Finn had realized, to be able to think things like this. For years, when he'd noticed a guy, he'd tied himself up in knots telling himself he was only appreciating objective aesthetic beauty, or was paying attention how the guy dressed or walked or acted because he wanted to emulate it. But now he understood it wasn't anything like that. Finn couldn't be Mustard if he tried. He had that laconic cowboy thing going on, but Finn had never seen a horse that wasn't pulling a carriage through Central Park. And Finn valued precision as much as any scientist, but he'd never have Mustard's soldier edge.

He didn't want to be like Mustard. He just wanted him. Coming to grips with that had opened up an entire world.

One that Mustard didn't want to live in.

"Are you just going to stand there, or are you going to come in?"

Finn started at the question. "I didn't know you'd seen me."

Mustard was still staring at the floor. "This is Blackbrook. I'd be an idiot if I didn't pay attention to people sneaking up on me."

Finn came a few steps into the room. "What are you doing?"

"Thinking." Mustard pointed at the stained floor. "Boddy was a big fellow. How did Mrs. White drag him in here all by herself?"

Finn drew up beside Mustard. "So you're thinking there might be something to Scarlett's theory."

"I'm thinking there's a lot more going on at Blackbrook than we thought," Mustard replied. "Vaughn and Oliver were both here, the night of the storm, and that was probably the least dangerous of the secrets they were keeping. Oliver admitted to stealing supplies, and you and I both know how much the Fain glue fortune is worth to the school. Headmaster Boddy discovering any one of those secrets is motive enough for murder—and each of the three is a lot more plausible than some kindly old grandma snapping because she might have to move."

Finn thought about this. He wasn't sure "kindly old grandma" properly described Mrs. White.

"But," Mustard added, "maybe that's just my *misogyny* talking."

Finn said nothing.

"So you think it's true." Mustard didn't look at him.

He hesitated for four and a half seconds before answering. "I think in the last thirty seconds you suggested that a woman who definitely kidnapped two girls and dragged them into the secret passages didn't have the strength to drag a corpse down a hall."

"Maybe she didn't do the kidnapping part alone, either." Mustard rubbed the back of his head thoughtfully. "There were two Greens and nobody knew it. That right there makes for an airtight alibi for pretty much anything that happened on this campus until the moment Rusty's car went over that bridge."

Finn thought about it. "If Oliver really murdered anyone, he wasn't exactly being subtle about it just now. I think he's just playing with us."

"He's certainly playing," Mustard agreed. "But what's his game? In the same conversation, he told us how upset he was that his brother thought he'd murdered Boddy, denied murdering Boddy, hinted that he had murdered Boddy, and cast suspicion on his brother for murdering Boddy."

Finn made a face. "When you put it like that, he sounds nuts."

And maybe Oliver had gone a little crazy. Finn didn't know what he'd do if he lost his whole family, if his brother had died suddenly and violently like Vaughn had. And he was quite certain that as close as his family was, none of the Plums had the bond that Oliver must have had with his twin.

Mustard nodded soberly. "The only thing I'm absolutely sure about is that he sprung Mrs. White from jail and that he sent those letters about Dick Fain to Tanner. And both of those things he did with the help of Orchid. Who is also a killer."

True. Finn would never forget the sight of her standing over that man with a bloody wrench in her hand. "But that was self-defense."

"That's what we all thought."

"You think there's another story?"

"I don't know!" said Mustard. "If we're going to rethink what happened to Boddy, then maybe we have to rethink all of it."

"I think *that's* his game," Finn said. "Remember what Scarlett said? If that really was Oliver that day in the storm, he's the one who got us all to suspect each other. He even got me to do it, too, with Beth." Finn wasn't proud of how he'd acted that day. He knew Beth better than anyone else staying in Tudor House, and he'd played right into Oliver's hands. Finn was the one Beth should have punched, not Mustard. "And look, he's doing it again. We were there when Orchid attacked that Keith guy. We saw what happened. And we saw her tonight, too. Whatever she might have done to help Oliver"—whatever she might have *done* with Oliver—"she clearly really regrets it."

"She's a professional actress," said Mustard. "She's an accomplished liar."

"We're all of us accomplished liars," Finn scoffed. With the possible exception of Beth. That girl could never keep a secret.

"What do I lie about?"

Finn stared at him. "Are you kidding me?"

Mustard scowled. "I don't want to get into this right now—"

"—or ever," Finn grumbled.

"I need to figure out what part I played in this!" Mustard insisted. "I sent Tanner to talk to that Oliver kid before I knew he was a total psychopath. And then he went home for the weekend and now he isn't answering his texts."

"Oh?" Finn asked. "Then it's something you two have in common!"

"Would you just stop?"

Finn considered this. "No, actually, I won't. What's going on with you and Tanner?"

Mustard's mouth dropped open. "Excuse me?"

"You heard me," he snapped. "You pushed me away, and you're all worried about Tanner, and Tanner broke up with his girlfriend—"

"Tanner is my *friend!*" Mustard said, flustered. "Wait. Are you—are you *jealous?*"

"Yes, I'm jealous, you moron! I *like* you."

"Shhh!" Mustard said, grabbing Finn's shoulder and pressing his other hand against his mouth.

Finn just stood there and let him. He met Mustard's angry gaze with a steady one of his own until they both became incredibly aware of the feel of Mustard's skin against his lips.

As soon as it happened, Mustard pulled back.

"I'm not into Tanner," he growled. "He's my friend and my roommate, and he's going through a really tough time. Besides, you're one to talk. What about you and Peacock?"

"Beth is going through an even tougher time, if you haven't noticed," Finn said. That glimpse of her murder board tonight was . . . something.

"Oh, that's why you have to go to her room every night to keep her company?"

Finn was astonished that Mustard even knew about that. Astonished, and a little thrilled. "Are *you* jealous?"

He stomped away. "No."

Finn's heart raced. *Yes.* "So I guess we are going to get into this right now."

Mustard was a few steps across the conservatory floor, breathing hard by the bare tables and the dead plants. This was how it had happened last winter, too, alone in an abandoned science lab.

"What do you want from me?" Mustard asked softly, roughly. "What? A date for prom? You want us to show up in matching tuxedos or something?"

Finn thought about Mustard in a tuxedo and his heart skipped a beat. "If you're asking me to prom, I accept."

"I'm not."

"What if I ask you to prom?"

"Don't you dare."

"Why? Afraid you'll want to say yes?"

Mustard said nothing, which was as good as admitting it, in Finn's opinion. And that's exactly why he didn't ask. Because he didn't want Mustard to say yes as much as he wanted him not to be afraid of doing so. Because that's all this was. Mustard wasn't angry at Finn—not for liking him, and not for coming out, either. He was angry at himself because he couldn't do it.

Finn had such a hard time wrapping his brain around that. Mustard was so much braver than he was about everything. But not this.

Something small, then. "Or we could start with—with anything. With you admitting you like me when we aren't standing in some dark room somewhere."

Mustard's face was downcast. His eyes were squeezed shut, his hands clenched into fists.

Okay, so not that. "What about you telling me something personal about yourself?"

Still nothing.

Finn took a deep breath. "Look, I messed up with Beth. I sabotaged her for my own ambition. And I lied to Scarlett, too. I don't want to repeat the same mistakes. And you—you're different. I was never able to lie to you, even during the storm. If I've learned anything at all at this stupid school this year, it's that life is short. Any one of us could die tomorrow. And I don't know about you, but I don't have an evil twin brother you can hook up with if you miss your chance with me."

He might as well have been saying it to an empty room, for all that Mustard responded. He stood still as a statue.

All right, then. That was his shot. Finn started to leave.

"It was freshman boot camp," said Mustard, and Finn froze. "They took us out into the high desert and they dropped us off with nothing but our wits and a multitool and told us to find our way back to the barracks."

What? He turned around. Mustard hadn't come any closer, but he was now looking at Finn.

"It took me two whole days, and I almost drowned in a river. But I got back first. I had a sprained wrist, a three-inch gash on my leg, and I was covered from head to toe in yellow river silt, but I won. They said I looked like I'd been dipped in a jar of mustard."

Mustard . . . Finn forgot to breathe.

"The older kids started it, but I wore it like a badge of honor. They couldn't stand that I beat the record. First time since 1988. You know who held it then?"

Finn knew the answer even before Mustard said it.

"J. C. Maestor."

His father.

"He thought it would never be beat. But I did it. I did it my first week at that hellhole. And when they kicked me out—"

"You had to keep the name."

Mustard nodded. "I earned it. They can't take that record away either, no matter what my father said."

Finn chuckled and risked coming forward. So it was another dark, abandoned room. It had Mustard in it, which was all that mattered. "I think you're ten times the man your father is."

He snorted. "You haven't met him."

"I don't need to. My dad would never belittle my brother or me like yours does. My dad would never tell me that I'm wrong for just being myself."

Mustard wasn't going to give in so easily. "Your father spoiled you rotten."

"Probably," Finn agreed. "But I'd rather be spoiled than—I don't know—*abused* like you have been."

"My father wanted to make me tough—"

"You're tough," Finn assured him. "Mission accomplished. I probably would have died in that boot camp."

One step closer.

"I wouldn't have let you die."

"As long as you could still come in first."

"Yeah." A small smile played across his lips. It was very hot.

This time, when Finn kissed him, Mustard didn't pull away. And he didn't rush things, either. He let Finn's mouth close over his, let Finn's fingers sweep his jawline and thread into his hair. Only then did he put his arms around Finn and press close.

Finn could have stayed here all night. His skin tingled wherever Mustard touched him; his blood rushed and his heart raced. And then Mustard made some kind of low, grumbling sound in his throat and Finn knew without a shadow of a doubt that they could not stay in the conservatory much longer. Still, he was afraid to stop—afraid if he interrupted them, they would return to their cold war.

And then Mustard broke contact and pressed his face into the hollow of Finn's collarbone, mumbling, "We need . . . to . . . leave."

"Yes!" Finn whispered, relieved. He didn't know what Mustard was offering him, if he was getting what he wanted, or if he was just getting deeper into this quagmire. But at the moment, he could not bring himself to care. His mind raced through the options. "I—don't have a roommate, he choked out. "Or a dorm proctor. Winkle hasn't slept here in days." For the first time, he was grateful for the way the school was falling apart.

Mustard nodded wordlessly against his sweater.

"Meet me there?"

Another nod.

Finn fought to catch his breath. "Promise."

Mustard lifted his head and met Finn's gaze. "I'm not going to wimp out again."

Finn smiled. "Right."

They were both being brave.

20

Orchid

Nobody followed Oliver when he left. There were a million things they each had to know, but not one of them wanted to stay in his presence for another moment. Still, as soon as he was gone, the meeting fell apart.

"Well?" Scarlett asked Orchid dryly. "Aren't you going to run after him? It's not raining or anything, but otherwise, pretty cinematic."

Orchid was not amused. "I don't want to have anything to do with Oliver Green."

"All evidence to the contrary."

"Stop it, Scarlett. It was a mistake, okay? A momentary lapse in judgement."

Her eyes widened. "Well! I guess he should consider himself lucky, then. The last time you had a lapse in judgement, you killed someone."

That was *not* a lapse in judgement. Orchid had never been so clearheaded in all her life as when she killed Keith. He was going to murder her—strangle her right there in the study! It was him or her, and Orchid wanted to live.

She wanted to live. That was why she'd risked everything all those years ago and thrown away her old identity. It was why she was managing even now to go on, after what she had done to Keith. After what happened to Vaughn. After all of it—

Mustard and Finn had already made themselves scarce by this point, and Peacock was pretending not to listen to them and had returned to her journal.

"Look, I've already wasted enough time on this tonight," said Scarlett. "Prom isn't going to plan itself. See you later, Beth."

Peacock murmured her good-byes and went back to work on her creepy murder-evidence board. As hobbies went, Orchid had questions.

The Vaughn meter dinged on Scarlett's phone again. Orchid put her hands over her ears. "Can you turn that thing off?"

"Gladly," said Scarlett. She hit the mute button on her phone. "Happy? Now we can ignore the fact that we're in a very successful business with a psychopath until the next time he asks for a check." She turned on her heel and marched out of the billiards room.

Orchid followed, shutting Peacock's door behind them. "You think I don't know that? It's been eating me up inside. I never would have let you produce Vaughn's music if I knew what we were getting ourselves into."

"Oh, I don't blame you for that part," Scarlett called over her shoulder as she swept down the hall. "Just the part where you sat on the news about Mrs. White for an entire day. What if she had come back here?"

Orchid stopped in her tracks. She hadn't actually considered that. Her lawyer had mentioned a restraining order, but she hadn't even wanted to think about it, especially not in that moment, with her clothes half off and Oliver responsible for making them like that. She just wanted to go bury her head under the covers, to disappear into her oversize sweater. She wanted to go back to when she was the anonymous student at the elite, unreachable school. "Honestly, I've been on autopilot ever since I found out."

"Shame you weren't on autopilot before you decided to hook up with your dead boyfriend's brother," said Scarlett. "What do you want me to say to the media if that part of the story gets out?"

"It won't!" Orchid insisted.

"Really?" Scarlett scoffed. "Did Oliver strike you as a guy who wanted to be quiet? About *anything*?"

"He won't go to the media. He'll want to protect Vaughn's music . . ." But Orchid didn't believe it, even as she said it. Oliver didn't care about the music. In fact, he seemed almost repulsed by it. He was happy to take their cash in the short term, but now that Orchid had provided him with the proof he needed to pursue his claims against Blackbrook and Curry Chemical, he wouldn't even need it anymore. The Fain glue was worth tens of millions of dollars. He could pull the plug on her and Scarlett's little online enterprise whenever he wanted. "He won't go the media because it's pretty clear that he doesn't want to talk about Vaughn."

That part was true enough. Whatever horrible things she could say about Oliver—and there were plenty!—Vaughn's death weighed heavily on him. Whatever had happened between them in the ballroom was driven as much by his own self-loathing as by hers. She didn't even need her therapist to tell her that part.

Orchid thought Scarlett was going to head up the stairs to her bedroom, but at the front of the hall, she kept going, right into the study.

Orchid stopped in her tracks. She couldn't go in there. "Wait."

Scarlett did not wait.

"Scar!"

She turned at the door. "Come in if you dare."

"Scarlett!" Orchid gripped her sleeves, glaring. She hadn't set foot in the study in months.

Scarlett narrowed her eyes. "I sincerely hope that Mrs. White feels just as awkward going into places where she's killed people."

And then she disappeared inside.

Anger bubbled up inside Orchid, red hot and choking, and the next thing she knew, she was standing in the study, and Scarlett was staring at her, flabbergasted.

"Wow," she said flatly. "I didn't know you had it in you."

Orchid very narrowly stopped herself from shooting back *You don't know what I have in me.* She was quite certain Scarlett would have had a grand old time with that one.

The study was just the same. Well, there was a new carpet on the floor, and the toolbox with the big, heavy lethal weapons in it had been removed—but other than that, not a thing had changed since the day Keith had trapped her in here. Since the day she'd killed him.

"Has it occurred to you," Orchid said through a clenched jaw, "that when you pull stunts like this, you're only making it worse?"

"Has it occurred to you," she snapped back, "That I'm the only one here trying to help you, and you sabotage it every time you keep me out of the loop?"

"I brought you Oliver as soon as I realized he existed!"

"Yeah, well, you could have waited on that, I think. We could have talked about it first. *Strategized* about how to fix our mistake. But no, you make all the decisions all by yourself. Give him money. Give him those letters. Give him *whatever he asks for,* apparently, and don't even pause to wonder why it is that he never revealed himself to us before?"

Orchid's eyes burned with unshed tears, because as much as she hated to admit it, Scarlett was right. Oliver had played them all, and she, Orchid, had helped him do it.

"You treat me like I don't matter at all," Scarlett cried. "You treat me like I'm just your employee. You treat me like you're the heroine and I'm the sidekick, and I'm sick of it!"

Orchid couldn't even deny it. And wasn't that exactly what Oliver had said about Vaughn as well? That the plan he and his brother had concocted to attend Blackbrook turned Vaughn into the primary twin—the only one whose wants and desires mattered. As much as Vaughn was known around campus, he was known as a musician, and Oliver said he didn't even play. He'd told Orchid all about how being forced to defer to Vaughn had eaten away at his sense of self.

"You made it perfectly clear that you were only helping me with Vaughn's music because you had experience with all this online stuff," Orchid said. "And I hate publicity. You *wanted* to do it. You love doing it."

"Oh, yeah, I love looking at pictures of aspiring rock stars' finger calluses." Scarlett rolled her eyes. "I was happy to do it because it seemed like the only thing that was going to tether you to Earth after what happened to you last winter. I care about *you*, Orchid. You just won't let anyone care about you unless you are paying them for the privilege. Your lawyers, your therapist—"

Now the tears did fall. "That's not true! Vaughn cared . . ."

"Yes, he did. And you made sure he made money off the love songs he wrote you, too. No wonder you hurried to pay Oliver off."

Not true, not true, not true. "It wasn't my money!"

"Maybe not, but there was a right way and a wrong way to handle it. And the wrong way was handing a check to some guy just because he had Vaughn's face."

She was right. Why was she always right? Orchid hated that.

"Look," Scarlett went on, "Vaughn wasn't my best friend in the world, but I can admit that he was talented. It's a perfect storm, what we're doing. I have the skills, you have the platform, and he has the content. I fooled around with streaming my gaming sessions or doing makeup tutorials, but I'm not an on-air personality. People think I'm harsh and bitchy."

Orchid snorted. Wonder why?

Scarlett gave her a withering glance. "But I know I'm good at the back end. I always thought I could make something huge if I had the right property and the right push, and now I know I can."

"Good for you. What a triumph."

But if Scarlett had ever demonstrated the skill of putting up with Orchid, the pretense had utterly dropped now. "I'm not *using* either of you. I didn't do any of this for me, which you can tell by the fact that I'm not the one in control of it. I couldn't write Oliver a check for ten thousand dollars, Orchid, and even if I could, I wouldn't have done it without talking to you first. And if I'd heard a word about Mrs. White, I would have called you three seconds later. You're my *best friend*!"

Now Scarlett was crying, too, fat tears rolling down her cheeks.

"I'm so, so sick of people on this campus pretending to be my friend and then not trusting me with whatever is going on with them. Have I ever given anyone any reason to think they couldn't trust me with their secrets? I thought you *did* trust me! You told me who you really were that day, in the storm. You told me about Keith, even when I threw it back in your face. But now you're back to keeping secrets. Just like Finn did. I can't *help* you if you *lie* to me!"

"Maybe it's not your job to *help* us," Orchid said. "You say I pay all the people around me, but you—you just do favors for them, and you call it friendship."

Everything went very, very quiet. And then Scarlett quite calmly reached into her pocket, pulled out her phone, and pressed a few buttons.

"There," she said, in a calm, dangerous voice. "I've deleted Vaughn's channel. If you don't want my help, fine. You won't get it. Not you, not your dead boyfriend, and not that serial killer who wears his face."

Orchid just stared at her in total shock. Vaughn's music!

His fans! She opened her mouth several times to speak, but could think of nothing to say. She was so ignorant of what Scarlett had been doing, she didn't even know the ramifications of channel deletion. Was everything they'd done over the last four months just . . . gone?

Scarlett observed the process Orchid was going through and then, as if satisfied with the effect her actions had had, said simply: "Huh. I guess I did have more control over things than I thought."

Orchid still didn't know what to say.

"Now, if you'll excuse me," Scarlett went on, "I have a lot of prom planning to do. You might not appreciate all I've done for this school, but there are still people at Blackbrook that do. And I'm going to throw them one hell of a party."

Orchid narrowed her eyes, finding her tongue at last. "If that's the kind of thing that makes you happy, Scarlett, then go for it. Have fun with your little Blackbrook prom."

"And you have fun with Oliver."

With those two barbs hanging in the air, Orchid left the study, and Scarlett slammed the door behind her.

Orchid ran upstairs to her room and did some of her own door slamming.

Then she sat down at her computer and pulled up Vaughn's channel.

Not found.

Her breath caught on a sob. All these months, it was like a part of him had still been alive. His words, his music, sung to her from beyond the grave. The more other people heard it and loved him, the easier it was to bear. But now . . .

With shaking fingers, she pulled up the original recordings, still saved on her phone. "Another Me," "Endless Blue," "Off on Another Great Adventure"—the songs she'd listened to and loved were still there, saved on her phone. They were probably saved on countless other people's phones, too, even if the channel was no more. Vaughn wasn't gone—just this outlet.

Maybe it wasn't all bad. They were Oliver's property now, these songs, and running the channel just put money in his pocket. They couldn't trust him, so why help him? If he wanted to produce Vaughn's music on his own, let him.

She remembered how he'd looked when Scarlett had told him about the newest hit. No, he wouldn't be producing these on his own. And even if he did try, he didn't have Scarlett's talent.

Orchid hated to admit it, but Scarlett had made the right move yet again.

Still, screw her. She said Orchid acted overbearing, throwing her money around? Please. Scarlett didn't know what she was talking about. If anything, Scarlett was the one treating Orchid like the helpless damsel, not letting her make any of her own decisions. For months—months!—she'd acted like Orchid was crazy, as fragile as the flower for which she'd named herself, incapable of taking charge.

She had no idea what she was dealing with. Scarlett didn't know what it looked like when Orchid really wanted to throw her money around and take charge.

Scarlett thought she could control every aspect of this school? Every aspect of prom?

She had another think coming.

21

Peacock

<u>**LIST OF POSSIBLE SUSPECTS**</u>
1. OLIVER GREEN
2. ORCHID MCKEE
3. TANNER CURRY???
4. MRS. WHITE? I GUESS?

I called Winkle. No one else seemed to think it was a good idea, but what happens if no one warns him about these things and then one of us ends up dead? Headmaster Boddy failed at keeping us safe on this campus. Dr. Brown did, too. How can Winkle even hope to try if we don't let him know what's going on?

Turns out he knew about Mrs. White, so that's good. He also didn't seem too surprised to hear about Oliver, so I guess those Green boys weren't being as sneaky as they thought with their whole "pretend to be Vaughn" scheme.

I think I did the right thing. I know I did. I would never be able to sleep nights if I knew that people responsible for the violence on this campus were still walking around.

I don't even care what the others say. They want to keep their secrets? Fine. But that's how folks end up dead. And honestly, they aren't taking this seriously. I thought they would now, but Scarlett and Orchid are in some all-out war over prom?

Actual murders going on, and they just care about prom! At this rate, one of them will be next.

22

Mustard

Mustard could probably count the times he'd overslept in his life on a single hand. But right now, that hand was currently trapped under a pillow, numb with the weight of Plum's big, stupid head on top of it.

The amazing thing was, he didn't care.

Imprisoned as he was, Mustard took this opportunity to look at the big, stupid head in question. The floppy, too-long curls that no one in military school would ever be allowed to sport, the high, sharp cheekbones, the tiny bruise marks on the bridge of his nose where his glasses pinched.

It was a nice-looking head. It contained an especially nice brain. Mustard had a few thoughts about both of them, but he should probably save them for later. He'd barely have time for a run before class at this rate.

Of course, he could always skip his run. For months, he'd been running to keep himself from thinking of this. This exact thing. Finn Plum a few inches away, breathing softly in his sleep. But Mustard was pretty sure not even a marathon would banish the memory this morning. And he didn't want to banish it.

Did he?

He waited for the usual panic to rise, hot and choking in his throat, but it did not, and he wasn't sure why. Was it that every time he breathed, he caught the scent of Finn's shampoo, or that his skin was warm from being pressed up against Finn's side? If he moved from this spot, if he filled his senses with something other than Finn Plum, would he be able to think straight?

He bit back a laugh. Nope. Not likely. But he should think about getting up, anyway. If nothing else, to go to the bathroom.

Carefully, he slid his hand out from under the pillow, and his body out from under the covers. Socks, shoes—wait, where was his shirt . . .

"Are you sneaking out?" Plum asked from the bed.

"No," Mustard said quickly. "Well, not sneaking."

"You probably *should* sneak," said Plum. "Winkle may not be sleeping in the dorm, but this place is still full of gossips."

Right. That. Mustard retrieved his shirt from the floor. Plum, meanwhile, retrieved his glasses from the bedside table, slipped them on, then watched as Mustard donned his shirt.

"I have class," Mustard said.

"I know. We all have class. This is a school. Supposedly."

"I meant," Mustard said, sitting down on the edge of the bed, "that's why I was sneaking—um, leaving."

"No, I get that, too."

"I'm not sneaking out *on you.*"

"Right." Plum looked at the clock. "It's only seven A.M."

"Yeah, I really overslept," Mustard said offhand, then started at Plum's snicker. "What?"

"I feel sorry for your roommate."

Mustard looked at Plum. "No you don't." Then he hooked

his hand around the back of Plum's neck and pulled him in for a kiss. Plum kissed him back quickly, then just as quickly pulled away.

"What is it?" Mustard said, alarmed. Morning breath? It was morning breath.

"Nothing." Plum shook his head. "I just remembered I still have to give Blackbrook my answer about the dye. Everything we've been through, and I'm going to lose the formula after all."

Mustard frowned. "What if I talked to Tanner?"

"What? He's got better connections at Curry than Winkle? They just want my formula, and they're going to screw me over to take it."

"Tanner's not like that," Mustard said. "The other day he was telling me all about his dad and Dick Fain. They were friends here at Blackbrook. He helped Dick Fain sell his glue to the chemical company that became Curry Chemical."

"Yeah, he set up the system that's screwing me over."

"Right, but Tanner understands that it's a bad system, even if it is his dad's. He's a good person. He was trying to help Vaughn with his claims before Vaughn died. Last I talked to him, he was trying to help Oliver."

"That's hardly a recommendation. Besides, I thought you said you haven't seen him around."

"He just went home to deal with the whole Dr. Brown thing. I'll call him. He hasn't answered my texts, but I'm sure he'll pick up if I call."

"Yeah," Finn agreed. "A call is an emergency." On the bedside table, Finn's own phone started to buzz.

"Speaking of . . ."

Finn looked at the screen. "It's Scarlett. It's not an emergency to anyone but her."

"You don't know that. This is Blackbrook. Maybe someone else has died."

"Fair enough." Finn answered the phone, his signature preppy, bored tone coming front and center. "Morning, Scar."

Mustard couldn't make any words out, but he could tell from the volume that Scarlett Mistry was very upset.

"Prom? No." Finn's eyes were wide. "What? No, Scarlett—"

Mustard started to back slowly from the room.

Finn looked panicked. He shook his head furiously at Mustard. "That's not going to work this morning—"

Mustard backed more quickly, ignoring Finn's hand signals to stop.

"I'll just meet you for breakfast in the dining hall. I could be there in fifteen minutes—"

Mustard was not having a chummy breakfast with Plum and Scarlett. He didn't care what new understanding they had reached last night.

"No—stop!" Finn exclaimed, and Mustard wasn't sure which one of them he was talking to. He just left.

The coast was clear in the hall, so he took the opportunity of ducking into the floor bathroom before heading down the steps and out the door into the spring sunrise.

Where he ran right into Scarlett Mistry, still chattering on the phone, and hurrying up the front step to catch the door before it closed.

By instinct, he held it for her.

"Thanks," she muttered unthinkingly and slipped inside.

Bullet. Dodged. He walked on. One step. Two.

"Mustard."

He cringed, and turned.

Scarlett stood at the top of the steps, looking like she'd stepped out of a fashion magazine. Her hair was pulled back from her forehead in some complicated-looking combinations of braids and clips that highlighted the red streaks.

"Just the man I was looking for," she said.

Uh-oh.

"You didn't tell Orchid you'd go to prom with her, did you?"

"What?" That was the last thing he expected to come out of her mouth after watching him walk out of Finn's dorm.

"Well, did she ask you?" It wasn't so much a question as an order, and unfortunately, Mustard was trained to respond to those.

"No."

"Okay, well then, do you want to go with Peacock?"

"I—" he was baffled.

"Me and Peacock and Finn. Like a group. I thought the heights would work best in those pairs," she said, as if that explained, well, *anything*. "Do you have a tux? If not, you're going to have to go out to the mainland to rent one—"

"You want the Murder Crew to go to prom in a group . . . but without Orchid?"

"Keep up," she said, her tone clipped. "She can't be trusted."

Well, Mustard didn't necessarily disagree with Scarlett there, but Orchid wasn't the only one he'd put on that particular list. There was also the boy who wasn't dead.

"You and Peacock are over that whole incident from the storm, right?"

Mustard rubbed the back of his head. He could still feel the scar tissue under his hair. "Um . . ."

"Fine, go with me, and Finn will take Beth. Though I don't know, they dated, so that might be weird, but really, no weirder than . . ." Scarlett trailed off. She stared at Mustard. Then slowly, she turned her head and looked at the building behind him.

Mustard felt some deep, primitive instinct telling him that a predator was about to pounce.

"This isn't your dorm," Scarlett said.

"Not yours, either."

That might have worked with some people. But not Scarlett Mistry.

"You wore that shirt yesterday," she went on.

The tiny prey animals far back in Mustard's evolutionary tree shivered. "Yeah," he said with forced jocularity. "I'm way behind on laundry."

She narrowed her eyes pointedly at him.

He stared right back.

She pursed her lips. "Whatever," she said at last, to Mustard's very great relief. "So, what about prom?"

"Um . . ."

"Do you want to go with me? And Peacock? And Finn?" There was a tiny, almost imperceptible emphasis on that last name. And the stare that followed her invitation was its own brand of punctuation.

"But what about Orchid?"

"Orchid is not my problem."

He couldn't help but laugh at that. "Since when? You've basically made yourself her full-time babysitter ever since Keith. Taking her to see her lawyer, making sure she ate, all that Vaughn stuff?"

"Not my problem," Scarlett repeated, with a brittle air. "Besides, haven't you heard? Vaughn's career is as dead as he is."

Mustard was confused. "I thought his latest song was the biggest hit yet? What happened since yesterday?"

"You tell me."

Well, he wasn't taking that bait. Mustard pulled out his phone, which was at a dangerously low charge. There were a few new texts from Tanner since yesterday, but he'd look later. He pulled up Vaughn's channel—or tried to, at least.

"It's gone."

Scarlett shrugged a shoulder.

"Did Oliver make you take it down?" That didn't seem likely, given how it was making him money hand over foot.

Another shoulder shrug.

Mustard sighed. "I don't really have time for this—"

"Neither do I! I can't believe I spent so many hours on Vaughn Green and his music. It's all over. Oliver and Orchid can do whatever they want. I'm done helping *both* of them. I have a prom to plan."

"And a murder to solve?"

"Huh?"

He stared at her in astonishment. She remembered what shirt he was wearing yesterday, but not that she'd floated several outlandish theories about how maybe there was a teen-age murderer walking around free in Rocky Point?

"Oliver."

"I told you, I don't care about Oliver."

Mustard groaned in exasperation. "Yesterday you thought he was a murderer!"

"No," Scarlett said, holding a finger in the air for clarification. "Yesterday, I *accused* him of being a murderer. And his answers were mystifying and evasive and—"

"Suspicious?" Mustard finished. This was not the Scarlett he was used to.

"Admittedly," she replied. "But not in the way I thought. He's doesn't seem to be afraid we're going to call the police with our suspicions, or go to Winkle. So I think his game isn't murder. It's chaos."

Mustard considered this. If so, he was winning.

"He thinks he holds all the cards, that he can manipulate me into doing his bidding? Well, he can forget it. I made him ten thousand dollars. I'm not making him another penny."

Wait, *Scarlett* had deleted Vaughn's music? Mustard glanced up at the building edifice and saw the pale oval of Finn's face against his window, watching them. God knew what he must think.

"And I'm not getting involved in any of this nonsense any-more," she went on. "Things started going downhill for me around here once I started on all this intrigue. Dr. Brown stripped my leadership positions, I bombed the SATs . . . I should be formulating a plan to fix all this, and instead I've spent the last four months helping people that clearly don't deserve it. Oliver. Orchid."

Mustard glanced behind her to the door and saw Finn outlined in the glass on the top half.

"So I'm back to doing what I know, and that's prom."

The door opened. "Oh, Scarlett!" Finn said in the least convincing tone imaginable. "You came. And, um, Mustard. Glad to see you, too."

Scarlett rolled her eyes. "Save it."

"What . . . What are we talking about?"

"Prom," Scarlett said at the same time as Mustard said "Oliver."

"Oliver," Finn agreed.

"No, I—" Scarlett fumbled.

"She deleted Vaughn's channel," said Mustard. "The one that was making Oliver a ton of money."

"You did *what*?" Plum turned to her in astonishment. "Scarlett, that dude's dangerous. He's possibly a murderer, remember? Why would you get on his bad side?"

"Because I'm done playing his games!"

All at once, Mustard understood. Scarlett liked to be in charge. The actual thing she was doing didn't matter to her nearly so much as that she had complete control over it. The appearance of Oliver meant her pet project was no longer hers. So why not get rid of it, even if the only thing she had in its place was Blackbrook's tiny school dance?

Plum seemed to have come to the same conclusion. He rubbed his temples. "You'd better hope Oliver isn't really a murderer."

"Please!" she snapped. "If he's really the heir to the Fain glue fortune, he won't miss Vaughn's music money."

That reminded Mustard of Tanner's texts. He looked at his phone, but as soon as he swiped over to his messaging app, the whole thing shut down. Great.

"I'd love to continue this," he said. "But I have to go charge my phone and get in touch with Tanner. I should have done it last night—" And then he shut his mouth before he said something dumb.

Plum blushed. Scarlett rolled her eyes again.

Okay, then. He waved and Plum waved, and then Mustard walked away and left the other boy to whatever prom-related horrors Scarlett was about to unleash. He consoled himself that Plum had known Scarlett for a lot longer than he did, and could probably deal with her plans better than he could.

As he walked back to his own dorm, he once again waited for the familiar panic. Scarlett knew where he'd spent the night. Scarlett *knew*.

And . . . she didn't seem to care. Not nearly as much as who was going with whom to prom. It was not at all what he had expected. But maybe he should have. Scarlett wasn't like the people he'd gone to school with before. Well, not entirely. She was power hungry, and ruthless, and would probably make an excruciatingly sadistic petty officer if she wanted to.

But she didn't seem to care a bit about the secret that had defined Mustard's life. Counted it no more important to her plans for prom than that Peacock and Plum had once dated. The mind boggled.

He remembered Finn, bouncing around and declaring himself bisexual to anyone who listened. Mustard thought he'd been crazy to do that. But Scarlett was his friend, and her reaction to Mustard had been a shrug and then a pivot to a discussion about tuxedo rentals.

He kept waiting for the cold, clammy slap of horror, and it never came.

Instead, he stood on the green in the bright spring morning in yesterday's clothes, after spending the night in Finn Plum's dorm, and no one cared. No kids were going to rat him out to the commander, no headmaster was going to call his father . . . no one cared.

After all this time, Mustard wasn't entirely sure what to do with that thought.

First thing's first, though. Get in touch with Tanner.

He took the stairs up to their room two at a time, and was surprised to find the door to their room unlocked. That meant Tanner had returned. And if he had returned, he might have been wondering where Mustard had spent his night.

Ah, there it was, that touch of dread. Funny that it chose now to emerge. Mustard braced himself for whatever comment his roommate had no doubt prepared. He thought about striking first, in an attempt to ward off questions he wasn't prepared to answer. Yes, he'd start. He opened the door, ready to ask where Tanner had been all week.

But the greeting never made it past his lips.

Tanner Curry sat in his desk hair, his hands folded in his lap, his head lolling back. His eyes were closed. His skin was gray.

He was dead.

23

Scarlett

S carlett Mistry had decided to storm the administration, but storming was taking longer than anticipated due to Peacock's mobility scooter. When they got inside, Scarlett headed naturally for the stairs to the second floor, but Peacock cleared her throat and pointed at the ancient elevator.

Scarlett groaned. "That thing barely worked before the flood."

"Trust me, I know," said Peacock. "But you would not believe how long it takes me to get up and down a set of stairs."

Actually, Scarlett did believe her. Blackbrook's astonishing lack of ADA compliance was one of her pet issues, back when there was still a campus beautification committee for her to run.

She shook her head. She imagined what their priorities would be now. Probably less worried about flower beds and more concerned with hiding the corpses.

They waited for the elevator. Scarlett clenched her fists. Waiting for the elevator was hard to do when you were storming. So was waiting *in* the elevator, as it wasn't exactly speedy.

And yet, what choice did they have?

Finally, they reached the upper floor, and as soon as the rickety doors ground open, Scarlett did storm into the corridor and down the hall to Winkle's office. Peacock wheeled stormily in her wake.

The headmaster's assistant was seated at the desk outside the door to the office that had once belonged to Headmaster Boddy.

"We'd like to see Mr. Winkle," she demanded of the assistant. "Now."

"He's very busy today," the assistant replied. "And shouldn't you two be in class?"

Scarlett snorted. "We have important information about the latest death on campus—"

The door opened and Perry Winkle stuck his head out. His expression was one of interest that immediately faded to annoyance at the sight of Scarlett and Peacock. "Oh," he said. "It's you."

"It's us, sir, and it's vital that we speak to you about—"

"Prom? Yes, I got your fourteen emails. I'm sorry, but—"

"No, it's about Tanner Curry." Scarlett made sure that she was speaking in a voice loud enough to echo up and down the paneled halls.

That did the trick. Whatever gossip was flowing through campus, Winkle didn't want to add to it. "Come in, then," he said, aggravated. "Hurry up."

They were ushered into Boddy's old office. It was odd, Scarlett thought, how little it had changed in the months since the headmaster's death. Everything else about Blackbrook had undergone so much alteration, but the headmaster's office seemed trapped in the Blackbrook Academy of the past. The fine wood paneling had not sustained water damage, nor had it been subject to the ravages of the piecemeal renovations. Portraits of headmasters past still lined the wall in gilded frames. The leather furnishings were burnished, the mahogany desk was neat, and the brass fixtures fairly sparkled. The May day was warm, but a fire glowed in the grate. Scarlett half expected to see Headmaster Boddy checking his pocket watch by the window and looking out on a quad filled with students.

But Boddy was dead, and instead they had Mr. Winkle, who shared Boddy's penchant for three-piece suits, and not much else. Where the old headmaster had been warm and professorial, Winkle was calculated and careful. From the moment he'd arrived on campus, Scarlett had gotten the impression that every word he spoke and action had been preapproved by some corporate policymaker. Or maybe he *was* the corporate policy maker. All she knew was, Blackbrook had been on shaky ground ever since the first person was murdered on the campus. If something wasn't done now, they had more things to worry about than dead students. The entire school would be toast.

Now, Winkle stood by his desk—Boddy's desk—and raised his eyebrows. "Yes? You said you had information?"

Yes, that was indeed the claim she made in order to gain admittance. "It's absolute chaos out there. Rumors are running rampant. The administration has to issue a statement."

"The statement is that Tanner Curry was found dead in his room yesterday morning," Winkle said mildly. "I cannot comment further on an ongoing investigation."

"Investigation?" Peacock repeated. "Murder or suicide?"

"Like I said, I cannot comment." He looked at Scarlett. "Do you have information or don't you?"

Not as much as she'd like. Not yet. "Amber Frye, Tanner's girlfriend—she lives in Tudor House with us."

"*Ex*-girlfriend," Peacock corrected.

"She's really upset."

"I can imagine," said Winkle.

"Like, we had to sedate her with some of Peacock's pain pills."

Winkle looked amused. "So you're here to confess to me your illegal drug use?"

"They aren't illegal," Peacock said, offended. "I had prescribed them by a doctor!"

"He means it's illegal for us to have given them to Amber," Scarlett said. "And go ahead, add another scandal to the rap sheet. That will be great for the school."

"I'm sure you only meant the best for your friend," Winkle said, his tone as measured and even as always. "I'm sure we can overlook a few small peccadillos during an emergency such as this. I commend your efforts, Miss Mistry, in keeping your classmates calm. On that note: how is prom coming along?"

"We're not here to talk about prom!" Scarlett slammed her hand against the table. Storming and slamming wasn't her usual modus operandi, but, like Winkle said, this was an emergency. "The student body needs answers. Peacock doesn't have enough pain pills to dose everyone."

"Mass sedation?" Winkle looked like he was considering this. "Or distraction? We could move prom up, I suppose—"

"What happened to Tanner?" Scarlett insisted.

"He died." Was that a shrug? A *shrug*? The bodies were piling up on campus, and the person in charge barely seemed to notice, or care.

"How?"

"That is, one hopes, what the investigation will show," Winkle replied.

"Okay, then, where's Mustard?"

"I beg your pardon?"

"His roommate. Samuel Maestor?"

Winkle's face smoothed out again. "Ah, yes. Mr. Maestor is answering a few questions for the local authorities."

"No one has seen or heard from him in a day."

"Perhaps they had a lot of questions." And that was definitely a shrug! Scarlett was incensed.

"Well, has anyone called his parents?"

"I assume Mr. Maestor has. I know I certainly would, were I a minor in police custody."

"Wait a second," said Peacock. "Are you telling us he's been *arrested?*"

Scarlett couldn't believe her ears. Headmaster Boddy would never have responded in this way to a student arrest, let alone a student death! And though she'd had her struggles with Dr. Brown, the woman had come in strong in support of Orchid after what had happened with Keith, and done everything in her power to help Peacock find a way to continue on at Blackbrook after the car crash.

"Don't you think that's the responsibility of the administration? At the school where he *lives?*"

"I believe we're done here," said Mr. Winkle. "You have no information of interest to me, and as I said before, I have plenty to do. So do you, if I'm not mistaken, Miss Mistry. That ballroom over at Tudor won't decorate itself."

"Stop talking about prom!" Peacock shouted. "We're not still holding prom!" She looked to Scarlett for backup. "Are we?"

"Er . . ." said Scarlett.

"Scarlett!"

"Life has to go on?" she offered weakly.

"Precisely," said Winkle. "I hired the band you wanted, I ordered the photo booth, and your classmate Miss McKee has graciously offered to supply dresses for every girl in your class. Something about having connections with some fashion designers . . ."

Wait. *What?*

"She can't do that!" Scarlett hissed, mostly to herself, but it's not like she cared who heard.

"Why not? Saves me at least a dozen requests for off-campus shopping trips to the mainland," Winkle replied. "Now. Out."

What choice did they have? They got out.

While waiting for the elevator, Scarlett asked Peacock: "Did you know about this?"

"About Mr. Winkle being completely useless to stop the carnage taking over this campus, just like every other member of the administration?"

Scarlett looked up at the other girl, who was kneeling one leg on the scooter, her back perfectly straight and her face staring straight ahead at the elevator doors. Amber had been hysterical, impossible to soothe, which Scarlett had understood implicitly after all those months dealing with Orchid's outsize reaction to Vaughn's death. At least Amber and Tanner had been an item for months. But Peacock and Tanner had always run in the same, sporty circles. Maybe this death was hitting her hard, too.

"Beth? Are you . . . okay?"

"No!" she blurted and looked down at Scarlett, her face a mask of incredulity. "Is anyone?"

Scarlett shook her head. "No, you're right." So it wasn't *special* trauma, then. Just . . . more of the same. Like everyone was feeling.

Or something like that.

The elevator still hadn't arrived, and after another long silence, she added, "So, what's this about Orchid and the prom dresses?"

Another incredulous look. "Are you serious? Yeah, I got a text from Orchid about getting a bunch of dresses shipped in. But that was before, you know, there was another dead body. Like I told Mr. Winkle, I kind of figured prom was canceled."

"And now that it's not?"

"I don't know, Scarlett!" The elevator doors finally slid open, and Peacock wheeled inside. "It feels really ghoulish to go now, doesn't it? But that's what everyone does at Blackbrook. Just keeps moving on, regardless of anyone else whose life has been destroyed."

Scarlett followed her into the elevator. "No, you're right."

They rode in silence to the ground floor. As the doors slid open again, Peacock shifted her scooter around. "But you're still planning it, aren't you?"

"I'm also still going to class," said Scarlett. "And I'm eating three meals a day, and I'm brushing and flossing. Life goes on."

"I thought that way, too," said her friend, "and then I fell off a bridge. Life doesn't always go on. At least, not the life you had before."

They headed out into a spring fog, which at least meant it was warming up.

"Nobody thinks anything about this is normal," Scarlett said. "But then isn't that why we should try to find happiness and beauty where we can?" Like Orchid and designer prom dresses. Scarlett might hate that Orchid came up with the idea without her, but she couldn't fault the combination of ingenuity and resourcefulness. Maybe Scarlett had finally managed to rub off on her.

"I used to love the dances here," Peacock said. "But I can't exactly dance in this."

Scarlett wasn't so sure of that. Peacock was twice as graceful, even in casts, than half the kids on campus.

"What if I did a sort of memorial thing—for Tanner and Vaughn?"

"And Dr. Brown and Headmaster Boddy?" Peacock considered this. "What are you thinking, a moment of silence in between slow songs?"

Scarlett made a face. "I think I can do better than that."

But right now, they had bigger problems. Finn Plum was waiting for them on the front steps of Tudor House. His hair was mussed into a cloud on top of his head, his eyes were rimmed in red, and he was pacing back and forth on the wide stone steps.

"Did you get in to see Winkle?" he asked as they approached. "Violet told me that's where you were going."

"We did," said Scarlett, not wanting to get into it until they'd retreated somewhere private.

"He seems more interested in prom than in what's happening on his own campus," Peacock added. "Totally blasé that Mustard is in police custody on suspicion of murder."

"WHAT!" Finn shouted.

Scarlett sighed. So here they were, getting into it. All the way into it. She shooed them both into the hall.

"And here I thought he cared," Peacock was saying as she wheeled across the parquet. "He certainly seemed to be listening the other day when I told him all about Oliver and Mrs. White. But now there's another student dead and *another* student responsible and—"

"Mustard did not kill Tanner Curry," Finn said in a low, dangerous tone.

"Would you two shut *up*?" Scarlett hissed, following them. Peacock kept wheeling across the floor, and Scarlett followed, beckoning to Finn, who had gone from anxious to fuming. Once they were inside the billiards room, Scarlett shut the door, turned around, and crossed her arms over her chest.

"Let's work this out."

"What possible reason would Mustard have to kill Tanner?" Finn asked Peacock, his tone frantic.

She shrugged. "I don't know what goes on between roommates."

"That's preposterous. They're good friends."

SCARLETT

"Are they?"

"Tanner is a Curry. You know, the same company that holds the rights to Dick Fain's glue?" Finn threw his hands up in the air. "Oliver Green stood in this room not two days ago and vowed revenge against everyone for what the school and Curry Chem did to his grandmother. Why would you think this has anything to do with anyone else?"

"Well, obviously the police do," said Peacock. "Otherwise why would they still be holding him?"

"Lots of reasons," Finn said. "The influence of the Curry family name—"

"Complete and utter dereliction of duty by the administration of this school," Scarlett added.

Peacock appeared unmoved. "If they arrested Mustard, I'm sure he called his parents for help. Maybe he's just waiting for them to get here from Texas."

Finn shook his head and ran his hands through his wreck of hair. "He didn't call his dad."

"Why not?"

"Because then he'd have to give him his alibi."

"So?" Peacock asked.

Oh. Scarlett buried her head in her hands. Things would be so much easier around here if everyone stopped making out with each other. There would still be all the murder to deal with, though.

Probably.

"*Finn,*" said Scarlett. He'd dated Peacock all freshman year. This couldn't be easy.

"*I know.*" He glared at her, then turned back to Peacock. "Beth, I know Mustard didn't kill Tanner. He was with me."

"When?"

"The night Tanner died."

"What? Studying?"

"No."

"Playing video games?"

"*No.*"

She shook her head. "So then what?"

Scarlett groaned.

"Beth," he said at last, very quietly, "we're together."

Peacock's eyes got very wide and her mouth made a perfect O. Then she turned, limped over to her bed, and sat down. Hard.

"Are you mad?" he asked.

"Why would I be mad?" she asked quickly, her tone brittle. "I dumped you years ago."

"Yeah," he said, "but we've been spending a lot of time together—"

"*Yes we have!*" She wasn't meeting his gaze. Her hands gripped the coverlet. "How long has this been going on?"

"Um . . . on and off for a while. Like, since the SATs."

"Since *the accident?*" Her voice got very shrill. "And you never bothered to tell me—*anything?*"

Scarlett stayed very quiet. Maybe they'd forgotten that she was here.

"We were all going to go to *prom* together!" Peacock was saying now. "When were you planning on telling me?"

"I mean—the prom thing wasn't really my idea."

They both looked at Scarlett. So much for them forgetting.

"Did you know?" Peacock asked her. "Did you know when you came up with this crazy prom idea?"

Scarlett grimaced. "I mean, of course I knew. I try to make it my job to know everything."

From the look on Finn's face, Scarlett realized that was probably the wrong thing to say.

"Get out," said Peacock. "I'm so annoyed with both of you right now."

Scarlett could understand that. They left.

"She's going to kill me," he said tonelessly. "Or maybe both of us."

"Nah. She's been complaining about the body count on campus. She's not going to add to it." Finn was still pretty wrecked, though, so Scarlett patted him on the shoulder. "She'll get over it."

He did not look like he believed her, which was one of Scarlett's worst pet peeves. She estimated fully half of the problems on this campus came from people not believing her. The murders she could do very little about, but she really could have made a difference with the rest of it.

Still, she took him upstairs to her room, where he immediately collapsed on the bed, his face pale.

"Have you slept?" she asked.

"No."

"How about food? When was the last time you had water?"

"Scarlett . . ." He threw his arm over his eyes.

"I'll fix this," she promised him.

"I don't care about prom."

She rolled her eyes. "Not that, silly. Mustard."

"You can't."

"Don't underestimate me, Plum," she replied, and pulled out her phone.

24

Peacock

ELIZABETH PICACH'S ~~RECOVERY JOURNAL~~
INVESTIGATIVE NOTEBOOK

<u>**POSSIBLE SUSPECTS**</u>
1. **OLIVER**
2. **ORCHID**
3. ~~**TANNER**~~
4. ~~**MUSTARD**~~

WHAT?????????

25

Orchid

The last thing in the world Orchid wanted as she tried on prom dresses were texts from Vaughn Green. Unfortunately, Oliver had other plans.

VAUGHN

> I need to talk to you.
>
> Please.
>
> Please, I'll do anything.

She'd do anything to talk to Vaughn, too. *Vaughn*. Not this imposter. And though she had a pretty good idea of what Oliver's "anything" might entail, she was no longer interested.

Orchid thought about blocking his number. Or at least changing the contact name. But for now, she just rolled her eyes and put the phone down. Like everyone else at Blackbrook, she was getting very good at ignoring what was happening right in front of her face. She turned to look at herself in the full-length mirror.

"What do you think of this one, girls?"

They were in the ballroom, which was only place on the

ground floor with enough mirrors for the activity at hand. Orchid had arranged for a few dozen designer gowns to be delivered to Tudor House, and she and her friends were "shopping" for prom.

Well, all her friends except Scarlett, but did she even count anymore?

Violet tilted her head to the side and examined the gown. It was sea green, with a ruffle that started at Orchid's knees and fanned out.

"You kind of look like a mermaid?" she said. "But . . . in a good way?"

Mermaid, huh? Orchid turned back to the mirror. Did she want to look like a mermaid at prom? Did she want to wear green, for that matter?

On a side table, her phone buzzed again.

No. Not green.

She stripped off the mermaid dress and looked for another.

Peacock was sifting through lace and tulle. "Not a lot of blue, huh?" At first, Orchid hadn't thought Peacock was going to show up. She'd heard the other Murder Crew members had banded together to attend prom as a group—without her, which Orchid supposed meant they'd picked sides in her current war against Scarlett Mistry. They all thought she was in league with Oliver, which she *so* wasn't. But what she'd realized is that it was Scarlett who'd really fostered friendships with each of the others. She barely knew Finn or Mustard, despite what they'd all been through together.

And she knew exactly what Scarlett would have to say about *that.*

But tonight, Peacock had come anyway, eyes blazing, and declared that she was looking for something—as she put it—*banging*. Orchid wondered if she, too, had had a falling out with Blackbrook's preeminent queen bee.

"Sorry," Orchid said to Peacock. "Though I think there were a couple near—"

"Wow!" Violet pulled another dress from the rack. "Do I remember this from the Oscars?"

"You do," said Orchid. "About three or four years ago. One of the best supporting actress nominees."

"Omigod." Violet practically ripped the zipper in her rush to get it on.

Amber began helping her. "Chill out. These dresses cost nearly as much as tuition."

Amber had consented to join them for this activity, but had yet to put a gown on herself. Instead, she was ensconced in an oversize Blackbrook Crew hoodie that must have been Tanner's.

Orchid couldn't exactly blame her. Tanner wasn't even cold in the ground. Orchid had been destroyed for months when Vaughn died.

Maybe she was still destroyed.

But there were ten other girls gleefully sorting through the available options, squealing with delight as they twirled and posed in front of the mirrors.

Orchid smiled in triumph. There were few perks to being an infamous ex–child star. Calling in favors from designers she knew, just so she could stick it to Scarlett, was definitely one of them. Scarlett might be micromanaging every aspect of prom planning, but no one would be talking about the decorations or the band this time. Most of the girls coming would be sporting runway fashions.

But not Scarlett.

Did Orchid feel guilty about this? Not really. Scarlett was more than happy to use Orchid's fame and fortune when it suited her, and then throw it in her face when it didn't. Just like her moneygrubbing *mother*. Scarlett had been the one to insist that Orchid trade in on her notoriety after Keith's death, after all. Orchid had wanted to hide in a hole again, just like she had been for the last three years. She didn't want to morph into a music producer. And then for Scarlett to say that Orchid didn't love her? Screw that. How was Orchid expected to love someone who saw her as a paycheck?

At least Vaughn was dead. Anything she had done to help his career wasn't something he'd ever know about. Besides, if he and his brother truly were the heirs to the Fain glue fortune, they were way richer than she was. Though, ironically, by giving Oliver those letters, she might still be the one responsible for helping him claim that fortune.

Orchid picked another dress off the pile. This one was white and a little too bridal for her taste. Or maybe too innocent. Or something.

"Ugh," said Violet. "I'm swimming in this one." She held up the excess fabric pooling around her ankles.

"Let me try it," said Peacock, holding out her hand. Orchid didn't know if she'd describe Violet's castoff as *banging*, though. Elegant, maybe. Timeless?

There was a sequined off-the-shoulder number she recalled

seeing, however. And it was shorter, too, which would be great for Beth since she was dependent on the scooter. She returned to the rack to find it, flicking quickly past a crimson raw silk whose boatneck and gold accents would be perfect for someone *not* in attendance—not that Orchid cared!—but then, her fingers paused on another dress. This one was a silky, iridescent black that shimmered with purple flames as the fabric moved under the light. She pulled it out. The material gathered on one shoulder, then fell in tight folds across the bodice to a spot on the left hip, where it exploded outward in unexpected ruffles sweeping into a short train.

She smiled. This was not an innocent dress. If she was taking on the queen bee of Blackbrook for her crown, she might need a gown to match.

Orchid pulled the gown off the rack and held it up to herself. Her hair, still mauve, made for an unexpectedly punk contrast to the shimmering black gown.

"Oh yeah," said Violet, nodding at her. "That's the one."

Orchid was zipping herself up when Amber called out from the corner where she'd left her phone. "Orchid, your phone is blowing up with notifications."

"I know." She rolled her eyes and turned in front of the mirrors.

Amber gasped and Orchid whirled around to discover the other girl with her phone in her hand.

She rushed forward. "That's private."

Amber was holding the phone out like a dead animal, her face a mask of horror. "That's *Vaughn.* Why is Vaughn texting you from beyond the grave?"

"It's not Vaughn," she said, and snatched the phone out of Amber's hand. "It's his brother."

Amber, Violet, and a few of the other girls looked at her, confused. "Vaughn had a brother?"

"Yes," Orchid said, her jaw clenched. "And he's been bothering me."

From her scooter, Peacock snorted.

Orchid glared at her. "He has!"

"Okay," said Peacock dryly. "If that's what you want to call it."

"Yes, that's what I want to call it."

Peacock shrugged. "Look, men suck. You'll get no argument from me."

"Is this about Vaughn's music channel disappearing?" This came from Violet, who was now in the bridal gown.

Probably. "When we made it, we didn't really think about the fact that Vaughn's songs all belonged to Vaughn's heirs. Or that he had heirs. So yeah, it was kind of a mess."

Amber looked on the verge of tears again. "No one from Tanner's family even reached out to me."

"Oliver didn't reach out to me," Orchid said. "I had to track him down. Talk about a mistake. He's—he's not a good person."

Amber spoke in a choking sob. "Well, he lost his brother and then had to watch his girlfriend make his death internet famous these last few months. I don't think I'd be a good person anymore, either."

"That's not what I did!" Orchid snapped. "It wasn't his death. It was his *music.*"

Amber shrugged, sniffling. "It doesn't matter."

"Yes it does!" She was shouting, and all the other girls were giving each other quiet looks.

Amber hugged herself inside her hoodie and sighed. "Orchid, I don't blame you or anything, and I certainly spent plenty of time listening to Vaughn's music, especially when Tanner had it on. But everyone knows the reason it took off like that was the whole 'gone too soon' angle you and Scarlett were pushing. People were moved by his story. I imagine that it must have been hard for Vaughn's brother to have to watch that."

"He didn't have any trouble cashing the check for it," Peacock said.

"I'm just saying," Amber went on, "for someone who went to the lengths you did to not be famous, it's weird that you turned around and did the same thing to Vaughn."

Orchid breathed in and out. "Take that up with Scarlett. The whole thing was her idea. The only thing I've ever done with my fame at this school is order these dresses." And then she lifted her train and ran out of the ballroom.

Upstairs in her room, Orchid slammed the door shut and pressed her back against it, panting. This was why it never paid to do nice things for people. Not once they knew who she was. Orchid McKee might be able to throw dress-up parties for her friends—might even have been able to have friends. Have boyfriends. Have anything without people constantly questioning her motives at every turn. But not Emily Pryce.

And it didn't even matter that Amber wasn't even using the dresses or going to prom. Scarlett was right—as usual—but she had it backward. It wasn't Orchid who thought she had to buy people's friendships. It was the rest of the world.

Her phone buzzed again. Against her better judgement, Orchid looked.

VAUGHN

> Orchid, please.
>
> I'm sorry about the other night. And the other, OTHER night.

Oh, she'd just bet he was.

VAUGHN

> I'll tell you everything, I swear. But not on the phone. Can we meet?

ORCHID

> The other day, you seemed pretty determined to convince us all that Mrs. White killed Boddy with your brother's help. How can you possibly think I'm going to listen to anything you say now?

Oliver didn't respond. Maybe she'd finally gotten rid of him. Then her phone buzzed again and Orchid didn't know if the pounding in her heart was from relief or fury.

VAUGHN

> Your loyalty to my brother's memory is moving, even if you're totally wrong about who he was.

And even if she wasn't particularly loyal. Loyal did not describe people who made out with their dead boyfriends' brothers.

ORCHID

Tell me you don't think that Vaughn had anything to do with the Headmaster's murder or we have nothing more to talk about.

VAUGHN

I think my brother and I had everything to do with Headmaster's Boddy's death.

She was holding her phone so tightly her knuckles had gone white. So Scarlett's theory was correct. Mrs. White hadn't killed the headmaster because of the Tudor House plans. She'd killed him because he'd realized the truth about the Greens.

As a motive for murder, it wasn't quite as good as Orchid's own.

ORCHID

How long have you known?

She could barely breathe. Her vision blurred as she stared down at the three tiny dots of Oliver's non-answer.

After an age, a new text came through.

VAUGHN

Can we meet?

"No!" she screamed at the screen. She'd been lied to one too many times, and alone with murderers two too many.

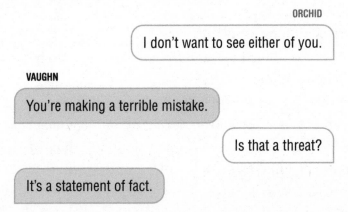

VAUGHN

Just me, if that helps. Not Linda.

Orchid let out a shocked bark of laughter. She hadn't been aware he meant Mrs. White at all. But of course. Mrs. White must be staying with Oliver at his house.

ORCHID

I don't want to see either of you.

VAUGHN

You're making a terrible mistake.

Is that a threat?

It's a statement of fact.

There was a knock at her back, and Orchid jumped. She wiped at her cheeks, which were wet with tears. When had she started crying? Why had she started crying?

"Orchid?" Peacock's voice came through the thick wood of the door.

Orchid sniffled, and opened the door. Peacock was leaning against the jam, holding up her casted leg as if it was part of her new exercise routine.

"Beth," she said, surprised. "I thought you couldn't make it up the stairs."

"It takes a while," Peacock replied. "So I save it for special occasions. Can I come in?"

Orchid shrugged and opened the door wider. As Peacock limped in, Orchid retreated to her bed, pausing only to stick her phone in a desk drawer. Let Oliver text her collection of highlighters.

"So that was quite a scene," Peacock said. She crossed her uninjured arm over the braced one and leaned against the cabinet. "You okay?"

"Don't I look okay?"

"Not for a long time, and less so than usual, lately."

Orchid sniffed. "Ditto."

Peacock laughed ruefully. "I suppose that goes for all of Blackbrook. Are you able to sleep? Do you want me to get you some of my painkillers? I know I shouldn't, but—it helped Amber the other day."

"No—"

"How about some tea? I have some great herbal teas. You should really let someone help you."

She shook her head. "I'll be fine."

Peacock appeared to take that transparent lie at face value. "So . . . is that the dress you've chosen? It looks great."

"I guess so." Orchid looked down at herself. The dress was great. It was everything else that was a mess.

"Let me take it. Violet's got a steamer and she's going to do all of them before the dance."

"Yeah, sure." She went over to the cabinet and grabbed some flannel pants and an old T-shirt to change into. She wriggled out of the gown, got into her comfy clothes, and blew her nose.

"I think you two should probably have a real conversation," Peacock said.

"Who, me and Oliver?"

"No, you and Scarlett."

Oh. That. Orchid sighed and flopped on the bed. "No."

Peacock frowned. "I saw the red-and-gold dress downstairs. It's perfect for her."

Orchid had seen it, too. "Then pull it out for her. I don't care."

Peacock's expression remained neutral. "It's starting to get difficult to tell who are the good guys and who are the bad guys."

"It was never easy," Orchid said. "Remember, this all started with us sitting around this house accusing each other of murder."

"Yeah, I kind of missed that at the time." Peacock pursed her lips. "Sort of a pattern of mine of not noticing who is dangerous until it's too late."

"Oh? Getting any better at that?"

"Yes." Peacock folded the dress over her arm. "You know who is really dangerous, don't you?"

Orchid couldn't help it. She glanced at the desk drawer. She should know. She really should.

Oliver was protecting Mrs. White. That much was clear. And Mrs. White was still a murderer, no matter why she had done it.

You're a murderer, too. I don't automatically hate you for it.

"I don't," she confessed to Peacock.

The other girl's eyes widened. "Then maybe you're the one who's dangerous."

Orchid bowed her head, and more tears fell on her cheeks. "Well, we knew that part already."

26

Mustard

Mustard hadn't been told much other than that his lawyer was here to speak to him. As he hadn't realized he had a lawyer, this was somewhat of a surprise.

But as soon as he saw who was accompanying her, the surprise vanished completely.

"Good evening," Scarlett Mistry said, grinning proudly, as he was shown into the conference room by the police. The attorney he remembered. She was the one who'd worked on Orchid's case, which boded well, given that Orchid brained a guy and never even saw the inside of a holding cell. Pretty, young, efficient, and a total shark.

"Mustard, it's good to see you again."

"Miss Landis." He nodded.

"You can call me Bianca. I'm sorry I'm here so late. This place is back of beyond."

He didn't actually know what time of day it was. There were no windows in the holding room, and none in this conference room, either. At Farthing, they'd been taught all the ways to mark time, in case they were captured. He'd been here for four sandwich-and-soda meals and twice as many escorted bathroom trips. He'd been here for six changes of shift. He estimated it had been about a day and a half.

She touched her perfect hair twist and sat across from him, opening a manila folder. "I've secured your release, and prepared the paperwork for the action we are taking against this department for the completely appalling treatment that you've been subject to for the last thirty-six hours."

Score one for Farthing education.

"As a minor, you never should have been questioned without your parents or other custodial guardian present. Since your father is currently in Texas and the acting administrator of Blackbrook Academy has abrogated all responsibility for this situation, any statement you have made in this facility is entirely coerced and should be stricken from the record. Please let me know what you have told them so I can get started on my statement."

"I didn't say anything," Mustard replied. "I'm not an idiot."

Bianca Landis smiled with too many teeth. "Very good. Of course you're not. Please sign where the tabs indicate."

Mustard looked at Scarlett, who nodded as if she'd explain it all later. But even if everyone else at Blackbrook was used to being managed by Scarlett Mistry, he was not.

"I don't have any money to pay you," he explained to the lawyer.

"It's taken care of. Sign." She shoved the papers forward.

"But—"

"My cut of Vaughn's music money," Scarlett broke in. "If we're using it to get people out of jail, I'd rather my percentage went to release someone who *didn't* kill anybody."

Mustard was overruled. He signed.

Bianca brusquely gathered the papers and stood to depart, adding only, "Don't go far. We've got more to manage."

After the tall blond lawyer shark was gone, Mustard turned back to his new jailer, the petite, black-haired student shark. "Where exactly does she suppose I'd go, Scarlett? Back to Texas?"

"Back to Blackbrook, silly. And you're welcome, by the way."

"I'm not suspended? Or . . . expelled?"

"Of course not," she scoffed. "That would take the administration, you know, actually *doing* something. I have no idea what Winkle's priorities are, but it doesn't seem to be running a school."

"Well, I can't get back in my room. It's a crime scene, isn't it?"

Wasn't that the whole point of this exercise—that they thought someone had murdered Tanner?

Scarlett folded her arms and gave him an amused stare. "I wasn't under the impression you'd been staying in your room, anyway."

His face burned. He'd like to be shown back into his holding cell now. Please.

Scarlett, miraculously, took pity on him. "If strictly necessary, I suppose I can swing a few nights at a hotel on the mainland. There are no Mistry properties in Maine, but—"

"It doesn't matter what I do if I can't go back to Blackbrook." His father had made it perfectly clear that the remote prep school was his last chance.

"Of course you're going back!"

"What, so we can double-date to prom?" He shook his head.

"Even if Winkle decides not to punish me, if my dad gets wind of what went down, he'll yank me out so fast my head will spin."

"Let Bianca deal with that. She'll nuke them like she's about to nuke this police department."

Mustard hoped so. Everything had happened so fast the other morning. He thought he was doing the right thing. When he first went to the police station, he thought it was just to give a statement, as he had when he'd witnessed Orchid killing Keith Grayson. By the time he realized what was really going on, staying silent and hoping to wait them out was the only option he had left.

"All I can think is that the Curry family wants a fall guy, and they have a lot of pull, and plenty of fancy lawyers of their own. How much money did you make off Vaughn? How many hours of legal counsel can we afford?"

Scarlett frowned. "Let me worry about that."

"How's Plum?"

She frowned harder. "Also on the list of things I'm worried about, if you want the whole truth. He's got this wild idea that he can offer Curry Chem his dye in order to get them off your back."

Mustard blinked. "That's ridiculous." He wouldn't let that happen. Couldn't.

"I'm glad we're in agreement." She gave him another one of those careful, level glances. "I don't know if you've noticed, but Finn is all about big, romantic gestures."

Mustard had, in fact, noticed. A few months earlier, he'd rescued Finn's project from the passages below Tudor House, and Finn had definitely seen it as a big, romantic gesture.

And maybe it had been. Mustard wasn't sure. He wasn't sure about anything right now. He'd spent an entire day turning it over and over in his mind, coming up with ever-more outlandish and upsetting theories.

The door to the conference room opened, and Bianca strode back in, looking mildly disgusted.

"I am amazed these people manage to clothe and feed themselves, they are so phenomenally stupid. This place should be razed to the ground, and every employee forced to attend remedial kindergarten. Let's go."

"What happened?" asked Scarlett.

"They have another suspect. Bringing her in now."

Amber, thought Mustard, horrified.

"Mrs. White?" Scarlett asked, and Bianca gave a curt nod.

Oh, right. The actual confessed murderer in their midst. The one who had so recently been released from prison, thanks to Oliver Green and the rest of the music money.

He wasn't thinking. Or maybe he'd been thinking too much. Though he didn't know why Mrs. White would want to hurt Tanner, either. Didn't know why anyone would want to hurt Tanner Curry, other than Tanner himself.

"We'll talk in my car. I've already got your things, Mustard." She held up a plastic bag holding his keys, cell phone, and wallet, and Mustard pulled himself together enough to take it and mumble a thank-you.

He was shortly after herded to the car by two of the pushiest and most capable women he'd ever met, and he was mildly surprised to discover that he was grateful for it. Maybe he was getting better on that whole misogyny thing Scarlett had mentioned. Either way, the Mustard of a few months ago would be shocked to discover that he was letting Scarlett Mistry make any kind of important arrangements for him.

The Mustard of a few months ago would be shocked about quite a lot of things, actually.

In the car, Bianca asked him a few quick questions, typing furiously on her phone the whole time. He told her what he knew, which was not much. Tanner was dead in his chair. No blood, no sign of struggle. Mustard hadn't thought murder; he'd thought—

"That's what we thought, too," Scarlett said, when Mustard found he couldn't keep talking. He stared out the window at the drab parking lot and the annoyingly bright sky. Scarlett, equally annoying, kept talking. "That he'd done it to himself. I mean, he's been acting so weird lately, right?"

"I'd really like to keep this out of the realm of speculation," Bianca cut in. "It's not our responsibility to figure out how Tanner died. Just our responsibility to tell the authorities what we know."

"Well, we *know* he dumped his girlfriend out of the blue, and we *know* he quit all his sports teams," Scarlett said. "And Amber and Finn told me he's been saying all this maudlin stuff—"

"Scarlett," said Bianca in warning.

Scarlett was not much for warnings. She looked at Mustard. "There must be something you didn't see. Because otherwise, why would they be pushing this idea that there was foul play?"

Exactly the question he'd been wondering himself, ever since it became clear that the cops weren't questioning him for information, but instead trying to get him to say something incriminating.

"I don't know," he blurted. "I've been trying to make sense of it all. Like maybe the Currys can't bear to think that things were so bad with him, so they want to blame someone else. Or maybe they've got some big insurance policy on him and it won't pay out for a suicide."

Scarlett pressed her hand to her mouth in horror.

He should stop talking. He knew he should. But he'd been silent for more than a day, with nothing to think about but this, and besides, it was Scarlett. Scarlett the fixer. Scarlett, who was always a couple steps ahead of everyone else. Scarlett, who wanted to be in charge so badly she'd actually hired a lawyer for him just so she could sit here and be smug about it.

"Or maybe something else. I don't know!"

"Precisely," said Bianca, her tone clipped. "You don't know. You don't know anything more than what you already told me. Who are you, Perry Mason? No. *I'm* the lawyer. Understand?"

No, but probably because he had no clue who Perry Mason was. But he nodded anyway, and went back to looking out the window. His cellphone, still dead, sat in a bag in his lap. He dreaded to think of the messages waiting for him. And then he thought about the messages Tanner had been sending him, back when Tanner was still alive. The ones he hadn't been able to look at.

"Hey, do you have a charger I can use?"

Bianca passed him a cord, then started driving.

"That's going to take forever," Scarlett observed, nodding at Mustard's dead phone.

He grunted noncommittally.

"I'm just saying, you could borrow my phone . . . if you wanted to call your father, or, like, Finn . . ." she trailed off, as if waiting for him to say something.

He didn't say anything. His father. Ugh, his father! Mustard already knew what his father had to say. The fact that he'd remained in Texas, even when his son was getting arrested— well, that said it all. His dad was done with him. If not for the Murder Crew, he might have rotted in that holding room.

Or maybe it had only been Scarlett who had come for him.

"Does Plum know you're here?" he asked her, staring resolutely out the window.

"Of course," she replied, sounding mildly disappointed that he'd even had to ask. "But Bianca didn't think it was a good idea to bring him."

"To be fair, I didn't think it was a good idea to bring *you*, either," said Bianca.

The phone booted up. A cascade of messages poured in—Murder Crew, his father, tons of private ones from Finn. He scrolled down to Tanner's name and clicked to open the conversation. The screen showed the last few messages they'd exchanged before he died.

TANNER

> Did you ever meet this Oliver kid?
> What a punk.

MUSTARD

> Only when he was pretending to be
> Vaughn. How did talk go?

idk. Weird? This whole thing is weird.

Then, later:

TANNER

Going home this weekend.

MUSTARD

Sounds like a good idea. Take care.

And finally, the new messages, all from the night before he'd found Tanner dead.

TANNER

On way back to Rocky Point. Things did not go well. Talking to my dad was like talking to a rock. He only cares that things look right, not whether they are right.

Mustard understood those kinds of fathers all too well. He wished he'd had the chance to talk to Tanner about this. He wished he'd had the chance to talk to Tanner the way he should have. Maybe things would have turned out differently. He scrolled down to look at the rest of the messages.

TANNER

Not really sure where to go from here. It's a total train wreck, and he knows it. Dr. Brown might have listened, but Winkle won't.

> Where are you?
>
> Text me back, man. Where you at?

And that was that. Mustard didn't know what he'd been expecting. A suicide note, maybe. Or a clue to what might have happened to Tanner in the hours between sending these texts and winding up dead in his desk chair.

Where you at?

What if Mustard hadn't been in Plum's room that night? If he'd been home, where he belonged, would Tanner have died?

"What is it?" Scarlett asked.

"Nothing." He put the phone down and went back to staring out the window.

"Those were texts from Tanner, weren't they? What did they say?"

"Nothing!"

"Well, they're about to be evidence—"

Mustard groaned, swiped the screen back on, and shoved the phone at her. "Evidence of what, exactly? That he got home that night and I wasn't there? That part we knew already. We even have witnesses."

He met Bianca's eyes in the rearview mirror. She gave a weary shake of her head.

"We're not detectives, Scarlett," he said to her. "Every time we try to be we fail miserably."

"Speak for yourself," she replied, as she scanned the texts.

"Oh yeah? Did you figure out Oliver?"

"I figured out *you*."

He snorted and went back to window-watching.

"Well, these don't sound like the texts of someone suicidal," she pronounced, and handed him back his phone. "And they must have some reason to suspect foul play."

"Other than *it's Blackbrook*?"

"Once again," chimed in their lawyer, "I will remind you that this is not your responsibility."

"See?" said Mustard. But even as he said it, he knew it wouldn't stop Scarlett, just as it wasn't stopping his own brain.

They'd arrested Mrs. White. But why? Why would she have killed Tanner Curry? Tanner Curry had been trying to help her surviving godson. Tanner was just a kid.

But Mrs. White had almost killed him. She'd almost killed a lot of them there in Tudor House that night.

He turned back to Scarlett. "That thing you said the other night about the Greens and Mrs. White and Headmaster Boddy—do you think it's true?"

"Oliver didn't exactly deny it."

"I was thinking . . . All that stuff we didn't know about how it was done—how Mrs. White dragged Boddy down the hall to the conservatory, or cleaned up all the blood while we were still asleep, or got Karlee and Kayla down in the secret passages—that could all have been her and Vaughn together. Or her and both the Greens."

"Excuse me?" asked Bianca. "Who are 'both the Greens'?"

Scarlett rolled her eyes and explained.

Bianca brought the car to a stop right in the middle of the road. She turned in her seat and looked back at the two of them. "This is information that I wish you had shared with me previously, Scarlett."

"Why?"

"Because it involves Orchid and what happened with her. Orchid is still my client. This could be a conflict of interest."

Mustard grit his teeth. "So what? We have to get out and walk now?"

Bianca took a deep breath. "No. I don't know. I'll take you both back to school and review. I may have to refer you to a colleague, but I hope you have no more legal troubles . . . Just—just sit there, and don't say anything, okay? Ugh." She turned around, and Mustard could swear he heard her mutter *Teenagers!* under her breath.

But they obeyed her and stayed quiet the entire way back to Blackbrook. Mustard wondered if Scarlett was going to explode, and figured it was only her hefty investment into his legal assistance that was keeping her lip zipped.

Mustard, for his part, just stared out the window and thought about Tanner's last words to him. He hadn't realized all this time being friendly with his roommate, he'd never grappled with what it meant to actually be friends. There was so much he couldn't say to Tanner, and so much—he now knew—that they should have said to one another, about their fathers, about expectations, and about the value of throwing them away.

Bianca drove them to Tudor House, which Mustard supposed made sense. He still wasn't sure where he was supposed to be going. His room was altogether out of the question. Plum's was an option, maybe? Once he talked to Plum.

As soon as the car pulled up to the edge of the lawn, the door to the house opened and Plum came out, moving at a pace somewhere between a hurry and a sprint. Through the front window, Mustard saw a cluster of girls' faces—Peacock and Amber he recognized at once. Amber—he hadn't even thought of what he might say to her.

By the time Mustard had exited the car, Plum was at the edge of the walk. He stopped short, as if realizing they had an audience.

"Hi," said Mustard.

"Hi," said Plum.

Mustard started right in. "Scarlett said you were trying to strike some deal with Curry. Don't do that—"

"Don't tell me what to do—"

"After all I've been through to protect your stupid formula—"

"Shut up!" Plum said sharply. He stepped forward. "We're not going to talk about that right now. Are you okay?"

"I'm fine." Plum better not touch him. Everyone was watching. Plum better not touch him. He couldn't bear it, after everything.

Plum didn't touch him. He did something far worse.

"I'm so sorry about Tanner," he said. "I know how much you cared about him."

And that's when something stiff and brittle crumpled up inside of Mustard, and he collapsed against Plum's shoulder as big, heaving sobs came bubbling up from a place he had hardly known was there.

27

Orchid

As it turned out, high school was not all that different from Hollywood. Both places loved their big, fake, fancy parties, no matter what kind of scandal or carnage they were covering up with the celebration.

When Orchid first escaped her old life and came to live at Blackbrook, she thought she'd freed herself from the expectation of such events. She'd never attended any of the other school dances, even if it meant hiding away in her room while they were happening just downstairs in the ballroom of Tudor House. She had her disguise of fake glasses and unkempt hair and oversize sweaters. Putting on a ballgown and partying was the exact opposite of the impression she was trying to convey.

Now, as she stood at the door of the Tudor House ballroom on the evening of the Blackbrook prom, her colorful hair styled in old-school Hollywood glam, the shimmering ruffles of her gown swirling about her high-heeled shoes, she couldn't help but feel the futility of all her efforts. All those years of hiding—behind glasses and sweaters, silence, and fake identities. And here she was, anyway, the scandalous starlet. And more scandalous than she'd been, even in Hollywood, because now she wasn't just a teenybopper movie star heading down a bad path. Now she was also a killer.

One of many, perhaps, on this campus.

Orchid couldn't imagine how one held a prom in the middle of all this chaos, but then again, she wasn't Scarlett Mistry. Scarlett, Orchid had to admit, might have outdone herself this time. Trails of spherical white paper lanterns led a ghostly path from the front door of Tudor House, down the dark hall, and into the candlelit ballroom. The mood was elegant but somber, fitting for a prom scheduled to include a memorial service for those Blackbrook had lost this year. At the door sat boxes filled with small white candles in individual candlesticks, ready for a symbolic candle lighting. The walls were hung with large, black-and-white portraits of the dead: Headmaster Boddy, Rusty, Rosa, Vaughn, Dr. Brown, and Tanner. In front of each picture was a small pedestal featuring a vase with a single white rose, another candle, and small cards and pens for students to leave notes with memories of the departed.

And then, in the corner, the band was setting up.

Orchid watched this all with a mixture of skepticism and begrudging appreciation. On one hand, she wasn't sure how much fun kids would have dancing alongside the memorials. On the other, she had no idea how Scarlett had managed to pull it all off, especially since she'd heard Scarlett spent most of the other day helping Mustard.

She'd also heard from Peacock that Scarlett had finally accepted one of the gowns from Orchid's stash. Orchid had expected to feel smugly triumphant about this, that for all Scarlett's posturing, in the end, she'd needed something from

Orchid after all. But instead, the knowledge left Orchid feeling more hollow and isolated than she'd ever been all those lonely years in disguise.

This was what came of trying to make friends. Well, Orchid had learned her lesson now.

She heard the squeak of the screen door by the kitchen entrance. Her date had arrived.

She took a deep, cleansing breath, squared her shoulders, and went to intercept him.

She reached the door just as he'd finally managed to turn the key in the ancient lock. The door opened two inches, then stopped as the chain pulled tight.

"There's a chain?" came Oliver's voice from the other side of the door.

"Of course," said Orchid, as she pushed the door shut and unlatched the chain. She opened it again and smiled. "It turns out all kinds of unsavory characters have keys to this house."

Oliver stood on the stoop and just stared. There was a rumble of thunder behind him, and the wind rustled the leaves across the yard. It would storm later.

Orchid was pleased to see he was wearing a suit. She hadn't been certain that he would dress for the occasion, hadn't even been certain that he would come. And she still couldn't decide how she felt about the fact that he had.

"Orchid," he breathed. "You look—"

"Can it," she blurted. "I know how I look. I know how I've looked every single day for my entire life." She couldn't bear compliments coming from this face, this voice. Because it wasn't *him*. It was Oliver.

But Oliver could not tear his eyes off her. "I—I just wish my brother were here to see you looking like this. I wish Vaughn were your date tonight."

Orchid swallowed, then clenched her jaw. No. She was not going to fall for it again. She'd seen behind Oliver's mask of kindness and charm. He said all the right things, because he knew she would fall for them. And then he used her vulnerability to do one of two things: try to get into her pants, or drive the stake further into her heart.

"Vaughn is dead, as you so enjoy reminding me," she forced herself to say. "And remember—you're only my date in the most broadly technical sense. Come in."

He held up his hands and stepped over the threshold. "Oh, I know. Look, I didn't even bring you a corsage."

She nodded stiffly. Good. Because this wasn't a date. She thought about the flower box up in her room. It didn't matter. If he didn't bring a corsage, she certainly wasn't going to give him a boutonniere. Because this wasn't a date.

It was probably just another one of his manipulations, but Orchid was betting on the fact that if she knew it going in, she'd be less likely to fall prey to whatever he was attempting.

"Seriously," he asked. "Why the chain?"

"Seriously," she shot back, "you know why." And then, in a rustle of taffeta, she turned on her heel and led him out of the kitchen and down the hall. "Let's get this over with, before people start showing up."

"Let's get this over with so you can see once and for all that I'm not lying to you," he said to her back.

She turned around, there in the hall. The lanterns cast

their pallid light over both of them, masking Oliver's scowl. For a moment, Orchid remembered the night of the storm, when the hall was similarly dark, and she and Vaughn had first started talking to each other.

"Let's allow for a second that I believe you," she hissed. "Let's pretend that I think you're telling me the truth. Has it ever occurred to you that Mrs. White might be lying—to *you?*"

"Mrs. White has no reason to lie to me," he said, staring back at her.

The candles flickered. With her heels on, she was precisely the same height as him. If this were a date, they'd look really good in pictures. If he were her date. If he were Vaughn.

"They're trying to frame her," Oliver insisted. "Just like they tried to frame Mustard."

In the end, that was what had convinced Orchid to give Oliver another chance. He'd texted again, begging her to help him. Mrs. White, he claimed, had been taken into custody again, this time on suspicion of having had something to do with the death of Tanner Curry. This information had been verified by Orchid's lawyer, Bianca, as well as Mustard.

Oliver was indeed a jerk, but there could *also* be a massive conspiracy afoot to defraud him of his rightful inheritance. The inheritance he would have split with Vaughn, had Vaughn still been alive. Both things could be true at once.

So, if you thought about it, she wasn't doing this for Oliver. She was doing it for Vaughn. At least, that's what Orchid kept telling herself. And the longer she stared at Oliver's face in the candlelight, the harder it was to keep the two of them separate.

"Show me," she said.

Oliver led the way into the study.

Of course. Of course it was the study. Orchid grit her teeth and followed him inside. Here, at least, they could avoid all the mood lighting. The desk lamps weren't exactly bright, but they weren't as romantic as the candles and lanterns in the hall.

Besides, this was the study. Orchid kept her eyes averted from the floor, where every shadow in the wood made her think of bloodstains.

Oliver crossed the room, then turned to see her lingering by the door. He smirked.

"Come in, Lady Macbeth."

"Get what you came for."

"I'm right, though, aren't I?" he scoffed. "The outfit, the orders . . . Emily Pryce's newest role is that of the evil queen."

She didn't so much as blink. "What does that make you?"

"The cursed prince, of course."

"Wow, Oliver, maybe you should have been the one writing murder ballads instead of Vaughn."

His eyes narrowed at her and he turned back toward the bookshelves. "Here." He pulled down a volume and held it out to her. "Look familiar?"

It did. Last winter, she'd sat in this very room with Vaughn and Mrs. White, looking through these old pictures from when Tudor House had been a girls' reform school. Mrs. White had been a student there. So had the Green twins' grandmother, Olivia Vaughn.

"How is this evidence?"

"I don't know. Linda said it was. Go ahead and look yourself so you know I didn't do any sleight of hand."

Orchid shook her head and took the book. She opened it to see the yellowed pages, the faded photos. She flipped through and a white sheet of paper slid out and fluttered to the floor.

She glanced down at the paper, which looked like a printout of an email. One that was covered in spatters of reddish-brown. She blinked, but the bloodstains remained.

Oliver leaned over and picked it up.

"It's from John Curry to Headmaster Boddy," he said. "It's from the day before the storm."

"Why is it covered in blood?" Orchid managed to ask.

"Why do you think?" And then he read: *"Thank you for this information. Too much to hope, I guess, that this whole thing died out three years ago. The scholarship was more than generous. I hadn't been aware you'd arranged for even that much. If she continues to be difficult, we will have to consider our options. With the new construction, perhaps it's best to make sure her final ties to the school are cut. If necessary, explain to her that the boy's promising future might be at risk if she keeps up the pursuit. There should be no problem getting you the funds required to begin work in the new term."*

Orchid bit back a sob. "When she killed Headmaster Boddy—it wasn't about tearing down Tudor House," she said. "Not really. And it wasn't about you and Vaughn."

"It was exactly about us," Oliver scoffed, "only not the way you think. It wasn't that Boddy found out that my brother and I were tricking them. Vaughn only ever wanted to be a student here—to be a good little Blackbrook kid. Look at this letter! They gave him that scholarship to shut us up, and it almost worked! For Vaughn at least. One scholarship, for the most *promising* of the grandsons, and maybe we would have been quiet forever. But I wasn't satisfied with that. I convinced Mrs. White to help me fight for what we were really owed. And this—this was the result."

Orchid remembered that horrible night of the storm, when Mrs. White had her cornered in the secret passage under the kitchen. It had never made sense, what she was saying about snapping and stabbing Boddy because they'd been arguing about his demolition plans. Orchid knew that Mrs. White had loved this house, but to kill a man over it seemed like madness. Maybe that's why she'd stuck to that story all these months— because casting herself as a crazy old woman was helpful for her defense.

"Don't you see?" Oliver strode forward, thrusting the paper at her face. "This proves that Curry Chem knew exactly who we are and what we're owed, and they were willing to do whatever it took to keep us from getting it!"

"So then why did Mrs. White hide it here in this book?" She would not be drawn into another of Oliver's manipulations. She was done being a victim. Victim Orchid had died in this very room four months earlier.

Oliver took a deep breath. "She told me—she told me that she saw the email with the Headmaster's things the night of the storm. She confronted him and—well, you know what happened next."

What had happened next was that Mrs. White had stabbed the headmaster.

"She told me that the next day she was in here looking at the paper and trying to figure out what to do when you and Vaughn came in the room. You were all looking at this book and she thought it was as good a place to hide it as any—and, then, she got arrested."

"Why didn't you retrieve it?" Orchid asked. "You've had a key to this place for months. You've been in this house plenty." He could have planted this letter, bloodstains and all. This whole thing could be another con, like the one he and his brother had been pulling off for years.

"She only just told me about it."

"I don't believe you."

His lips turned into a thin line. "I suppose I deserve that. But I am telling you the truth."

"I don't," she repeated slowly, "believe you."

Oliver had cried wolf far too many times. She didn't know what to trust. If Vaughn were here, it would be different. Maybe. Orchid wasn't even sure anymore.

"Well, that's a problem, isn't it, Orchid?" He shook his head. "Because I'm going to need a lot of people to start believing me, and very soon."

"She was your partner in crime. She'd been helping you gather information about your past—"

"Yeah, from jail!" He made a disgusted sound. "You might not realize this, having never actually gone to jail for killing someone yourself, but it's not as easy to communicate with the outside world as you think."

Orchid's face burned. "Watch yourself. What I did, I had to do. He was going to kill me. Your brother saw it. They all saw it."

He stared at her, and in his eyes there was something desperate and terrible, and when he spoke again, it had crept around the edges of his voice, too. "You're right. They all saw it, and I didn't. I was not there that day, and so I can't judge you for what you did."

I can't let you become a murderer. Vaughn's half-whispered plea to her, just before he drove off, had ricocheted inside her mind for months. Their voices sounded the same. They sounded exactly the same.

"But maybe," Oliver went on, softly, "we can't judge Mrs. White, either. Because none of us were there when she killed Boddy. None of us know what he said to her." He took a deep, shuddering breath. "Except I think she killed him not for a house, not even for a scholarship. I think there was a bigger threat going on here, and they've been lying to us all along."

They were standing very close now, there on the carpet, in the room where she'd killed the last man who'd tried to hurt her.

"Mrs. White knew the truth about Dick Fain. Gemma—our grandmother—obviously did. But they never told us, for whatever reason. They only told us that Gemma had invented the glue and Fain took the credit. And Gemma died without even fighting for what was hers. I thought maybe she didn't have the proof, but I wasn't going to roll over like the rest of them. I was looking for proof that she'd invented the glue. I don't think Mrs. White had any idea what we'd discover in those letters."

"We—"

"My brother and me, the night before he died. We found those letters to our grandmother underground, in the passages. I was the one who put them in the boathouse, the night before the SATs."

Orchid swallowed. With the rest of the things he'd stolen. "So your brother was your real partner."

"I had no real partner," he said through gritted teeth. "Vaughn—Vaughn wanted to forget it all, just like Gemma did. He wanted to finish out Blackbrook and get scholarships to college and stay quiet. And besides, he thought I was evil. The night before he died, we fought—we fought like we had never fought before. He accused me of murdering Rusty. Do you know how hard that was?" His voice broke. "He was the only person I had left, and he died thinking the most horrible things about me."

He dropped his head on her shoulder, and Orchid was shocked to find that his face was wet.

I can't let you become a murderer. Finally, Orchid understood what Vaughn had meant. *I can't let you become a murderer . . . too.* Vaughn thought that Oliver killed Rusty, and it was destroying him.

"Help me, Orchid," he begged her. "I'm just fighting for what is right, and you know it."

She did. It was just like with Vaughn's music. Once she realized Vaughn had an heir, she understood the music wasn't hers. The glue couldn't be Blackbrook's or Curry Chem's, either.

"Help me, Orchid," he said again. "If you won't do it for me, do it for Vaughn."

She drew in a shuddering breath. Maybe this was all just another lie. A beautiful, terrible lie, and they could pretend that neither of them were evil. They were just cursed characters in a haunted castle. A murder ballad sung by a dead boy.

She tilted his face up toward hers and nodded. "Deal."

"Deal," he whispered, and kissed her.

28

Peacock

ELIZABETH PICACH'S ~~RECOVERY JOURNAL~~
INVESTIGATIVE NOTEBOOK

POSSIBLE SUSPECTS
1. **OLIVER GREEN**
2. **ORCHID MCKEE**

FACTS

1. She is the only confessed murderer on campus.

2. She provided the money to help him spring Mrs. White, also a confessed killer, out of jail.

3. They are both way deep in whatever is going on with the Fain glue fortune.

4. Which Tanner was also obsessed with before he died.

5. AND I JUST SAW THEM KISSING IN THE STUDY!?!?!

29

Plum

The key to a good scheme was making sure your enemy was unaware of your real plans. Plum thought that was probably Sun Tzu or something, because Scarlett loved to quote Sun Tzu at him, and he always nodded sagely as if he, too, had memorized some two-thousand-year-old book by a Chinese general. Still, though he could not quote chapter and verse of *The Art of War*, some of the lessons had to have sunk in over the years. How else to account for the fact that not one of them, friend or enemy—not even Scarlett—had managed to figure out his real plan?

Right now, they were probably all gathering at Tudor House for Scarlett's carefully scheduled prom. All afternoon, Finn had helped her with the final preparations—picking up the giant portraits of the deceased, making sure the band had all their audio equipment, even stringing paper lantern lights. According to Scarlett, it was the least he could do after she'd spent an entire day springing his boyfriend from the clink.

And Finn *had* been grateful. That he could not deny. After all, Finn had been prepared to do something extraordinarily desperate in order to make sure that Mustard was safe. Finn had been prepared, to his horror, to capitulate. And that was something of which he was sure Sun Tzu would never have approved.

Not to mention Scarlett.

Now, though, Mustard was free, and probably about to text Finn to find out where he was. He basically had that phone glued to his hands these days, rereading Tanner's last texts as if they held any clues. Due to Scarlett's responsibilities at the dance, she had told them all just to meet at the Tudor House ballroom. Beth had said it made no difference to her, since she was only down the hall, anyway. Finn had told Mustard that he was getting ready with Scarlett, and Scarlett that he was getting ready with Mustard.

He'd told a lot of people a lot of things.

From the shadows beneath the colonnade, Finn watched the students hurrying across the green toward Tudor House, dressed in gowns and suits, cocktails dresses and rented tuxes. They'd be lucky if they made it to the building before the rain started. Already he could feel the change in air pressure that indicated the gathering clouds had bigger plans in store. Probably, he should have brought an umbrella.

There weren't many students headed toward the dance tonight, because there weren't that many kids left at Blackbrook, and some of those remaining thought it was bad form to hold a prom in the midst of all this death. He'd gotten an earful about it from Amber, and he hadn't entirely disagreed with her. But he still hoped that most of the students and the faculty were present, at least for the memorial part of the evening.

He didn't want to risk anyone catching him in the act.

When the coast was clear, he crossed to his favorite window, the one with the broken latch, and pushed it open. From there, it was a quick jaunt through the quiet, unused storeroom, up a flight of marble stairs, down a dark hall, and up to a door that they really should have installed better security on. He knelt before the lock and got to work. Above him hung a carved wooden plaque with the Blackbrook school crest and motto:

To Make Men of Knowledge and Integrity.

Finn had always thought it was a dumb saying. The first part was right, but every Blackbrook kid knew that you never got anywhere worrying about the second. Men of integrity at Blackbrook were people like Dick Fain, who had shared the fruits of their labor with the school. Men of integrity were people like Tanner, who played by the rules so long that it broke them into pieces. Integrity was for suckers.

A-ha. The door swung open into darkness beyond. Finn smiled and slipped inside.

Scarlett always said that Finn was a total idiot about any-thing that didn't come in a test tube, but that wasn't entirely true. He had some other skills. Jimmying locks, for example, or figuring out where people hid their passwords, or rooting out secret files or deleted messages on their personal comput-ers. A hacker he wasn't, but he knew enough to have gotten access to school records for himself and Scarlett, back when that sort of thing mattered.

Not everyone was as lax with security as Headmaster Boddy had been, though. That man had kept a note in his desk drawer with his passwords scrawled on it. He printed out his emails. He didn't use a lock screen.

Dr. Brown had been much more careful, locking down internal school systems as well as the secret passages. Winkle's priorities weren't on the school at all, which was fair. Neither were Finn's, anymore.

Because here was the thing about integrity. Whether a person thought you had it depended very much on the person in question. To some, it meant playing by the rules. To others, honesty. Vaughn Green had looked like the picture of integrity. Then he died, and everyone discovered all his rule-breaking, all his lies.

And Finn? No one at Blackbrook, even the people he was closest to, thought he was a man of integrity. He'd betrayed Beth, lied to Scarlett, double-crossed half the people on campus. Mustard had told him once that he'd asked around about Finn, and every last person told him that Finn was not to be trusted.

Which was true. Or at least, it had been true before Finn met Mustard. Because *Mustard* was a man of integrity, and he made Finn want to be a better person. And that was why Finn was skipping out on prom to do his sneakiest—and most honorable—thing yet.

The headmaster's office was tidy, without the stacks of books and file folders he remembered from when Boddy had still presided over this room. Finn had anticipated as much. He was hardly expecting a giant neon arrow pointing to a convenient scrap of paper announcing what Winkle—and, by extension, his sketchy Curry Chem overlords—were up to.

That's why Finn needed time, as well as plausible deniability. If Scarlett knew his plans, she'd probably volunteer to help him, and if she went missing from prom, people would be sure to notice. If Mustard knew what he'd be up to, he'd try to talk him out of it. He'd probably make some point about all the other times he or Plum had gotten caught trying to sneak around campus. But he had no idea the extent of Finn's sneakiness.

Besides—Perry Winkle had broken into his room first.

The locks on the desk drawer posed little problem, but they also revealed little of value. Finn remembered Boddy's old filing system—sections for admissions and academics, extracurriculars, financial, and residential issues. He and Scarlett had spent plenty of time familiarizing themselves with the inner workings of Blackbrook.

He didn't want much today—just enough to nail Winkle to the wall. Something, anything that he could hold over the man's head to make him leave Mustard alone, leave Finn alone, leave his dye alone. If Blackbrook was imploding, so be it, but Finn wasn't going to let his invention get trapped in the event horizon.

Nothing. The files were months old, as if they hadn't been touched or updated since Headmaster Boddy's death. There were a few recent items, mainly requests for student records from kids who were transferring to more functional schools, or resignations from longtime faculty members. Finn paused briefly on one from his freshman science teacher, his flashlight bouncing over the phrase *no longer even pretending to run an institution devoted to academics, let alone student well-being. I cannot in good conscience participate in such a corrupt system, and therefore tender my resignation.*

Well, then. He took a picture of the letter, wondering if he could talk any of these ex-teachers into being whistleblowers.

Kids complaining to their parents about conditions at Blackbrook resulted in transfers. This was fine for the average student. But it didn't solve his problem. According to Winkle, even if he left the school, they could sue him if he ever tried to sell the glue anywhere.

And it didn't solve the situation with Mustard, either. Since he'd gotten back to campus, the only word from the administration came in a tersely worded affirmative response to Mustard's request to the residential staff to be allowed to transfer to Finn's room, since his was still a crime scene. Under supervision from campus security, he'd been allowed to pack up his computer and overnight bag. Scarlett might be confident in the skills of the fancy lawyer she'd managed to hire, but that didn't mean that Mustard was in the clear.

Scarlett had grilled Mustard about what he'd seen in the room while he'd packed, but Mustard hadn't gained any great insight during the ten minutes the guard had given him to throw some spare socks and a few T-shirts into an overnight bag. After they were finally left alone in Finn's room, Finn hadn't wanted to bring it up again. Mustard was already so upset. He couldn't stop talking about the texts that Tanner had sent him that night, sent apparently when Tanner had gotten back to their room and found Mustard missing. Mustard kept wondering aloud whether—had he been there that night—his roommate might still be alive.

Blinking neon arrow, any time now.

Of course, if Perry Winkle had any sense at all, he wouldn't just leave incriminating evidence lying around. Finn never would, that was for certain. He might accidentally leave his most precious possession underground in a flood, but he wouldn't write down directions to it anywhere.

Maybe this was all simply a fool's errand.

He turned to go, and stopped. There, right next to the door was a coatrack, on which hung Perry Winkle's raincoat and a small leather satchel.

Hello, blinking neon arrow.

Of course Winkle wouldn't keep sensitive information in his desk. He'd keep it on him—unless, of course, he was going to a school dance, where he'd look weird carrying an overcoat and a bag, or leaving such things in a coatroom, where anyone could find it.

In a flash, he'd crossed to the coatrack and had his hands in the coat pockets. Nothing—no cell phone or incriminating notes. Next, he tried the satchel. He flipped open the leather flap holding the bag closed and shined his flashlight inside, examining the contents.

For a moment, Finn wasn't sure what he was looking at. But when realization dawned, his blood ran cold and he just stared into the bag as if rooted to the spot. Because Perry Winkle wasn't just hiding evidence of corruption at Blackbrook. If this meant what he thought it did, then what Winkle was really covering up was murder.

Lightning flashed in the room. Seconds later, thunder rumbled. The skies opened and it began to pour.

Finn started at the noise, and it was as if he'd come unfrozen.

The dance! He had to get to the dance, before it was too late.

30

Scarlett

At last, it was prom. The ballroom of Tudor House danced with glittering points of candlelight, and the somewhat upbeat melody of one of Vaughn Green's cheeriest tunes emanated from the speakers. The band, the Singing Telegrams, was tuning up as the attendees arrived. Students in colorful finery and the best corsages the lone florist on Rocky Point could muster lit memorial candles and left notes underneath the large portraits of the people the school had lost this year. The many, many people.

Once again, Scarlett Mistry had managed things. It was funny. Back before the storm, she'd flattered herself that she ran this school, but now it was really the truth. Without her efforts, there would be no prom. Without her management, there would be no music, no decorations, no memorial service, no—

Two girls walked by in designer gowns.

Well, okay, the dresses had been Orchid's idea. In fact, Scarlett was wearing a designer loaner, too. Peacock had dropped it off for her, claiming that she'd set it aside without Orchid's knowledge, an argument that Scarlett found faintly ridiculous. But the dress was a stunner—a red, raw-silk number that Scarlett had paired with gold strappy sandals and styled with a vintage pair of gold earrings and her hair in a sleek twist. As much as she hated to accept anything of Orchid's right now, she would not let herself be upstaged on her big night by wearing a substandard gown.

Speaking of her latest nemesis, the ex-starlet had yet to make an appearance at the dance. Probably wanted to be fashionably late. Scarlett rolled her eyes.

Also M.I.A. was Finn, a source of increased stress to Mustard, who kept positioning himself in the most shadowy corners of the ballroom and glancing at the door, as if planning his escape. Scarlett didn't blame him. It must be awkward to attend a dance featuring a five-foot-tall photograph of the roommate the school administration suspected you of murdering.

Mustard's erstwhile date, Peacock, was no help, but that wasn't her fault. Scarlett had stationed her on her scooter by the door and given her the task of handing out memorial candles to the arriving students, a job she was undertaking with the utmost solemnity. Breaking with tradition, Peacock was not wearing a dress in her signature color. Rather, her gown was black—a somber velvet affair with long, pointed sleeves and a high lace collar. With her hair pulled severely back and her face framed in shifting candlelight, she looked a bit like a sorceress inviting people into some occult ceremony.

Lightning flashed outside, and thunder rumbled. The ancient electrical systems of Tudor House flickered and, like clockwork, all the students screamed. Great. A power outage was all they needed.

But the lights held. In the silence following the shouts, Scarlett could hear the rain begin. She thought about all those ruined updos and water-stained silks of the people still making their way across campus to Tudor House. The audio restarted the Vaughn Green track—no, it started another one entirely—the annoying, creepy murder ballad. Scarlett grimaced. She thought she'd removed this one from the set list.

Let me in, the soldier cried
Cold, haily, rainy night
Oh let me in, the soldier cried,
For I'll not go back again, no.

Scarlett was easing through the attendees over to the phone resting on the speakers when she heard party conversation give way to gasps and astonished murmurs. A moment later, the crowd parted to let the newest arrivals in, and Scarlett finally got a good look at them.

Ah, of course. Never let it be said that either of them would miss a chance for attention.

Orchid McKee glided across the polished floor on the arm of Oliver Green. Her dress was black, too—or not black, exactly. An oily, iridescent purplish black, the color of bruises and broken promises. Her eye makeup was smoky and dramatic, as if she'd already been crying. And Oliver . . .

Oliver looked like the image of an angry god. Other people might have come to this dance to party, or even to mourn. Oliver Green had come to *smite.*

Scarlett swallowed and turned off the music. She had been the one to delete Vaughn's channel. Maybe Oliver had come to smite *her.*

But if he had, there was no indication on his face as he and Orchid swept up to where she stood near the now-silent speakers.

"Good evening, Scarlett," were the first words Orchid had deigned to speak to her in days. "It looks lovely in here. You did a wonderful job."

"So did you," Scarlett replied, her tone every bit as cold. She touched the silk on her skirt. "Thank you for the dresses."

Orchid lifted a shoulder in what may have been an acknowledgement or a shrug.

"I see you made sure the *entire* Murder Crew came," Scarlett went on, nodding at Oliver.

"I figured if my brother is going to have a memorial after all this time, I might as well attend."

Scarlett looked over their shoulders. They were drawing a crowd of gobsmacked and even frightened students. "Feel like identifying yourself before we add *haunted* to the list of Blackbrook's worst qualities?"

"Where's the fun in that?" Oliver replied with a smirk.

As always, he was impossible. She turned to Orchid. "Did Peacock tell you what we want to do with the memorial service?"

"She did, but I'm not sure why you want me to be the one to make the announcements."

"It's a nice gesture. I'd asked Amber but she couldn't bring herself to do it, or even to show up tonight. You were close with both Vaughn and Rosa, and besides, I know I can count on you not to flub your lines." She handed Orchid the prepared script.

Orchid rolled her eyes. "I'm shocked that you're okay with anyone stealing your spotlight."

"Don't be silly, Orchid," said Oliver. "Scarlett would never settle for a spotlight. Not when she could have the whole stadium."

Scarlett turned to face Oliver, but she did not contradict him. After all, he was right. Funny that someone she hadn't even realized existed a few weeks ago turned out to be the person on this campus who knew her best. "Unless you think that you would do a better job leading the ceremony, Oliver? You have even more performance experience than your date—or is it your *girlfriend?* Now that I think about it, I'm not sure either of you have much business speaking about how much you miss Vaughn."

"You'd be surprised," said Oliver cheerfully, as if they were discussing the weather.

"Scarlett," Orchid broke in. She'd been looking at the script and probably missed the latest volley entirely. "What is this?"

"The memorial service. Why, are there typos?" Though she knew quite well that there were not.

"The *second* page." Orchid held it up and made a face.

"What?" She lifted her shoulders. "They always do class superlatives at prom. Didn't you get my email with the survey attached?" She'd sent it out to the entire class. It was hardly her fault that there were so few responses.

"You're really doing it at *this* prom? After the memorial service?"

"I thought it would lighten up the mood."

"*Most Helpful: Scarlett Mistry,*" Orchid read disdainfully. "*Most Likely to Succeed: Scarlett Mistry.*"

"Don't read it like *that,*" Scarlett said.

"Best Hair: Scarlett Mistry!"

"I didn't win them all." She pouted. If people didn't vote, they shouldn't be upset with the outcome. Besides, her hair was awesome.

"You're ridiculous, you know that?"

"And now *you* know why I can't emcee." She urged Orchid toward the podium at the top of the room. "Come on, let's get going."

She guessed Finn was going to be a no-show. Despite all his posturing, maybe he'd chickened out about appearing in public with Mustard. Although, if that were the case, why couldn't he have just gone with Scarlett's group date configuration? As Orchid called for attention over the microphone at the podium, Scarlett saw Mustard drawing closer, alongside Peacock on her scooter.

"Thank you all for coming tonight," Orchid said, reading obligingly from the script Scarlett had prepared. "I know it's been quite a year here at Blackbrook. It may even seem odd for us to be holding a dance in the midst of all of this catastrophe. How can we celebrate when there are so many who are not here to celebrate with us?"

"Who is that you brought?" shouted someone in the crowd. "You hire a lookalike, Emily? Why didn't you get him a tux?"

There was a ripple of laughter through the room.

Orchid chewed on her lip, and then she folded the paper and put it on the podium.

Oh no.

"That's Oliver Green," she said evenly. "He's the twin brother of Vaughn Green, and many of you know him, even if you don't realize it. He's been in your classes, he's been cleaning your halls and bathrooms and cutting your lawns. You see, it turns out that Vaughn and Oliver have both attended Blackbrook for years. He's here . . . because this is his prom, too."

Scarlett pressed her thumbs into her temples as more exclamations of shock circled the ballroom. She should have included an entry for Oliver on the class superlatives list. *Most Likely to Stab You in the Back.*

Nah, too much competition.

"Just like it's the prom of all the people who are missing," Orchid went on. Scarlett couldn't help but be impressed. She knew the girl could act, but she didn't realize she could improvise. "Which is why we thought we'd take a moment—right up front—to honor them, faculty and students. Their lights shine on, even though they are no longer with us."

Okay, that part was Scarlett's line. Orchid was pivoting back to the script. And right on cue, the Singing Telegrams began playing a soft, instrumental cover of Vaughn Green's "Off on Another Great Adventure," Scarlett's personal favorite of the catalog.

Orchid began to talk about Headmaster Boddy, and there was an appreciative murmur through the crowd as she recounted times the administrator had been ready with a kind word of guidance for his students. Scarlett noticed more than one student nodding in enthusiastic agreement.

She moved on to Dr. Brown. "Dr. Brown was with us for far less time, but she still devoted herself to helping the school get through the double challenges posed by the storm damage and the scandal of her predecessor's murder. The stress of these monumental tasks probably contributed to her death, and we owe her our thanks for everything she did for us."

The ballroom door slammed open, bringing in a gust of wet wind from the hall. The candles sputtered and for a moment the ballroom smelled like the night of the storm.

People were murmuring, but Scarlett couldn't see through the crowd to tell who had come.

And then he pushed his way up to the podium and she saw it was Finn, soaked to the bone, his hair plastered all over his face in floppy wet curls, his clothes dripping. He grabbed the microphone out of Orchid's hands.

"I have something to say!" he shouted.

Even the band stopped playing.

"We all know it's been a rough couple of weeks here," he began. "Dr. Brown, and then Tanner, and then this ridiculous witch hunt, trying to blame Mustard—of all people—for Tanner's death!" He ran a hand through his hair and then shook the water off. "Mustard and Tanner were friends! I saw it. And I couldn't stop thinking, you know, couldn't stop asking myself why it was that this school was so determined to believe that Tanner was murdered, so eager to blame it on my—" He cut off and his gaze landed on Mustard in the crowd, standing next to Peacock.

His eyes narrowed.

"But they were right. Tanner was murdered! And not just Tanner—Dr. Brown, too. I have the proof right here." He reached into his jacket pocket, pulled out a few folded sheets of paper, and slammed them down on the podium.

You could have heard a pin drop in the ballroom.

"These are toxicology reports. Two of them—one for Dr. Brown and one for Tanner Curry. And they both show an overdose of the same medication. Dr. Brown never died of a stroke, and the administration knew it!"

There was a commotion in the back, and Scarlett saw Perry Winkle pushing his way through the amassed students toward the podium. "Mr. Plum, that is quite enough!"

"Oh, I'm just getting started!" Finn exclaimed.

"That information is part of an ongoing investigation, and this little outburst of yours—"

"An ongoing cover-up, you mean!"

"Just because we don't release information to the students does not mean—"

"The investigation is over, Mr. Winkle," Finn said, and there was a note of sadness in his voice. "I know exactly who killed them."

That stopped Perry Winkle in his tracks.

"I just don't know why." He shoved his hair back again, and looked like he was about to cry. "Why did you do it, Beth?"

There was a murmur of confusion from the crowd, because hardly anyone called her that. But not for Scarlett. Her gaze shot to Peacock.

"I don't know what you're talking about," said Peacock. She knelt on her scooter, her back as stiff as a board.

"Yes, you do," he went on, now staring at Peacock as if they were alone in the room. "How many nights did I give you that exact medication after your surgeries? I read the bottle. I remember how careful we had to be with the dosage—"

"Oh, yeah, you took such great care of me," she mocked. "I thought it meant something. I thought we were getting back together—"

His eyes widened. "Is that why you set up Mustard? Is that why you killed Tanner?"

Mustard, who had been standing beside Beth, now took a big step away. "What?"

Peacock pursed her lips and seemed to think for a long moment. "No," she said at last. "That was just a lucky bonus."

Everyone gasped.

"What the hell, Beth?" Finn demanded.

"Nobody listens to me!" she shouted, throwing her hands in the air. "I've been saying for weeks that something bad is going on here, and no one listened."

"But—*you're* the something bad?" Mustard spoke the words they were all feeling. "You were the only one who thought Dr. Brown was murdered."

"I certainly didn't expect the school to cover it up, no. I guess Winkle really did want that headmaster job. This place is appalling."

"You've been keeping an investigative notebook of suspects!" Mustard said in disbelief.

"It's called diverting attention, duh." Peacock rolled her eyes.

Scarlett felt sick. Peacock was delusional. The things she was saying were beyond terrifying. That she was saying them in a room full of people was next level. Scarlett thought of the massive murder board in Peacock's room, her refusal to see a therapist, her dogged insistence on an imminent murder spree. She was a lot worse off than Scarlett had suspected. Far sicker than she could have possibly imagined.

Finn stood before her, still fighting to get through. "But why, Beth? I don't understand. Why did you kill Dr. Brown?"

"Because she let this happen to me! To all of us!" Peacock gestured to the photos of the dead, to Rosa and Vaughn. "It was on her watch that all this happened, and the most she could say was too bad? Remember what Rosa said, before she was killed? The security at this school is a disgrace. If Dr. Brown had been doing her job instead of making special rules for some Hollywood starlet, Keith never would have gotten into our house. He never would have tracked me down, used me to kill a girl. Vaughn would still be here. I'd still be playing tennis. And day after day she'd stop by room and ask if I was okay. If there was anything she could do. But she was too late to do anything that might have actually mattered. I . . . . *hated* her . . . *so* . . . *much.*"

Scarlett was baffled. Truly at a loss, for possibly the first time ever. "But why did you kill Tanner? And . . . how?" Scarlett added. "He's—I mean, you're—"

Peacock leveled a glare at her and all of a sudden Scarlett wondered if she was next on Peacock's hit list. "I'm what, Scarlett? *Crippled?* Please."

Scarlett cowered. If she were smart, she'd keep her big mouth shut as Peacock confessed her crimes to the entire ballroom. Truth be told, Peacock got around fine. Scarlett even remembered her saying that it took her a long time to get up stairs, not that she couldn't do it at all.

Peacock, in fact, was now confessing to method. "We all learned last winter how easy it is to get someone to drink a poisoned smoothie. He'd had a long train trip. No chance to eat dinner. He had it coming. Spoiled brat. He had no idea how lucky he was. Can you believe he just quit his team? I'd kill to be able to play. I *did* kill, and I still can't play."

"You killed him for quitting crew?" Mustard asked, horrified.

"No, you loser," she sneered. "He saw me. He saw me meeting with Dr. Brown before she died."

"That was why you have been trying to pin the blame on him this whole time!"

She shrugged. "It worked when you all wanted to blame me for Mr. Boddy last year. What better way to get suspicion off me than to put it on him? But after that meeting we had, with Oliver, I knew you guys wouldn't blame Tanner anymore. And if you talked to him about it, it might all come out."

But . . . . It *had* all come out! Peacock was telling her audience of shocked but finely dressed Blackbrook kids what she'd done as if it was part of the evening's festivities. On one hand, Scarlett wanted to warn her about that. On the other, she felt that the wisest move at the moment was to become part of the background.

Orchid didn't have the same sense of self-preservation. Her giant, movie-star eyes were overflowing with tears. "Beth," she said in a tone full of heartbreak. "They aren't to blame for what happened to you, to Vaughn . . ."

"Yes they are," Peacock replied, coldly staring at Orchid. "But not as much as *you*."

Orchid shied back, but Peacock wheeled forward, her eyes blazing. Even on the scooter, Peacock towered above her. "You killed Keith and barely got a slap on the wrist. You stole your dead boyfriend's music and hooked up with his brother. Ash was right about one thing: you're a monster, Orchid—Emily—whatever. But I can't get you to borrow my meds or drink the things I give you, and believe me, I've been trying for weeks. So we'll have to try something else."

And then, with reflexes that had made her feared on tennis courts throughout New England, Peacock snatched up the candlestick from one of the other guests and dropped it, still burning, onto the train of Orchid's gown.

The slick material went up like an oil-soaked rag. Orchid shrieked, but her cries were mostly drowned out by everyone else screaming. People were running in an attempt to back away from the flames. In the chaos, even more candles dropped.

Oliver tackled Orchid to the ground and began batting out the flames with his suit jacket. Finn and Mustard tackled Peacock. Scarlett started toward the door and was quickly tripped. Little fires sprang up everywhere.

Scarlett had just managed to push herself back up on her elbows when she heard the roaring gush of a fire extinguisher. White foam sprayed across the dance floor, spattering her and soaking Orchid, Oliver, and the spreading fire until every last flame sputtered into smoke.

She lowered her hands and stared up at their rescuer,

blinking. This was a mirage, maybe. Or a hallucination. "Mrs. White?"

"Scarlett," said Mrs. White, in a tone reminiscent of the time she had caught her charges not putting glass bottles in the recycling box. "I'm surprised at you! Surely you know that fire extinguishers should be kept in any room where there is an open flame, let alone one hosting several dozen teenagers with candles." She turned to Orchid. "Are you all right?"

Orchid nodded dumbly. "Just . . . singed. And confused." She looked over at Peacock, who was still struggling under Mustard and Finn.

"Get off me!" Beth cried. "What do you think I'm going to do, run?"

Scarlett stood on shaky feet and turned to their savior. "What—what are you doing here?"

"That would be my fault," volunteered Oliver. "We had this whole . . . revenge scene planned." He shrugged. "Guess that will have to be postponed. Where is that weasel Curry Chem exec anyway?"

Perry Winkle, it turned out, was crouched in fear behind a settee.

The police, ambulance, and fire trucks got to Blackbrook much more quickly this time. Perhaps they'd learned the route. Even after Peacock was taken away, however, Scarlett felt strange, as if this was all some terrible dream. The storm had passed as quickly as it had come. The students had mostly scattered, except for a few who were still giving statements, and the remaining members of the Murder Crew stood out on the wet, breezy lawn with thin blankets wrapped around their formal wear.

"How could I not have seen it?" Finn asked no one in particular. "She was clearly hurting so much more than I realized, and I had no idea. I saw her every day, and I had no idea."

"None of us had any idea," Mustard said, his hand on Finn's shoulder.

Scarlett swallowed. She'd known Peacock was traumatized by everything that had happened, but had accepted it as the totally reasonable response to what she had gone through. She'd focused all her attention on Orchid, who seemed far closer to the edge, and hadn't noticed how Peacock had gone right over it.

Mustard and Finn still had their heads close together, and Scarlett gave them privacy. She headed over to Orchid and Oliver, who were standing together near a stone wall. After all that had occurred, maybe it was time for a truce. Not just with Oliver, but with Orchid, too. Right now, Scarlett needed to know who her friends were. Who they *really* were.

"How is he?" Orchid asked as she approached. She nodded toward Finn.

"Messed up," Scarlett said. "You never want to think someone you care about is capable of that kind of thing."

"Yeah," said Oliver. "I get that." Orchid smiled ruefully and squeezed his hand.

"She was wrong, you know," Scarlett said. "You're not a monster."

"Maybe." Orchid shrugged. "I don't know, though. Beth and I have a lot more in common than I thought."

Scarlett hugged herself tighter inside her blanket, but she didn't know if she would ever get warm. "I don't know what's going to happen now." Should she call Bianca? Was that a conflict of interest?

"Justice," suggested Orchid tonelessly.

Oliver snorted. "At Blackbrook? Dream on."

Scarlett wondered if that was true. Every round of violence just seemed to lead to another and another. She knew too much to believe it was ever really over. Especially as she stood here next to a girl who had killed someone, and a boy who might have.

"What *was* your revenge plan?" she asked him.

He shrugged. "Publicity. I was going to ruin your prom."

She looked down at their burned outfits. "Well, at least you got that part of your wish."

"I planned to force Winkle to recognize my claims. Use guilt over Tanner Curry's death to get his father to do what's right."

"That's all?" And here she'd thought he was some criminal mastermind. "Oliver, you should have told me."

"Maybe I didn't want your help, Best Hair."

Scarlett smiled. This might be the beginning of a beautiful friendship. "That's usually people's first mistake."

That's how it could have
happened.

But how about this?

30

Orchid

At last, it was prom. The ballroom of Tudor House danced with glittering points of candlelight, and Orchid could hear a Vaughn Green tune coming from the speakers. The band, the Singing Telegrams, was tuning up as the attendees arrived. Students in colorful finery and the best corsages the lone florist on Rocky Point could muster lit memorial candles and left notes underneath the large portraits of the people the school had lost this year. The many, many people.

Orchid had expected stares when she arrived on the arm of Oliver Green. She'd steeled herself against them, retreating into that place inside her brain she reserved for such occasions, like she used to back in Hollywood, when her manager would send her to parties filled with flashing cameras and handsy men.

Fortunately, Oliver drew most of the attention, as much for his resemblance to his brother as for his overall demeanor, which was as stormy as the sky outside. Peacock, dressed in a severe, black lace cocktail dress, gave them both a dirty look as she took their tickets and handed them their memorial candles, and then waggled her eyebrows at Orchid behind Oliver's back as he bent to sign the guest book beneath his brother's portrait.

What? She mouthed at Orchid, who could only give her an apologetic shrug.

She glanced at what Oliver had written on the book. *For us.*

He looked at her. "Ready?"

Then he strode into the ballroom as if he owned the place, and—if his claims about the way Blackbrook and Curry Chem had stolen his inheritance proved to have merit—he basically did. All Orchid could do was keep up. His face was set, determined, and if Orchid had seen that look on Vaughn, she might even have been frightened.

But Oliver wasn't Vaughn. Where Vaughn seemed powered by melancholy and poetry, Oliver was fueled by anger and vengeance. Orchid understood both, and tonight, she had promised Oliver she would help him.

Oh let me in, the soldier cried,

For I'll not go back again, no.

A murder ballad was an odd choice of song for a party, Orchid thought. She spotted Scarlett in the crowd, messing with the speakers, and figured Scarlett thought so, too. As the music died, Oliver steered Orchid up toward the podium in front.

Scarlett's expression held nothing that could be mistaken for happiness upon seeing them. She looked great, though, in her red dress, her hair swept into a sleek updo. "I see you made sure the entire Murder Crew came."

Orchid was spared an answer as Oliver and Scarlett traded barbs like they'd been doing so for years. Which, Orchid realized, they kind of had.

Peacock had told her that Scarlett wanted her to deliver the remarks at the memorial. Not exactly a role she relished, but she admitted it probably should be her job. After all, she was tied to at least two of the deaths. Besides, how could she say no to Peacock? She was indirectly responsible for her accident, too. But when Scarlett handed over the script, she saw only a few scant notes about the dearly departed, and several pages of class superlatives, most of which seemed, suspiciously, to have been awarded to Scarlett herself.

"Are you serious with this?" she asked Scarlett. "Best Hair?"

Scarlett patted her updo. "What? It's not wrong."

Orchid rolled her eyes. Scarlett went off to confer with Mustard and Peacock about Finn's absence from the festivities, and Oliver drew close.

"I wouldn't worry about it too much," he said, his voice low and confidential. "We're not going to get that far. I'm going to blow up this little shindig long before we have to give out awards."

She gave him a weary smile. "Maybe people wouldn't be so quick to think you're dangerous if you didn't use phrases like that."

"I don't care what people think." He gestured to the crowd, many of whom were still staring. "They think I'm a ghost or an avenging angel. I don't care. There was only one person whose opinion of me mattered, and he's gone."

Orchid knew if she blinked fast enough, the tears gathering in her eyes would be swept away before they had time to ruin her makeup. "You wanted me to help you for Vaughn's sake. What are you going to do for Vaughn's sake?"

"I'm going to help *you*." He took her hands in his. "I know you want to be free of this nightmare as much as I do."

Did she? What she really wanted was to go back in time to before all this, when she was just mousy Orchid McKee, flirting in the dark halls of Tudor House with Vaughn Green. She wanted to be the girl Headmaster Boddy said was a promising young scholar, but she feared that girl—that anonymous Orchid McKee—was gone forever.

"I just want justice, like you said," she reminded him. "I want you to get what you deserve from Blackbrook."

"Absolutely," he agreed. "Let's get started."

When Orchid turned, she saw Scarlett watching her. And she had to admit, her hair really did look quite nice. She was standing with Mustard and Peacock, and their expressions were all ones of distrust as they watched Orchid and Oliver up at the podium. Finn was still nowhere to be found. So much for Murder Crew forever.

Orchid adjusted the microphone on the stand and got the room's attention. The memorial service, as Scarlett had written it, was pretty standard. A reflection of all that had befallen Blackbrook this year, a call to remembrance of those who had passed. She started listing their names, but when she got to Vaughn, there was chatter among the crowd.

"Oh yeah?" someone called. "Then who is that?"

Oliver leaned in and spoke into the microphone. "My name is Oliver Green. You all know me, even though you don't think you do. Fact is, I was a student here, too, right alongside my brother. Blackbrook thought they could shut us up by—"

The ballroom door slammed open, bringing in a gust of wet wind from the hall. The candles sputtered, and Orchid remembered the darkness of the winter storm, when everything had started to go wrong here at Blackbrook.

"Wait!" screamed Finn Plum. He pushed through the crowd up to the podium. He was completely drenched from the storm outside, his clothes sticking to his skin, his hair hanging like wet snakes around his face. "I have something to say!"

He snatched the microphone out of Oliver's hands. "I thought it was crazy, that the administration was going after—people—and trying to make a case that Tanner was murdered. But they were right! Look!" He pulled a piece of paper out from his jacket pocket. It was damp, but the ink had not run. "This is the forensic report on Tanner Curry. It says he wasn't killed in his dorm room, but brought there after his death."

Orchid pressed her knuckles to her mouth.

"But he texted me from our room looking for me," Mustard said.

"Did he?" Finn asked. "Is that what he texted you?"

Mustard reached for his phone.

"Don't bother—I have those texts memorized from looking over your shoulder the past few days. He said he was on his way back to Rocky Point. *To* Rocky Point."

"Yeah, coming back from his home . . . to school." Mustard said.

"Or from his room on campus, to the village" said Finn. "Maybe after he texted you, he went to visit someone in Rocky Point. *Again.*"

Orchid turned to Oliver, eyes wide. "Tanner only knew one person in Rocky Point."

"Tanner didn't know me," Oliver snapped. "He barely knew Vaughn."

That wasn't the point, and Oliver knew it. He was very good, she realized, at not giving a straight answer while making you think that he had.

She decided to be direct. "Did Tanner come to see you the night he died?"

"Yes," Oliver said, as if taking a dare. "He told me his father was exactly the kind of person I always knew he was. That no one at Curry Chemical was going to give me the time of day, and that there was nothing else he could do."

"So you saw him!" Finn broke in.

"Yes."

"Then what?" asked Mustard.

Oliver gave a dismissive shake of his head, as if the question was too stupid to contemplate.

"Oliver," Orchid whispered. "Do you know what happened to Tanner?"

He turned to her, blinking, a disbelieving smile on his face. "What are you doing?" he asked under his breath.

What was *she* doing? What was *he* doing!

Oh, God, what was he doing?

"Oliver," she whispered again, and never before had she been so entirely certain of how different he was from Vaughn. "Did you kill Tanner?"

That same, small, flabbergasted smile. "How can you ask me that? I thought we understood each other. You and me. Killers."

She took a few steps back, the hem of her train tangling in her heels. "No. Stop."

"Orchid," he said, offended. "I was always going to get my revenge. There are two choices: help me, or get in my way."

She shook her head, as fear seemed to freeze her voice in her throat. *Run*, she thought. But she didn't scream it.

She should have screamed it.

"Tanner knew, but he wasn't willing to help. He had to pay. Dr. Brown, Boddy—even Rusty Nayler. They got in my way, so they had to go. It's not like I *wanted* to."

She took a shuddering breath. Vaughn had been right all along! "You—you said Mrs. White killed Headmaster Boddy."

"Mrs. White is on my side. She does what I tell her to do. She wants justice for me, and for my grandmother."

Scarlett let out a gasp of horror. "So it was you all along? You murdered all of them!"

"No," he corrected her. "I simply got justice. I didn't kill you, did I? Because when you were presented with the proof of my rights to my brother's music, you handed over the cash. I'm not a monster, Scarlett."

"Yes," she said. "You are."

He shrugged. "Okay, fine. I am." And then he lifted his voice to call over the crowd. "Door!"

On the other side of the ballroom, the heavy wood door slammed shut. The crowd began to shout.

And Oliver very casually took his memorial candle and lit the long velvet drapes on fire.

The shouts gave way to screams as people stampeded toward the door, dropping their own candles as they went.

Smoke rose, first in tendrils, then in great billows as drapes, upholstery, and dresses caught flame. Students pounded on the exit. Perry Winkle grabbed the fire extinguisher off the wall, but couldn't seem to get it to work.

"Let us out! Let us out!" people screamed.

"They won't get out that way," Oliver observed.

Orchid whirled on him. "What are you doing?"

"Being a murderer. I thought that was obvious."

The flames licked higher. The air was getting smoky, and the coughing, shouting crowd at the other side of the room grew obscured through the haze.

"And you would have murdered me, too, if I hadn't given you that money?" Murdered her, instead of made out with her?

"This has gone on long enough!" Mustard ran up to Oliver. "You let them out right now!"

"Me?" He pressed a hand to his chest. "I didn't lock them in. Look, I'm in here with you. It's tragic, isn't it?"

"So, what?" Scarlett choked out. Her eyes were watering from the smoke. "We all die in here together?"

"Tragic." Oliver let out a little cough. "Guess those Blackbrook kids had it coming."

"Screw that," Mustard said. He turned to Finn and Peacock. "There's no alternative. We're just going to have to break the door down."

"On top of it," said Peacock, wheeling off.

"I'm sure no one else thought of that," Oliver drawled, but the others had already run after her. Everyone but Orchid. Over the sounds of crackling flames and coughing, there came huge bangs, as something heavy bashed itself into the door over and over. Must be Peacock on her scooter.

She turned to Oliver. "You don't want to do this."

"What, die? I'm not so sure about that. Are you?"

"Yes!" And the second the word burst from her lips, she realized it was true. She had survived Hollywood, survived Mrs. White, survived Keith. She was not going to die tonight. She gestured to the portraits around them, bubbling and burning in the fire. "Look at them! They never had a chance. Look at Vaughn!"

Oliver looked, but his focus seemed far, far away. "Yes. Bet you wish it was him with you now."

The fire roared, the heat singed her eyes, and she could barely breathe. "Stop it. We have to get out, now!"

"What's out there for me, Orchid? I just confessed to several murders in a room full of people. If any of them survives this, there's no future for me. Not even your fancy lawyers could get me out of this."

"So you'll kill us all?"

A great crash rocked the room, but Orchid could no longer tell if it was the door going down or the ceiling giving way. A wall of flame divided them from the rest of the room.

There was no way out now, even if the others had managed to break the door down.

"Not you," he said. She turned to look at him, though her eyes watered. "You never got in my way. You stood by me, despite knowing what I was. You're like Vaughn. He wanted to give up on me so many times. But he never did."

Vaughn couldn't have known his brother was this much of a psychopath, could he? Then again, she was the one who had brought Oliver to the dance. She'd trusted him that all he wanted was justice. But the word had a different meaning for someone like Oliver. It meant Armageddon.

"Please," she begged, but she didn't know what for. It was over. After all this time, she was going to die in Tudor House at last.

"You Blackbrook kids," he said, almost sadly. "You never even bother learning the secrets of the place you live. All these years in Tudor House, and you don't know?"

"What?" she sputtered.

"The ballroom," he replied, "has two doors."

And with that, he pushed aside one of the heavy velvet drapes lining the walls and revealed a small, plain door. Kicking it open with his foot, he grabbed Orchid by the elbow and shoved her through.

She fell to the ground in a narrow passageway between the kitchen and the ballroom, one she had thought existed purely for a window well from the back of the house into the hall. From this side, the door she'd just passed through looked like a part of the wall paneling. Coughing, she blindly stumbled into the hall. The large ballroom door still held firm, but black smoke was pouring out from underneath. She lunged for the lock, the metal scorching her hands, and turned it. The door exploded outward, all heat and smoke and burning people.

Orchid went down under the onslaught, and as the roar of the fire grew and the world turned red and black, she thought she heard the distant strains of music, and under it all—impossibly—Vaughn's voice:

It is the game I'll never win
My only secret shameful sin . . .
I want to be
Another me.

But here's what really happened.

30

Scarlett

At last, it was prom. The ballroom of Tudor House danced with glittering points of candlelight, and the somewhat upbeat melody of one of Vaughn Green's cheeriest tunes emanated from the speakers. The band, the Singing Telegrams, was tuning up as the attendees arrived. Students in colorful finery and the best corsages the lone florist on Rocky Point could muster lit memorial candles and left notes underneath the large portraits of the people the school had lost this year. The many, many people.

But despite the death and the obvious pall over the festivities, Scarlett could not be disappointed in tonight's turnout. More than three dozen students had shown up at the party, which meant almost the entire remaining junior class was here, with assorted dates. Even Amber had shown up, claiming she was planning to stay only for the memorial service and leave the moment the dancing started. She was also dressed in black pants and a sweater.

Of course, Scarlett would bet that more than a few girls decided to come solely because it gave them access to Orchid's stash of designer dresses. Even Scarlett had capitulated eventually, and was wearing a gorgeous red gown that Peacock said Orchid had picked out especially for Scarlett. Her hair was swept into an updo, and she'd accessorized with gold shoes and her grandmother's earrings.

Outside, thunder crashed, and the electric lights flickered. Everyone in the room did that annoying but obligatory shout at the lights going out, and the music coming from the speakers skipped as the app hiccupped and began playing another Vaughn Green song entirely.

Let me in, the soldier cried
Cold, haily, rainy night
Oh let me in, the soldier cried,
For I'll not go back again, no.

Scarlett remembered the first time she'd heard this song—Vaughn had played it all for them the night of the big storm. A murder ballad, he'd called it. And it had ushered in months and months of murder.

At the door of the ballroom there was some sort of commotion. Peacock, in charge of taking tickets and handing out memorial candles to all the attendees, wheeled back on her scooter. Her height made it easy to get Scarlett's attention from across the room. She was gesturing furiously with her eyebrows.

A moment later, Scarlett realized why: Orchid had arrived, on the arm of Oliver Green.

Well. Never let it be said the ex-actress was lacking in drama. Everyone was openly gaping at the ghost of Vaughn Green as the two of them made their way across the polished ballroom floor, every inch the goth king and queen of the world's most mournful prom. Orchid looked striking in a dress that billowed like some mysterious sea creature through an iridescent oil slick, her hair a violet-pink halo framing a movie-star face. Oliver, too, had emerged from his grubby townie chrysalis. He walked straighter and more assuredly, as if feeding on the attention from the crowd. And over it all, the voice of Vaughn Green, singing about death.

Scarlett sighed and switched tracks.

"Aww," said Oliver with a sneer as they approached. "I like that one."

"You would," Scarlett said. She turned to Orchid. "Thanks for the dress. What is he doing here?"

"You're welcome," she replied with the same energy. "It's his prom, too."

"Technically," said Scarlett. "Murder Crew forever, and all that." She refused to give him the satisfaction of causing a scene.

"Speaking of, where is everyone?" Orchid craned her neck to see over the heads of the attendees. "I got my candle from Beth, but I don't see the boys."

"Mustard is avoiding Winkle." Which was perfectly understandable. Who wanted to be anywhere near the man who'd had you arrested on suspicion of murdering your roommate? He was also keeping his distance from the photograph of Tanner, and any of Tanner's friends who might be milling around near it. "And Finn, I don't know. He flaked."

"I thought you were double-dating." Orchid's tone was charged.

"You know Finn. Can't count on him." She pulled out the script she'd spent half the night concocting. "Peacock told you about the presentation, right?"

Orchid nodded. "Yes. Bold of you to assume I'd come running when you asked, after everything."

"Is it?" Scarlett handed over the script. "Then why are you here?"

Orchid scowled and snatched the pages out of her hands.

Scarlett just smiled. Whatever else Orchid might say about her, they both knew that Scarlett understood how to manage things. There'd be plenty of people to speak of Tanner and Headmaster Boddy—even Dr. Brown—but Orchid had been the only one to know Rosa, and nearly the only one to know Vaughn.

Except, of course, his brother, who was looking over Orchid's shoulder.

"I didn't know we were doing class superlatives at this shindig," he said.

"It's tradition! I sent out a survey." Most people had ignored it—which was unfortunate, as it had ever-so-slightly skewed the results.

"Is it a tradition to give all the awards to the same person?" He sounded innocent, but Scarlett knew better.

"Aww," she said, with mock sympathy, "Don't see your name under *Most Sociopathic?*"

"No," he replied evenly. "You won that one, too."

"Fine!" Orchid said, stepping between them. "I'll do it. But Scarlett, you and I both know that you do not deserve to win Best Hair."

Scarlett squeaked in indignation. "Who could beat me?"

Orchid rolled her eyes and swept past her to the podium. "Please," she said, her tone withering. "Everyone knows it's Finn Plum."

Well, that was . . . accurate. Scarlett hadn't even considered male students in that category. This was the problem with so few respondents. Neither Finn nor the person most likely to appreciate his floppy brown curls had answered the survey. Of course, Mustard had been getting over his time in jail, so she couldn't really fault him. It was a miracle he'd even managed to dress in a suit.

Oliver hadn't moved from her side. He just stood there, a pained look on his face as the next track started up. Scarlett never cared for this song. It was called "Sequel."

We're so quick to cancel it, cry that it's no good,
Put it on a list, say that it's the pits, and we were
     always fools
For daring to love something unfinished, something that all
     went wrong.
Held its secrets to the end, strung us all along.
Am I all alone in thinking that we each took part
In the creation of this vicious sequel, this evil work of art?

"Not a favorite?" she asked him. "I can't blame you. I always thought it was dumb for Vaughn to make a whole song about how he was disappointed by the end of a TV show."

He glared at her. "This song is about me, you idiot."

Scarlett blinked. Oh. *Oh.*

"They're all about me. About us. Vaughn was screaming out his confessions in verse and no one heard it."

Scarlett went over a few more choice lyrics in her head. Now that she thought about it, "Another Me" probably wasn't about Vaughn wishing he was a different person, either. How had she missed that? She looked at the girl at the podium. "Does Orchid know?"

"You know what I've learned, Scarlett? Everyone only hears what they want to hear. To see what they want to see. Vaughn, Orchid, and you and me, too. When you look at me and think I'm a psychopath, I'm a psychopath. When she looked at Vaughn and saw a sweet poet, that's what he was. Maybe the point Vaughn was making in this song is that neither of us were any of those things."

"If that's the case," said Scarlett, "then what he was really saying is you can be whatever you want to be."

"That's where you're wrong. My brother is dead, and I have to be both of us."

Scarlett was spared having to come up with a response as Orchid picked up the mike and got the room's attention. The memorial service was . . . not a success, and Scarlett could blame it on neither her script nor Orchid's performance. The fact was, no one was really paying attention to either. They just wanted to know the identity of the ghost of Vaughn Green, standing next to her in the front row. The shouts and jeers got louder and more insistent until finally, Orchid looked at Oliver and held out the microphone.

He sighed, waging some interior battle, and then took it. "Hi," he said to the assembled crowd.

Wow, he sounded more like Vaughn than ever through the speakers' amplification, or maybe that was just because she was beginning to forget what Vaughn had really sounded like, and only remembered his singing voice.

"My name—my name is Oliver Green. I was Vaughn's twin brother. Some of you know me, only you don't know that you do. We were tricking you, my brother and me. We were—going to school here, both of us, for years."

The shouts gave way to gasps of surprise.

"We though Blackbrook owed us, because a long time ago, a Blackbrook kid hurt our family, and the school helped him do it." Oliver took a deep breath. "All I ever wanted was revenge, justice. It's all I could think about, especially after my brother died. You see, everyone in my family is dead now. My brother, my parents, my grandparents. They all died without realizing their dreams. I thought maybe, if I finally got what belonged to us, I could move on. But the truth is—"

The ballroom door slammed open, bringing in a gust of wet wind from the hall. The candles sputtered, and the air smelled like the night of the big storm.

"Wait!" screamed Finn Plum. He pushed through the crowd up to the podium, his clothes dripping with rainwater, his beautiful hair plastered to his face, his glasses fogged up. "I have something to say!"

He reached for the microphone, but Oliver held it away from him. "I'm in the middle of something, man."

Finn shook his head, and droplets of water flew about. "There's a conspiracy, Oliver—" He made another lunge for the mike.

"I know that!" Oliver hissed, wrestling with him. "I'm trying to—"

"And I know who did it!" Finn promptly let go and Oliver went wheeling backward. Finn stuck his hand inside his jacket pocket and pulled out a cell phone in a black shatterproof case. The beat-up sticker on the back said *Blackbrook Crew.*

"This is the cell phone of Tanner Curry," Finn announced in as loud a voice as he could muster.

"Give that back, young man!" Perry Winkle strode forward now. "That is police evidence."

"If it's evidence," Finn said, "Then what was it doing in your satchel in your office?"

"I was taking it home to the family—"

"I thought you said it was evidence," Finn sniffed. "Let's just see what it's evidence of." He crossed to the nearby speaker, unplugged Scarlett's phone, and plugged in Tanner's. As it booted up, Finn called out, "Amber? Where's Amber?"

"Right here," Tanner's ex spoke up from the crowd.

"What's Tanner's lock code?"

"Seriously?" The girl asked. She mumbled something and there was a titter of laughter from nearby.

"What?" Finn asked.

She groaned. "It's six-nine-six-nine."

Finn closed his eyes for a long moment. "Of course it is." He punched the number into the phone. "Now, let's see what we have here that's so terrible that Perry Winkle thought it was worth stealing evidence off a dead man."

"Enough is enough," said Winkle. "Hand over that phone at once—"

Mustard stepped between him and Finn. "Don't try it."

"You want to get arrested again?" Winkle asked him. "How about expelled?"

"We'll see," he replied.

"I know a lot of things about you, Mustard."

Mustard looked him steadily in the eye. "And I think we're about to find out a lot more about you."

Finn spoke up again, his eyes still glued to the screen. "Here! These are texts Tanner sent the night of his death. The ones he sent to Mustard, and then some to—"

"Me," Oliver broke in. "He sent a bunch of texts to me."

"You!" several of them exclaimed at once.

"You killed him?" Orchid asked, stricken.

"No, I yelled at him." Oliver looked offended. "I do that. Get in fights with people right before they end up dead."

"You should be careful with that," Peacock said, her eyes narrowed. "People will think you're a murderer."

"People *do* think I'm a murderer," he pointed out.

"So this is from you?" Finn started reading. "*'You're either willing to help or you're not. But I'm not giving you any more information without a commitment.'* And then Tanner responded, *'It's more complicated than that. I'm not going to speak out against them unless I'm absolutely sure.'* And then you wrote, *'Sounds more like you are waiting to see if they make it worth your while to lie. Watch your back, Tanner. I'd sure be watching mine.'*" He looked up at Mustard. "The time stamp on these are before he sent his last messages to Mustard."

Scarlett was appalled.

"Looks like the cops arrested the wrong townie," said Winkle, glaring at Oliver. "Is this game over now? I don't think it's respectful of Tanner's memory to invade his privacy like this." Again, he tried to push past Mustard, and again he was stopped.

"There's one more set of messages," Finn announced. "Not a recognized number."

Scarlett frowned. Finn could cut the drama any time. "What does it say?"

Finn started reading again. "*I'm not talking to any of you again until you answer these questions:*

"*1. How did Emma Brown die?*

"*2. How did Olivia Vaughn die?*

"*3. How did Dick Fain die?*"

Silence fell over the room. Probably because most of the people had no idea who Olivia Vaughn was, and a lot of them probably didn't recognize Dr. Brown by the first name of Emma, either.

Scarlett's mind raced. Why would Tanner be curious about the deaths of those three people in particular? What did they all have in common, besides, you know, being dead? Dr. Brown had been a board member of Curry Chem, one who was keeping files on her computer about the "Vaughn Financial Claims." Olivia Vaughn, Vaughn and Oliver Green's grand-mother, was the one of the only people who knew Dick Fain had heirs, and Dick Fain—well, he was the one whose inven-tion and enormous fortune had been co-opted by Curry Chem and Blackbrook after he'd died young.

All of that together spoke to a cover up by Curry Chemical. One that would guarantee the glue money stayed where they wanted it.

"I don't understand," Oliver said. So much for the criminal mastermind being quick on the uptake. "My grandmother died of a stroke over three years ago."

A-ha! A stroke? Just like Dr. Brown!

"Three years ago!" Orchid said. "You mean right before Vaughn got accepted to Blackbrook? Right before he got that scholarship that Boddy and John Curry thought would make the whole thing die out?"

Wait, what? Yet another piece of information Scarlett didn't have.

"Dick Fain also died of a stroke," said Finn. "I remember because I thought it was a weird thing to happen to someone so young."

That was a lot of strokes. A lot of dead people. And every single one of them knew that Curry should not have the rights to that glue. The pieces all snicked into place, like a puzzle coming clear.

Mustard frowned, putting it together seconds after Scarlett. "That's what Tanner was talking about! He kept going on and on about how weird it was that everyone in Vaughn's family kept dying off . . ."

"This is a conspiracy theory," said Winkle. "Tanner was a very disturbed young man—"

"Oh, it was definitely a conspiracy!" said Finn. "But I think we're well beyond theory. Now why do you have this phone?"

"No," said Winkle. "Why do *you* have it? As far as I can tell, you've stolen the private property of a dead man and hacked into it—"

"Call it," blurted Scarlett.

Finn turned to her. They all did.

"Call the number that Tanner texted those questions to. Whoever Tanner was asking knows the answers, which means they're part of the conspiracy."

Finn brightened. "Great idea!" But as he pressed the button to call, Winkle clearly decided he was tired of playing nice. Instead of trying to go through Mustard again, though, he picked a smaller target.

He picked Scarlett.

Before she knew what was happening, he'd thrown an arm across her body and was dragging her backward through the crowd. Instinctively, she started to struggle, but then felt something hard poking her in the side.

"It's a gun!" someone screamed. "Oh my God, he has a gun!"

Her breath froze in her throat, and for once in her life, Scarlett had nothing to say. In the impossible stillness that settled over her, she felt a buzzing against the back of her thigh, as if—

Yes. Winkle's cell phone was going off.

Did that mean he did it? For once in her life, Scarlett couldn't think.

"Where do you think you're going!" Oliver demanded.

"Someone call the cops!" said someone else as Scarlett was dragged across the floor. Any moment now, he'd be out the door.

"By the time they get here," Winkle's voice rumbled at her back, "I'll have vanished."

"You're not getting away!" Oliver said, advancing. "You can't shoot us all! You don't have enough bullets in that gun."

He had enough for her. Shut *up*, Oliver!

And then Oliver charged. It all happened so fast. Winkle pulled the barrel of the revolver out of her side and lifted it to aim at Oliver. Out of the corner of her eye, Scarlett saw Peacock, her unbraced arm raised above the crowd. Something silver flashed through the air over Scarlett's head.

There was a loud *thonk* and an infinitely more earsplitting *crack*, and all three of them went down.

"Get him!" someone screamed.

"Get the gun!" corrected someone else.

Scarlett lay on the floor in a tangle of limbs. What had just happened? She scrambled off of Winkle as several members of the Blackbrook Crew team pinned him down. There wasn't much need, though, as he lay unconscious on the ballroom floor, a small wound on his forehead at the center of a blossoming bruise. Next to his head lay the heavy silver candlestick that Peacock had been using to help light the smaller memorial flames.

Scarlett fought to catch her breath. "It was him," she said. "His phone was going off in his pocket."

"Yeah," said Mustard. "I think we figured that out what with the whole hostage thing."

The students were all standing around in horrified clumps; even the teachers looked at loose ends. The Singing Telegrams all held their instruments awkwardly and stared. This was quite possibly the worst prom in history.

Peacock wheeled up to Scarlett. "Are you okay?"

Scarlett nodded and let the other girl pull her up. "You have a great arm."

She smiled. "I know. Believe me, when I want to throw a candlestick to hurt someone, my aim is impeccable."

Finn asked at her. "You're never going to let me live that down, are you?"

She smiled at him. "Nope. Never."

He touched her arm. "You're okay, though? Beth?"

"Are you kidding?" she replied. "I'm great. I've still got it."

Finn shook his head and turned to Scarlett. "You all right?"

"Fine." She was fine. She hadn't been the one to get shot at, in the end.

"I don't understand," Oliver was saying. "All this time, she was murdered? They all were! All because of me. All because of glue." He was still on the floor, his hand pressed to his head. Blood dripped down over his temples.

"Oliver!" Orchid knelt next to him. "You've been shot." She pulled his hand off his face. "Let me see it."

"Gemma . . ." he was saying, his voice low. "She never . . . she never wanted to fight for the glue. Never wanted us to, either. Is that because she knew Dick Fain had been killed? Had he promised to make things right for her, and then got killed before he could?"

"Someone *has* called the police, right?" asked Finn. "And, like, the FBI?"

Mustard had a phone in his hand. Thank goodness someone else was on top of things for a change.

Orchid had managed to get Oliver's hand away from his

face and was wiping up blood with a gorgeous pashmina that someone must have dropped on the ground.

"This doesn't look—" she frowned at him. "I can't find the wound."

Oliver barely responded. His eyes were unfocused, staring off at someplace a thousand miles away. The teachers had finally gotten their acts together and were rounding up the students and herding them out of the ballroom. The crew team had already dragged the unconscious Winkle off into a corner to wait for the police. Only the Murder Crew was left, a small, sacred knot in the center of the ballroom, surrounding the wounded Oliver.

Scarlett drew closer, staring down at him. It was true, under the smears of blood on his face, there was no injury. Her gaze traveled down to his hands, splayed in his lap.

There. She grabbed his hand and turned it over. A long gash ran the length of his palm, as if the bullet had grazed his hand. "Oliver," she said. "Your hand!"

She examined it more closely—the bloody wound appeared to be his only injury, except for a series of deep grooves across every callused fingertip.

Scarlett's grip tightened, and her mouth opened wide.

He blinked up at her, and then his eyes widened too as he saw what she was staring at. He tried to jerk his fingers away, but Scarlett held firm.

"No," he begged her.

"You—" She dropped his hand and stepped back, babbling as her brain did the math. *No way. No. Way.* "You need to get that looked at."

"Don't."

"You—" It *wasn't possible.* "You can't ignore it."

"Please!"

But when had Scarlett ever listened to him? To either of them? "You—you're Vaughn."

31

Green

Maybe no one had heard her.

"Oh my god," she said. "You're Vaughn."

"What are you talking about?" he snapped. Snapping was good. Snapping served him well. His brother always said he had anger issues, but maybe it was a trait they both claimed.

"Or—I don't know!" She threw her hands in the air. "Who was the musician? You said it was Vaughn. But you're a musician—I know those fingers. I had to look at so many stupid pictures of finger calluses on the forum—on Vaughn's forum. On *your* forum—"

"Okay," he said quickly. He had to shut this down. "I lied. I do play the guitar. But you know—I didn't want to do it after my brother died—"

"What brother!" she shouted. "What brother was that?"

His hand really stung. Right then, he wished Perry Winkle had shot it clean off. He clenched it into a fist, feeling the flesh tear even more. The pain gave him clarity. "What are you talking about?"

"Why would you lie about being able to play music?" she demanded.

"Scarlett, calm down. You both have just been through a lot." Orchid's tone was firm. Beautiful Orchid. He'd almost messed up with her. He'd almost lost her.

Again.

But Scarlett had never once been calm. "You're Vaughn Green, and you've been lying to us again. You've been lying all along."

Orchid was pulling away from him. He looked around to discover they all were, staring at him in shock and confusion.

Those were emotions he understood well. But none of them had ever really known him, not with the part he'd been forced to play. He could say anything now, and they'd never know the truth. They'd never really known Vaughn. They'd never really known Oliver. That was the only reason this had worked.

It had been so much harder to fool Mrs. White. But he had to make her believe—her above all others—or she never would have helped him. And he had to give his brother the dream he wanted. The dream he'd died without ever seeing come true.

He looked at them, the five of them—the Murder Crew. Peacock on her scooter, her leg cast at the level of his eyes. Finn, who had unraveled it all. Mustard, who had lost Tanner. Scarlett, who'd produced the music despite her dislike. And Orchid . . . Orchid who made him dream of impossible things. Thanks to them, he was finally, finally going to get justice. Justice for Gemma. Justice for Oliver. He couldn't keep lying.

"Yes," he said, at last, the words like an avalanche through an ice shelf. "I'm Vaughn." But even as he said it, it felt wrong. Impossible. Was he? Who was he anymore?

And still, it was the wrong answer.

"No . . ." Orchid drew back even farther. She stood and stared down at him, like a bug she'd just smashed on the pavement. "You're not. You can't be—"

"I'm sorry."

"You were *dead*! All those months . . ."

"I had to," said Vaughn Green. He struggled to his knees. Blood flowed freely from the wound in his hand. "I had to finish things for my brother. That part was true. He died helping you. He died thinking I hated him. I couldn't let his dream—"

"I have been *hating* myself," hissed Orchid, seething, backing away. The others spread out, giving them space, but Vaughn felt like he was falling into a deep, black hole. "Hating myself because of what I did with you. Because of the way I felt. And this whole time, you knew. You *knew*! And you *played* me."

"No, Orchid. I lo—"

"Don't you dare!" She held up a hand, her head shaking back and forth as if on its own accord. "You loved the *game*. You got revenge. You made us feel terrible. You were Oliver, and you were bad, and you *enjoyed* it."

He saw a few of them nod in agreement.

"You're dead to me," she stated. "Both of you."

And then she turned and walked out of the ballroom. Vaughn didn't know if the others followed or not, because he put his head in his bloody, bloody hands, and wept.

Six Months Later

The campus of Blackbrook lay still and silent, shrouded beneath the pallid November sky. A few resolute leaves clung to the branches of the trees, and shredded caution tape whipped about the unkempt lawns in the salty wind off the sea.

"Still a lot of water damage to fix," said Vaughn's lawyer, Tony Pratt, flipping through the portfolio on his lap. "This place is a real money pit."

"We'll start small," Vaughn said, staring out the window of the car. Others had managed solely with Tudor House. "The bones are all that matter."

The lawyer shrugged and slipped the paperwork back inside his leather briefcase. "It's your money, I guess. Or it soon will be."

Vaughn folded his hands in his lap, the scar tissue on his palm brushing against the soft cashmere-wool blend of the fanciest overcoat he'd ever owned. It seemed appropriate for the occasion, though he'd still stuffed a thick pair of mittens in the pockets, preferring those to the sleek leather gloves Pratt had on. You could take the boy out of Maine . . .

And he *had* been gone from this place, so removed it had been somewhat of a shock to see it looking the same, if slightly more ragged, and a lot more abandoned. In many ways, it felt like longer than six months. Years, maybe. Decades. He hadn't really been counting it like that, though. Instead, he'd counted it in songs (five), subscribers (two million), lawsuits (eight), and indictments against the people who had hurt him and his family (sixteen and counting, primarily against Blackbrook board members and Curry Chem execs).

Perry Winkle was being held without bail on multiple murder and conspiracy to commit murder charges, not to mention his assault on Vaughn and Scarlett. John Curry, Tanner's father, had tried to flee the country, but his plans were foiled by Tanner's mother, for whom loyalty to the Curry family stopped right where a plot to silence her son by killing him began.

Of course, both men claimed they had nothing to do with Tanner's death. Perry claimed he was under orders from Curry execs to silence their wayward son. John Curry and the rest of the Curry Board said Perry acted alone. Vaughn had started deep-diving into all their statements and defenses, but his therapist, Lynn, advised against it. He'd be better off, she told him, keeping his interest in this topic focused only on when he could expect the final settlement from Blackbrook and Curry regarding the Dick Fain estate.

Vaughn trusted Lynn, but he couldn't help keeping tabs on things, anyway. He didn't want anyone else to get blamed for things they didn't do, least of all people he'd once thought of as friends. Still, from what he could tell, the rest of the Murder

Crew had their cutthroat lawyer Bianca on retainer, and she shut down any movements the Curry Chem people tried to make in Mustard's direction.

Or anyone else's.

He could count the time that had passed in other ways, too. Specials about Emily Pryce (two, plus nearly fifty online videos) and him (several dozen online videos) and the two of them together (hundreds of fanfics). These caused Lynn to make uncomfortable sounds in the back of her throat, which Vaughn had learned was therapist code for "bad idea to engage." And he was, really, getting better at not engaging. He hadn't looked at anything in at least two months, not since he'd heard about the true crime documentary.

He had also not kept count of how many times he'd thought about texting Orchid.

Blackbrook had closed for good two days after the prom. Between the lawsuits and the damage to the school's reputation, there was no coming back. Now all that remained were a few assets to sell off.

Which was what Vaughn was doing here today.

They hadn't expected a lot of competition at the auction. The property was too remote. There were a few eccentric billionaires, of course, and some chatter about a guy who wanted to build a theme park, but Vaughn's team had told him there was little to fear.

That was, until the camera crew rolled in.

Vaughn's sense of dread rose as he stood on the lawn of Tudor House, letting the frigid Maine wind blow right through his fancy coat, and watching them freeze their fingers off setting up equipment. Once they were done, another car rolled down past the square: this one a long, black limousine.

Vaughn's stomach sank. He shouldn't have stayed. He should have just sent an agent to bid in his stead.

It was no surprise at all when the chauffeur opened the door and the Murder Crew started to emerge. First was Scarlett, dressed to kill, who immediately beelined to the crew member Vaughn guessed was the director. Peacock followed, back in her signature blue, this time using only a pair of crutches. Her little move in the ballroom with the candlestick had proved a turning point in her recovery, both mental and physical. He'd seen more of Peacock than anyone else the past six months. Deprived of control of Vaughn's music, Scarlett had turned her attention to Peacock, and was transforming her into an adaptive fitness guru. Though Vaughn knew that social media was hardly reality, she looked as happy and well-adjusted as he'd ever seen her, making videos about smoothies and strength training. Maybe she, too, had found a good therapist. His favorite videos were the ones of her out on the tennis court again, wheeling around and whacking balls.

The boys got out of the car after that, and Vaughn couldn't even focus on them. He clenched his hands into fists inside his mittens, steeling himself for who was coming next.

The first thing he noticed was her coat, a rich dove gray that fell to her ankles. Then her hair, which was a color Vaughn had never seen on her before—not the red of the heiress films, nor the mousy brown of her original Orchid disguise, nor the lavender pink she'd worn the last time he laid eyes on her. No, Orchid's hair now was burnished gold and long, well past her shoulders. She had on a thick white scarf and matching beret.

The Murder Crew huddled near their limo and sneaked furtive peeks at him.

He lifted his hand and waved. No point in pretending, right?

After a moment, he saw Orchid start his way. Scarlett clearly objected to this, and he heard her outraged squeak even over the wind. Orchid turned back and some kind of conversation took place that resulted in Scarlett sticking her hands in her pockets and stomping off, and all the cameras being dramatically swiveled away from him.

Orchid made her way over.

Vaughn stood rooted to the spot.

At about ten feet away, she stopped. "Hi."

He took a deep breath. "Here for the auction?"

"Of course."

"What does a starlet want with a school?"

She gave a rueful laugh. "What does a rock star?"

He turned and looked away—anywhere but at her pretty face, or at the people who had made all this possible, then cut him out of their lives. "What happened to *I'm dead to you?*"

"Call this a seance." She took a few steps closer, until one could almost describe them as standing side by side, then put her hands in her own pockets and joined him in staring over the campus. "Plus, I have a lot of experience talking to dead Greens." There was no rancor in the accusation, though.

Sometimes, missing Oliver was an open wound. Sometimes it was just an old scar. Always, he wanted to ask Orchid what exactly his brother had said to her on his final morning, and how he'd looked as he said it. Vaughn knew every micro expression Oliver had ever worn. He would have known sincerity by the exact position of his eyebrow or lip, the flare of his nostrils. But Orchid would have no way to tell. She hadn't even known who she was talking to, which boy it was who was about to die in an attempt to keep her from killing someone else.

"Vaughn," she said softly, and it almost did him in, "I'm glad you're doing well. Honestly."

Yeah, he was doing great. He might break off all his molars in a second. "You too. I finally took your therapy advice."

"Oh!" She sounded surprised, but pleasantly so.

He ducked his head into the collar of his coat. "Turns out it's not very healthy to pretend to be your dead brother in order to get revenge on a whole bunch of people. Who knew? I'll probably be working this out for a while."

It wasn't until he'd made himself over as Oliver that Vaughn truly got a sense of how much his brother had been suffering under their previous arrangement. There had been times, all those years at Blackbrook, that he thought he hated Oliver, and more that he thought Oliver hated him. It wasn't until he became his brother that he understood why, and began hating Vaughn, too.

Now, he wasn't sure who he was. But he was trying pretty hard not to hate either of them.

She considered this. "Well, then you'll have years of material for your songwriting."

Against his will, he brightened. "Have you been listening?"

She hesitated. "Sometimes, when I really want to torture myself." She looked down at the ground. "Like 'Morningfall.'"

He grunted. "I guess it's obvious that one's about you." The five he'd written since prom were about Oliver and death, mostly. Well, "Kingdom of Heaven" was about Orchid, but he dared not ask her if she listened to *that,* especially not after the internet had dubbed it the "makeout song of the summer."

Her tone was clipped. "It should have been obvious to me last spring that *Oliver* never *found* it. I torture myself with how gullible I was."

"I'm sor—" No. No apology would cut it here. And "Morningfall" had almost destroyed him. When Scarlett had posted the song and it went viral, it cut Vaughn in a way that watching all his other music produced without his say-so had not. It was then that he'd realized that he'd never really be able to make music again. "Oliver" couldn't keep "finding" missing tracks . . . and he had to be Oliver.

Plenty of people out there who still thought he was Oliver pretending to replace his brother, and that his music sucked now that he wasn't really Vaughn anymore. At least, that's what he gathered from internet forums before Lynn had convinced him to stop reading the comments.

Orchid gestured to the others. "Scarlett didn't want me coming over here until we got permission to film our conversation."

"Yeah, well you can forget it." He'd had his lawyer communicate as much to their team.

"I know." She stuck her hands in her pockets. "But Scarlett told me to tell you there was a bidding war. Three different streaming services."

"Good for her. I don't care."

"The contract is really generous—"

"Do I look like I need your money anymore?"

That shut her up. Vaughn could have bitten off his tongue. When he could bring himself to look at her face again, he saw her eyes were closed, her long, movie-star lashes fluttering on her windswept cheeks.

"It's sometimes hard for me to remember," she said at last, "That even when I thought you were Vaughn, you never really were."

That was something he had talked through a lot with his therapist, but he hadn't realized until just this second how much he longed to talk about it with her.

"Those months I had to be Oliver, I knew I was playing a part. But now I realize that I had always been playing one. That maybe we both were. We'd internalized this narrative of good twin and bad twin. I tamped down so many parts of myself to distinguish myself from him. My anger. My own desire for revenge. I pushed every negative aspect of myself onto Oliver, and he took it. He was happy to play the part, too."

Orchid nodded. She probably understood what that was like more than anyone. Orchid McKee was also a role. Before he'd stopped following news about her, he'd seen rumors she was going back to Hollywood, to acting. Or maybe she was just going to do this documentary with Scarlett.

Vaughn wished he knew. He wished he had the right to ask. But even though he'd just blabbed about six months of hard-won emotional growth, she shared nothing in return.

Probably wanted to save it for the cameras. Well, he wasn't going to give them the satisfaction. They could cover his part

of the story if they wanted, launch another ten thousand internet conspiracy theories about his true identity, but he certainly
wasn't going to help them. Not when Pratt and the rest of the
lawyers were still working out whether he had, in all of his
machinations, committed an actual, prosecutable crime.

He had defrauded Blackbrook, he and Oliver, but
Blackbrook didn't exist anymore. He had signed Oliver's
name to a few checks, but the money had been Vaughn's
to start. Pratt had advised him that even if he had engaged
in slightly less-than-legal activities, a prosecutor would be
unlikely to bother, since no real harm was done. Not by him,
anyway.

"We went by the cemetery in Rocky Point. That's a nice
stone you put up for him."

He'd redone the stones for all of them—Gemma, his parents, Oliver—even Rusty Nayler. "Yes, well, the funeral was
small. Oliver didn't have any friends."

She took a deep, shuddering breath. "I brought him flow-
ers. I wish I'd known him. He died because of me."

Vaughn was struck with a flare of unexpected jealousy,
the kind he hadn't felt since Orchid had hooked up with
him—with *Oliver*—in the ballroom the night he'd bailed Mrs.
White out of jail. Vaughn hadn't known who he hated more
that night—Orchid or himself.

"He died because of *me*," he said under his breath. "Because
of what *I'd* said to him. Because of what *I'd* accused him of . . ."
Oliver had died because Vaughn had thought he was a murderer. Then Vaughn had become Oliver and turned him into
the monster he'd imagined him to be. And then, when the

truth had come out, he'd gone ahead and written five hit songs about the issue.

He buried his face in his hands. He needed a lot more therapy.

"What are you doing here, Orchid?" he asked. "I haven't bothered you in six months. Why are you bothering me?"

"Oh." She stiffened. "If I am bothering you, I'll stop. I just—we didn't know if you had anyone."

Who was *we*? But he didn't dare ask that.

"I have a monthly call with Mrs. White from prison." Or at least the last two months he had. When she discovered his deception, she, too, hadn't spoken to him for months. He deserved that, too.

"How is she?" Orchid asked.

"Fine." He'd been able to hire her much better lawyers, who'd helped her leverage her information about the nefarious deeds of Blackbrook and Curry Chem for yet another reduced sentence. "She might even be up for parole before she dies."

If Oliver had died for him, Mrs. White had killed for him. Some days, he teetered between those two abysses.

"She didn't want to be in the documentary either." Orchid smiled ruefully. "We're working around it."

"You talked the others into it," he said. "Even Mustard."

"That took a lot of talking," she admitted. "Finn, mostly."

"Are they still a thing?" That had been one of the more surprising revelations to emerge in the days after the prom. Vaughn had been so wrapped up in his own twisted love triangle, he hadn't even noticed that two other members of the Murder Crew had a romance of their own going on.

Last thing he heard, Mustard and his father had finally made their peace with each other, eased in no small part by the fact that the elder Maestor sat on the board of a military contractor who licensed the formula for Finn's state-of-the-art black dye. And so the cycle began again.

They were all going to get filthy rich, before long.

She laughed. "Not really, though I don't know whether it was Finn wanting to spread his wings or Mustard wanting to put on the brakes. But they're still close. We all are."

"Not all of us."

Another long silence, with nothing but the wind blowing between them. "Vaughn—"

"No!" he snapped. He couldn't bear to hear her call him that name. "You're just here because you want me in your stupid show."

"That's not true!" She hesitated. "Okay, well, maybe it's true for Scarlett. You know she thinks she can move us around like pieces on a game board. But I'm here because I've been thinking a lot. I know a little bit about what it's like to cut yourself off from your own identity, to try to live another life. To lie about who you are. I'm here because when you were Oliver, you told me that you didn't judge me for killing Keith. And maybe because you were acting evil, you were the only person who could tell me I *wasn't* evil and make me believe it. And I needed so badly to believe it, back then. I know it was a lie, but—"

"It wasn't a lie," he said softly. "Not that part. Because

there's still a part of me that doesn't know what Oliver was capable of, that doesn't know what he did, or could have done. And I still love him."

And then he stopped talking. Both of them stopped, for a full minute. That one word hung in the air, the one she wouldn't let him say six months ago.

"You know," he said finally, because if this was the last time he ever saw her, he needed to get it off his chest, "I convinced myself that if I lost you to Oliver, it was only fair, since he'd lost so much to me."

"But you were Oliver."

"Yeah, it was really screwed up."

She nodded thoughtfully. "That's comforting, in a way."

"In what way?"

She looked at him, and there was a ghost of a smile on her face, "That you were lying to yourself every bit as much as you were lying to me."

The door of Tudor House opened and Pratt stepped out, pointed at his watch, and then raised his eyebrows.

"I, um, have to go in and buy all this now," he said to Orchid. She nodded. "I get it."

"You guys aren't going to stunt bid or anything to drive the price up, are you?"

Her lips pinched. "It was discussed."

Freaking Scarlett. He turned to go, but stopped when she spoke again.

"Can I ask what you're planning to do with it?"

Funny, he thought he'd been walking away, but they seemed to be standing as close as ever, listing toward each other like they had long ago on this very lawn, on another morning, back when everything seemed wonderful and possible instead of broken. He'd kissed her then.

He could barely look at her now.

"I'm going to make another school. One that's free. One for townies like me, where scholarship aren't payoffs and no one looks down on the kids who have them."

"That sounds wonderful." She beamed. "Blackbrook 2.0."

"Hell no." That sounded horrific. "The Oliver School. Thought I'd name it something with *slightly* less connection to murder."

"Even better." The listing continued, but Vaughn wouldn't give in. "Good luck, Vaughn. With—with whatever you do next."

He could think of several things he wanted to do next, and at least one of them would make for really good television, if Scarlett had sneaked the cameras back on. Somehow, he refrained.

"Why don't you all come along and watch anyway?"

Her eyes widened. "Really?"

He shrugged. "Murder Crew forever." And then he held out his hand.

She took it. Distantly, he thought he heard Scarlett groan and bark an order to the camera operators. But he didn't care. Orchid was holding his hand.

She beckoned to the others, and they came forward as a group across the lawn. Scarlett and Peacock, Plum and Mustard. Orchid squeezed the hand of the last Green, and together, the six of them ascended the steps to Tudor House.

Acknowledgments

You're probably not supposed to fall in love with characters you plan to kill off, so that's on me. But it's also on you, dear reader. I've cherished all your emails and messages begging me to get Plum and Mustard back together, all the capital letters and exclamation points wondering about the true identity of Oliver, or whether or not Vaughn was really dead. I hope this book gives you the opportunity to decide for yourself.

Thank you so much to the entire team at Abrams and Hasbro for allowing me to play in this madcap sand box, and for rising to meet all of my wild ideas with enthusiasm and *art*. Russ, you've been a dream to work with, and not just because you love Scarlett as much as me. Thank you to Jessica Gotz for coming in clutch. Thank you to Erin Slonaker who thought of places to stick movie quotes even I hadn't, to Brenda Angelili who made the text messages and "silent movie cards" come alive, and to Kevin Tong who totally nailed my spooky prom, as well as working with "Candlestick."

Shout out to Kate Testerman, for finding me this amazing project; Khristine Hvam, who brings my characters to life in such delightful and devious ways; and as always, to everyone involved in the *Clue* movie, who I feel I know (even if I never got the chance to meet you), and who have lent me so many great lines (and character names!) for this series.

To my daughters, my life would be so low flying solo. I love you. To my parents, who let me hide out in their house and finish this book for the price of a visit with the grands and some cocktail recipes: cheers!

And finally, thank you beyond measure to my fellow writers: Kyla (who convinced me to *go there* with Orchid and Oliver), Marianne, Leah, Lenore, Kelley, Pintip, Mindy, Carrie, Sarah, and many more who kept me sane while writing about death and isolation in a time of death and isolation. If only Mr. Green had friends like you. Murder Crew Forever.

Diana Peterfreund is the author of fifteen books for adults, teens, and children, including the Secret Society Girl series, the Killer Unicorn series, *For Darkness Shows the Stars*, and *Omega City*. She has received starred reviews from *Booklist*, *School Library Journal*, and *VOYA*, and her books have been named among Amazon's Best Books of the Year. She lives outside of Washington, D.C., with her family.